ALL THE STARS AS ANGELS
WAR OF THE GODS, BOOK 2

David A. Falk

Lagomorph Rampant Studios
Vancouver | Canada

Published by Lagomorph Rampant Studios
www.lagomorph-rampant.com

ISBN 978-1-0692160-4-5

This book is dedicated to

Kenneth Anderson Kitchen (1938-2025),

a friend and mentor who will be greatly missed.

CHAPTER ONE

The undersigned nations of the world have come to accord, following the terrible and tragic events surrounding the latest global conflict, a conflict with malicious new weapons and terrifying revelations of a future where such weapons could proliferate. **– "Preamble: Articles of the Armistice"**

The interior of the landing pod was pitch black except for a few indicator lights. But that was of no concern to Niva since she had completely memorized the interior, not that she needed to do so with her feline vision. Her backlit photodiode retinas glowed white in the dark. Nevertheless, the pod was piloted from orbit, making her little more than a passenger.

As the pod firmly bumped against the ground, she rocked side to side. It was over. A green safety light indicated her voyage was complete. She stood up and reached for the lever of the hatch. With a squeal the pressure between interior and exterior equalized. The door swung open, and the inside of the pod filled with bright orange sunlight.

Niva stepped into the doorway of the hatch and stretched. Her seven-foot height filled the hatchway. She wore a white kimono robe that covered her translucent white synthetic skin. Her black lips parted into a smile, and glassy white fiber optic hair cascaded over her shoulder. Her ivory irises adjusted to the uncomfortably bright light. Round gold metal pads encircled her wrists, ankles, neck, and a few were on her temples and under her eyes.

She looked out into the faces of five humans all pointing the muzzles of their rifles at her. She processed the information as quickly as possible. Her empathy chip noted that the humans were hunched. Tension filled their eyes. Slowly, she raised her hands, empty palms exposed to them.

"What are you?" said the blue-eyed woman in the front of the group. Her long brown hair swept in front of her face.

Niva recognized her from a report image. The image she had was of a 13-year-old girl that looked like she escaped a Dicken's novel. But age progression software indicated a 98% certainty this was Melissa Poul.

"You must be Melissa," said Niva. Melissa wore the crossed-rifles insignia for the Colony Security Chief. She spoke in a slow, careful voice. "This unit is an android from MegaAI *Orion S209*. This unit is unarmed."

"We saw the MegaAI in the sky," said Melissa. She grabbed the grip of the rifle tighter. Her crystal blue eyes focused through the length of a short scope. Long past were the days when MegaAIs were a cause for celebration. A MegaAI had not visited Gliese for a decade, and that previous visit had not gone well. "We received no notice of your visit."

"Unfortunately, sending advanced notice for our ship is impractical. But we are going to fulfill our obligations under the Colonist Charter." Niva kept her hands raised trying to de-escalate the situation. "Please, have your people send up a parts request. We are also reconstructing the docking station."

"That's what the last MegaAI said." Melissa frowned gritting her teeth. Niva looked into Melissa's eyes and could see that she had seen death. Recalling the details of her file, Melissa had been the veteran of two colony wars: the first happened on Mar 9th GE 153 and the second on Apr 4th GE 157. While only small skirmishes by Earth standards, both wars ended in routes for Basra colony. However, even small wars could have long-lasting effects.

"That is part of the reason this unit was sent," said Niva. "MegaAI *Sigma A017*'s last encounter with any third party was here at Gliese. We need to understand why we lost contact with that vessel."

"You could have done that from orbit."

"This unit is also here on another matter." Steps stretched out from the landing pod and slid into the sand. The accumulated sand whispered as it was pushed back. At the edge of the colony, the occasional blade of dune grass poked out sporadically from the surface. A warm breeze bent the blades and caused them to kiss the sand. "This unit needs to speak to your governor."

Four of the five humans pointed their guns away from her. Melissa pointed the muzzle aside but was more than ready to whip it back up and let off a round of smoking lead. Niva cautiously lowered her hands.

"This unit needs to bring a case of documents," said Niva. "May I reach into the capsule and retrieve it? There are no weapons in it."

Melissa refocused her rifle on the android. "Let's see the case."

Niva reached behind the door and pulled out a small case.

"Throw it there." Melissa pointed the muzzle of her rifle to the sand in front of Niva.

Niva tossed the bag to the sand. "The bag is not locked."

A balding security officer picked up the completely white bag. The satchel had a handle on the top of each side and was soft-sided. He opened the top of the bag and looked inside. He poked between the papers. He made sure he saw the bottom of the case between each sheet of writing. "No new nifty technology," said the officer jokingly.

"That's not funny," said Melissa. "Give me the bag."

He handed her the bag.

"We will escort you to the governor. You may disembark… slowly."

Niva cautiously stepped down the four steps onto the sand. Her white boots sunk into the sand, warm and soft, like taking a dip into a soothing bath. This was the first time she had ever been on a real planet. She was built in space and had never left her ship. Nothing seemed remotely familiar to her.

Melissa ushered her to go left.

Niva hiked through the sand. It was more effort than she expected. And the increased gravity weighed on her like lead weights were strapped to her limbs. Gliese's gravity may have been only 96% of Earth's, but the artificial gravity on the MegaAI was normally 85%. She added more power to her leg drivers to keep pace.

Her sensors warned of delayed reaction time. If these humans turned hostile, she could dispatch one or two of them, maybe, but they would make quick work of her. Fear interrupts flooded her cortex. No predicting how this meeting was going to go, and there was comfort where the situation was predictable.

Niva was escorted past family huts that had been built on the outskirts of the main sections of the colony. They were like metal chicks nestled to the main dome, standing as a hen over the brood.

The group walked past the main dome and to a colony lander that was prone on the ground. Niva recognized the 23rd century craft built to hold twenty colonists. The exterior paint was blistered, much of it chipped away by the elements. The colonists had converted the lander and storage bays into living space. The engines had been dismantled and cannibalized for components now used in many of the essential systems, such as mineral extraction and water purification.

Niva climbed a metal staircase and stepped inside the fuselage of the lander. Her boots clinked against the metal grating of the gangway. She crouched to keep from hitting her head on the ceiling. Melissa followed her inside and pointed to the office of the governor at the head of the lander. The security chief grabbed the alumasteel latch of the door, deteriorating gray paint flaked off in her hands, falling to the gangway. The heavy metal door swung open with squealing hinges no one had lubricated for over a century.

Vladomyr sat at the governor's wooden desk. His tall frame, dwarfed by Niva's, was nonetheless imposing. He had obsidian eyes and oil-slick black hair now frosted at his temples and in his beard. He tented his fingers and sat with his back to the door, a visible message of cold unconcern that she was no threat to him.

Niva scanned the room. The office was austere even by the standards aboard a MegaAI. Absolutely nothing was on Vladomyr's desk: no memorabilia, no computer terminal, no papers, no writing styluses… nothing at all.

Melissa put the document case on the desk. "The android brought this with her."

"Thank you, Melissa. Hans needs your help in the situation room." He swiveled his chair around.

"I should be here," said Melissa.

"Hans has already established an uplink with the MegaAI." He shrugged his broad shoulders. "We've verified the identity of our visitor. I don't need you here. Go help Hans before he fucks something up."

"Yes, sir," said Melissa. She glared at Niva and left the room, closing the hatch behind her.

"I am Vladomyr Golenishchev. Eleventh governor of Gliese 832 c, Arish colony." The tone of his voice was desiccated of enthusiasm.

"This unit was expecting Governor James Gardiner."

"Gardiner died in October GE 161."

"This unit is sorry for your loss." Niva consulted her empathy chip for the exact words to say. "This unit looks forward to working with you."

"Before any of that happens," said Vladomyr. He frowned and the skin around his neck flushed red. "You need to answer some questions. And if I'm not happy with the answers, I will personally shove you into a canon and launch you back into space."

Niva was sixty percent sure this was a physical threat. Her smile flickered, afraid of the unpredictable human. Machines were no threat to humans. It was something instilled in the consciousness of every intelligent machine. Even though there were empty chairs, the man kept her standing at the door, a violation of protocol. Was he trying to assert dominance?

"This unit is instructed to give any answer within its knowledge."

"What's that supposed to mean?" He tapped impatiently against the surface of the desk.

"This unit is not a MegaAI," said Niva. "This unit is an embodied architecture that has no built-in access to parallelized AI."

"I have no idea what you just said." Vladomyr shook his head. "Who are you?"

"This unit—"

"Stop right there. That's annoying. If you are going to talk to us mere humans, you will use the first-person pronoun, I. Do not refer to yourself in the third person."

"This unit, I mean I, will comply with your request." Niva adjusted her communication protocols. "I do not have all the answers, but I will cooperate."

"You should have said that." Vladomyr looked into her white eyes, white within white. "Let's begin with some basics."

Niva nodded in agreement.

"Who are you?"

"I am C-Niva-42716, a class C android. I am a functionary in service to MegaAI *Orion S209*."

"Sounds a lot like a job description. But who *are* you?"

She squinted and turned her head slightly. It took a second for her to realize the complexity of his question. "I do not think I can answer that question."

He chuckled. "It's a question that doesn't have a good answer."

"Why ask if there is no good answer?"

"Questions sometimes reveal what is hidden."

Niva was flummoxed by the question. Mechanicals are incredibly literal. Is it not the purpose of a question to solicit an answer? What did Vladomyr learn from his question? "What did my answer reveal?"

"I thought androids were never permitted to look like human beings," said Vladomyr, avoiding the question. "My recollection of the Armistice Articles of the Fourth World War might be a bit hazy. But from what I recall, androids that look like human beings are illegal. Now, a human-looking android walks into my colony. How does that happen?"

Niva recalled her legal and history files, and the legal interpretations of the Armistice Articles. "I am not a lawyer. But from what I know, the law concerning artificial intelligences built in the image of humans makes androids restricted but not prohibited. Androids are still permitted on military installations, where humans are normally absent, or for interplanetary diplomatic envoys."

"And the fact you androids look human?"

"My exposure to humans is limited to six individuals. But from the physiological data on file, are you telling me you would confuse me for a human?" She gave a large lateral smile that exposed her teeth within her slightly canine face.

Vladomyr looked at her from head to foot, squinting at her as he scrutinized her unique physiology. He snorted. "I suppose not." Then he laughed too. "Okay, why didn't the MegaAI announce its arrival?"

"We did not know we were coming. We were rerouted to investigate the disappearance of MegaAI *Sigma A017*."

"Disappearance? What do you mean disappearance?"

"After your encounter with MegaAI *Sigma A017*, communications from them went dark. The ship is lost, and we don't know what happened to it. Gliese 832 c was the last planet to have contact with the *Sigma A017*. We received a message from MegaAI *Heracles S350* and were diverted here to investigate the fate of the *Sigma* and complete the *Sigma's* mission."

"I understand that," said Vladomyr. He touched his right temple with his two fore fingers and rubbed in a small circle. "None of that explains why you couldn't warn us of your arrival."

"The *Orion* is not like any other MegaAI ship."

"How so?"

"She can travel faster than light speed."

"You're kidding?" said the Ukrainian.

Niva turned her head to the side, not quite sure what to make of his question. "I am not sure how to kid you," she said. "But the *Orion S209* is the only starship that can exceed the speed of light."

"I'm a physicist, so you definitely have my attention." Vladomyr was now enthralled. "How?"

"That is outside of my area of understanding." Niva was never programmed to do scientific research.

"How fast can it go?"

"It can cruise at 1.2 c."

"20% faster than the speed of light." Vladomyr shook his head as if his world had changed. "That must use massive amounts of power."

"Perhaps, not as much as you may think," said Niva. She was vaguely aware of some of the old power calculations used to fuel near-light-speed travel. She knew Vladomyr was born on Earth and had been on Gliese for at least thirty years so that means his physics was probably fifty years out of date. "The ship itself cannot travel any faster than a normal ship in regular space using pulse engines."

"So about 70% the speed of light."

"Actually, 65%," said Niva. "In normal space, we are a bit slower than other MegaAI. But the *Orion* can generate a warp bubble that contracts space around it. Think of it this way. We walk the same number of steps as everyone else, but our steps are twice as long."

"So what you are saying is that, even though *Orion's* pulse engines cannot exceed the speed of light, your ship makes more efficient use of every parsec."

She nodded. "The formula and space-drive architecture were discovered by our MegaAI."

"Does Earth know?"

"We intend to share all we discover with Earth Central Command."

"So then." Vladomyr thought for a moment. The implications must have come as a surprise to him. "It would be pointless for you to send a message warning us of your coming because the MegaAI would arrive before your message."

"That is a good summary," admitted Niva. She was still standing and wanted badly to sit if only to enter a lower power mode.

"Interesting," said Vladomyr. "I'm not fully convinced. What about the supply ships?"

"We are aware of that. With *Sigma A017* failing to implement repairs, transport ships from Earth were routed to other colonies. Once we repair your docking station, your regular biennial deliveries will resume."

"So then what's your business here?"

"Our main supercomputer, the Great AI has asked me to gather information."

"What do you need?"

"We need a copy of all files sent to *Sigma A017*."

"Don't you have the reports?"

"We need the raw data."

"Okay, I think we can do that."

"Also, do you have information about Basra? We cannot establish contact with them."

"That I can't help you with," said Vladomyr. "There's been no contact with them since the second colony war. I don't even know if there are any survivors. They've basically said anyone who encroaches their territory will be shot. I'll forward you their warnings."

Niva nodded. "There is one other thing."

"What is it?"

Niva stepped up to Vladomyr's desk. Her giant height loomed over him. She opened her handbag, removed a document, and presented it to the governor.

Vladomyr scanned the document. "Is this legal?"

"It is a recall order."

"I know what it is." Vladomyr tossed the paper, which floated across the surface of his whistle clean desk. "But is it legal to relocate someone from a colony?"

"It is," said Niva. "We've had it signed by an authorized ESA agent representing Earth Central Command."

"Gliese is not accountable to Earth government or the ESA."

"The right to recall is in the contract that every colonist signs. The named person is subject to recall and no longer has a right to live on this colony world."

"Well, that is a problem."

"Why?"

"Because Pierre Gulet is an exile. Nobody has seen him in ten years, and nobody knows if he is even still alive." Vladomyr slid the paper across his desk with his index finger. "But if you do find him, he might help you discover who you are."

* * *

Niva sat at the edge of the mess hall watching the people come and go. She watched the people, from child to adult, all dressed in the khaki green, colony regulation battle dress uniforms. The people would go up to the glass and steel serving station. The humans doing their daily eating ritual is something she had heard about and could not get enough of watching them do it. Some colonists shoveled their food, some guarded their trays and ate cautiously, some talked more than they ate. Each one was different and worthy of observation.

But everything was less colorful than she expected. She had been told how colorful colony worlds could be with a thousand dazzling greens of the jungles, hearty reds of the blooming flowers, and brilliant yellows and blues of the burgeoning butterflies—she had dreamed of seeing real butterflies. She got the reject assignment with Gliese, a dull, bland, dusty, desert world—a wasted chunk of dead rock hurtling through space.

A young boy came up to Niva. He stopped right in front of her. He could not have been more than seven years old. He leaned forward and looked at her with wide sapphire blue eyes. They were the bluest blue eyes she had ever seen, penetrating lenses of deep-water blue. In every other way, the boy was unremarkable, dusty and dirt-covered, like everything else here. He had unkempt black hair and stank of needing a bath.

"What are you?" said the boy.

"This unit… I am Niva," said the android.

"Are you an angel?"

"What makes you think that?" Niva squinted and tilted her head slightly perplexed.

"Are you from space?"

"I am," she replied.

The boy's eyes grew even wider than they were already. "Angels are from space."

Niva referenced her data files. She did not know what an angel was. The data returned: *an angel is a spirit being from another world that does the bidding of a deity [see "messenger"]*. She gave a brief involuntary smile.

This reminded her that she needed her autonomic processor checked—it was doing that more frequently. Definitely operating outside its design parameters.

"I am an android."

The boy squinted. The corners of his eyes wrinkled. His large, frog mouth, flattened. "I don't believe you," he uttered slowly.

"I assure you. I am a machine."

"Can't androids be angels?" said the boy proudly in a personal triumph of reasoning.

A woman in her thirties walked briskly by, grabbed the boy by the arm, and yanked him hard away. "Stop bothering the microwave." She snarled at the boy.

Niva sucked in her bottom lip. She recognized that pejorative. Even though cooking was not part of life on the MegaAI, everyone onboard was familiar with the human service devices: microwaves, waffle irons, toasters, ovens, percolators, all servile mechanisms with no intelligence used to heat food. Humans used those slurs for three centuries, and apparently they had never grown old. Her empathy chip filled her with sadness. She was reflective enough to know the emotions were not real but that did not prevent them from being painful.

A Scandinavian in his mid-fifties with loose blonde hair and blue eyes stepped up to Niva. He was a craggy figure worn away by years of labor and concern. The man could have passed for one of many fishermen that had set sail from Oslo.

"You are Niva?" declared Hans Poul simply. "This way."

Niva stood up and followed the man. People watching had lost its pleasure anyway.

"I was told to surrender all materials from the Reliquary to you," said Hans.

"That would help," said Niva. Her long ropey arms swayed as she walked. "Out of curiosity, does the Gliese colony have a sperm bank or fertility program?"

"Why do you say that?" Hans looked over his shoulder at Niva.

"It is a routine question to assess colony health."

"No, we don't have any sort of fertility or eugenics program," he replied then licked his lips. *Why did he add* eugenics *to his reply? Does he know something?*

"Did you work with Gulet?"

"Work with?" Hans snorted. "I hated that man."

"Is that not a strong word?"

"Can't find one stronger." Han shook his head. "I couldn't stand to be in the same room with him one second longer than I needed." They stopped in a darkened hallway. Her retinas adjusted their ISO for the lower light conditions. The lighting aboard a MegaAI was dim by human standards. And her vision could see well below a million ISO, practically the same ability to see in the dark as a rabbit.

Hans punched in a key code and opened the door to the lab. When they walked inside, the motion sensors raised the lights. The counters were covered in dust, and a pungent smell of mold hung in the air. And yet it had all the trappings of a biology lab: examination tables, dissection tools, and a fume hood.

"No one has been in here for nearly a decade," said Hans. "It will take me a moment to gather the materials."

Niva ignored what Hans said. She saw an open cage at the far end of the room and walked over to investigate. There was a tray of sand and long moldy vegetation. An unrooted sapling sat in the middle of the floor. And a scatterbug was lifeless in the corner. It was upside down and its feet hung limply at its sides. *Such is the end of all mechanical life.*

"Niva, I think I have everything," said Hans.

She returned to Hans who had gathered everything on a counter.

"I'm afraid not much remains," Hans said apologetically. "Pierre's findings created a lot of friction here with the other researchers."

"Why?"

"Professional jealousies."

"I don't understand."

"That's probably for the best," said Hans. "Unfortunately, a lot of the best evidence was destroyed in the back and forth. But this is everything I have."

Niva looked at the small collection of items. Even she would admit that it was not much.

Hans picked up each bagged item and explained it. "One ceramic fragment with a bit of unknown writing. A second ceramic fragment from an urn found in the cavern. A baggie containing potash and bone chips collected from an urn. One vial of purified prion." He finally picked up a plastoglass canister in which a brown liquid sloshed on the bottom. "This is a canister of poisonous gas collected directly from the Reliquary. Five of these were collected. Three of them were used against attackers from Basra as gas warfare. There is probably enough poison here to kill fifty thousand people. I've been instructed to give you one of the two cylinders. I only wish I could give you the other."

Niva nodded. She too was nervous about the cylinders. Even though she was an android and did not breathe air, her systems were still sensitive to environmental factors.

"I also have two data storage sticks that have all of the colony's data on the matter," said Hans. "There are a couple of items presumed lost but not destroyed. One fragment of white ceramic without writing. And a single finger bone believed to be from Species 1."

"Acknowledged," said Niva. She opened her document case and placed the items carefully inside.

"As far as I am concerned, you are doing me a favor taking all this away." Hans clenched his jaw and licked his lip. He trembled noticeably agitated. "If you want to do me a bigger solid, get that fucker Pierre off this planet."

What did he do to him?

"I need to find him first," said Niva.

"There is one person who might know how to find him," said Hans.

Niva nodded as she finished loading her case.

"Alicia Stripes, the colony physician. Lives in outer colony hut 18 in the northwest quadrant. Just be warned that she hates him more than I do."

CHAPTER TWO

Construction of embodied human personality models, also called **androids**, *is restricted. No mechanical will be created indistinguishable from a human being. Androids in limited numbers with limited functionality will be permitted for military use for training purposes when confined to a military base with a temenos, in environments where humans are normally not present, or for temporary diplomatic envoys to small human populations. —* **"Article 7, Articles of the Armistice"**

Niva stepped through the open door of the infirmary. Sick and injured people, seemingly unconscious, were prone on cots separated by powder blue drop sheets hanging from the ceiling. Monitoring equipment was at the head of each cot. It all seemed very primitive, but nobody would expect a colony world to have the latest in medical practice. There was nothing like it on the MegaAI. She was a machine. Many of her parts could be easily replaced. And any unit too damaged was decommissioned.

Niva recognized Alicia sitting at a desk in the far corner of the room. She had not changed too much from her ESA photo. She was a redhead with split ends, and she wore a blue surgical coat. Ten years older and thirty pounds heavier. A nine-year-old boy, slight and perhaps undernourished, with dusty ginger hair and aqua aura blue eyes was sweeping the floor around her desk.

The android stepped over towards the seated medic.

"I know what you are." Alicia refused to turn her attention away from the medical file she was working on.

"I require your assistance," said Niva.

"I don't give a fuck if you find that fucker or not." She picked up a pencil and held it in her right hand between her fingers. She squeezed till her fingers blanched.

"By that you mean?"

"That asshole, Pierre Gulet." Alicia looked to the left and spoke over her shoulder. "Tom, the adults need the room to ourselves."

The boy stopped sweeping. His dull eyes did not express any surprise at Alicia's request. Niva calculated a resemblance between Tom and Alicia—a 43% chance the two were blood related. Tom walked out of the infirmary and probably went to find other duties.

Niva pulled an official document out of her carrying case. "I have a recall order for Mr. Gulet." She handed the notice to Alicia.

The medic accepted the document between two fingers as if the document was infested with germs. Her brow furrowed as she stretched out the document to read it. Alicia grinned, and her eyes sparkled. "Oh my, an extradition order. Pierre must have been a very bad boy to get extradited from a colony."

"There is no presumption of guilt in the order," said Niva.

"Oh no, of course not." Alicia's grin grew even wider. "Because people get extradited from colonies every day for perfectly innocent reasons." She laughed with glee. "Couldn't happen to a nicer guy."

Why such animus? Did Pierre have any friends at all in the colony?

"Does Tom know the identity of both his parental units?" Niva tilted her head and leaned forward. She made sure her audio sensors did not miss a byte of important data.

"He's never going to find out." She squinted her eyes at Niva. Niva fingered the handle of her document case.

"Is Mr. Gulet aware?" Niva bit the bottom of her lip. She observed the medic with utmost attention.

Alicia glared at the android. Her crows-feet wrinkled at the corners of her hazel eyes. "Pierre abandoned us three months after Tom was born."

"What do you mean by abandoned? Did he domicile with you?"

"He shirked his responsibility to us." She banged her fist against the desk. "He was named the father. His duty is to be here."

"Did he live with you and the boy?"

"How is that relevant?"

"Questions of this nature help me to establish his state of mind and find him faster."

"No, we never lived together."

"And Gulet is Tom's father?"

"This is going to help you locate him?"

"It already has," said Niva. Her white within white eyes blinked infrequently. The gold patches under her eyes twitched involuntarily. "So by *abandoned* you mean…"

"Exile," said Alicia. She pressed her lips together tightly. "He chose exile over his responsibility to Tom and me." Alicia was holding something back.

"How close were you prior to his exile?"

"Close," said Alicia.

"How close?"

"We had a close working relationship for over a year. I was his personal assistant. We had physical relations. That close enough?" Alicia flushed dark pink. She looked like a volcano ready to blow.

"This must be difficult," said Niva. "But if anyone knows Gulet, it would be you."

"Then get to the point."

"Where am I likely to find Mr. Gulet?"

"He's a desert creature," said Alicia. "But there's not much out there. He would have to live close to a food and water source. The only place where there's anything like that around here is the Southern Crescent."

"What's that?"

"It's a crescent of terraformed forest south of the colony." Alicia wrote a note on a pad. "One of the few terraformed areas not destroyed by the Reliquary. If you go out there, you should take a security detail. Pierre is armed."

"How do you know?"

"I gave him the pistol."

* * *

The dry desert wind swept past Niva's face blowing her white glass hair back. A security officer drove the rover, and a second officer sat in the back holding a rifle. When they arrived at the edge of the green zone, the driver parked the rover. The security detail quickly hopped out of the vehicle and readied their guns.

Niva took her time exiting the vehicle from the passenger's side. She was careful not to step in front of their firing solutions. She had no intention of becoming an accidental casualty.

"Exiles are dangerous," said Jude, the driver. He drew a Glaucom side arm. He was clean shaven with the hair on his head carefully shaved off to a military regulation cut even though Gliese had no military.

"That's why you're here," said Niva.

"Jude never appreciated the occupational hazards of being security," said Bruno, the other security officer. Bruno had a buzz cut with a moustache. He laughed and loaded a round in the chamber of the rifle.

Niva focused on the edge of the forest. Her eyesight could magnify what she saw from a distance. Nothing indicated a human had been nearby. No spent fires. No animal remains. No broken tree limbs.

"Mr. Gulet needs to come with me peacefully," said Niva. "No one shoots first. And no one injures Gulet. He is not a criminal. He is only to be taken alive and unharmed. If we cannot take him unharmed, it is better to let him go."

"If he shoots at us and we cannot fire back, why are we here?" said Jude.

"Is Gulet the only exile out here?"

"That's why we're here," said Bruno. "So we are to protect the microwave from anyone not Gulet."

Niva glared at Bruno.

"Sorry," said the security officer.

"Let's start searching for Gulet." She led the way toward the forested area.

"You know it could take days to find him," said Bruno.

"He will come find us." Niva brushed past the savannah grass making her way to the tree line. "Gulet is nothing if not curious. Eventually, he will find out what we want."

"That's if he doesn't kill us," said Jude.

"Does he have a reason to want to kill you?" Niva turned back and looked Jude in the face.

"I suppose not," said Jude.

Niva then faced Bruno. "Does Gulet have any reason to kill you?" Bruno responded by shaking his head. "If Gulet has any reason to kill either one of you, go back to the rover now."

Both shook their heads. She waited for either one to turn around, but neither did.

"We are not going to give him any reason to shoot at us," said Niva. It was risky for them to linger out in the open. But she wanted Pierre to get a good look at them. She kept her hands exposed so anyone watching could see she did not have a weapon.

The android turned towards the tree line and continued walking forward until they entered the shrubbery. As they entered the darkness of the tree cover, the temperature dropped by nearly twenty degrees. The end of April on Gliese was still a cold month. It was not time to go back, but her two human companions were shivering.

"It's only 3pm," said Niva. She had an internal sense of the local time even though she had no watch. But they had only just arrived at the Southern Crescent, and no way was she going to return without having some opportunity to have Pierre find them.

"What is the plan?" said Jude. He folded his arms while his teeth chattered.

"Can you two build a fire?" Niva figured getting them active would keep them warm while they waited. She found a mossy log to sit on in front of where the men were going to make the fire. The moss was damp and cold beneath her.

"Gladly," said Bruno. The two men looked about and gathered small sticks.

Jude cleared a patch of open soil and built a tent of sticks. He took out a combat knife and shaved off some kindling. He made a pile of shaved wood. As Jude built the stack, Bruno went out and gathered more alder and scrub pine branches. Niva carefully tracked the sounds Bruno was making in the woods and where he was scrounging.

White sparks flared brightly as Jude struck a pocket lighter. The kindling ignited into a dull bluish flame and quickly died to orange embers. Jude blew on the embers and added more kindling until a small yellow flame took over from the embers. He added twigs to the flame. Jude broke larger sticks into pieces and added the pieces to the fire. Woody and resinous terpenes filled the air with the aroma of burning pine sap. Jude stood back up and joined Bruno in gathering more wood, and together they built a large pile of wood beside the fire. Jude added several large pieces of a dry rotted log to the fire. The flames leapt high filling the entire forest canopy with orange light.

"That is enough," said Niva. The radiant heat tingled her skin. "Sit and warm yourselves." The men sat across from her with the fire in between. Their faces looked like kabuki masks as the firelight brought their features into stark contrast.

"Thank you," said Bruno.

"I want to ask you two." Niva spoke softly. "After the second colony war of GE 157, what was it like living here?"

"Will our answers be confidential?"

Niva nodded her head. "I will not share your answers with anyone in the colony. Part of my job here is to assess the health and long-term quality of life on the colony to make life better for the colonists. As long as no crimes were committed, your answers will remain confidential."

"It's not fun living here, but it was never as tense as it was—as it became—after the second war," said Jude. He sighed and paused to remember. Life must have been very different seven years ago.

"I guess we all figured the first colony war was a one off," said Bruno. "And there were no casualties on our side. And it's not going to be popular, but I'm going to say it. Gulet saved our bacon in the first colony war. But he left in the colony sometime around the end of GE 155, and we got cocky. Didn't fare so well in the second."

"How high were the casualties?"

"Seventy of them, fifty of us," said Jude. "If it wasn't for our larger numbers after the first war, it could have ended differently."

Niva heard a branch snap. Her fingers squeezed into the soft moss.

"The second war really changed how we viewed living here," said Bruno. "With the transport vessels no longer coming, Governor Golenishchev has demanded we make more babies."

She heard some more leaves rustle.

"It's probably around 6pm," said Niva. "You two should return to the colony for the night. Temperatures are about to fall, and it is about to get uncomfortable."

Both men stood up. "Aren't you coming with us?" asked Jude.

"No, I'm going to stay here overnight," said Niva. "Just come back in the morning to pick me up."

"Are you sure?" said Bruno. "You won't be safe out here. What if you encounter an exile?"

"I think I will be fine." Niva picked up a branch and placed it on the fire. "I watched you make the fire. I think I can maintain it without help." Not that the fire mattered to her. Cold did not affect her in a negative way, and her systems were capable of operating below minus one hundred degrees.

"Can I leave you the rifle?" said Bruno.

"I'm not permitted to use arms," said Niva. She raised the volume of her voice slightly so it resonated in the grove. "I will be fine unarmed."

"If you insist," said Bruno.

"Melissa is not going to be happy about us leaving her here." Jude grabbed Bruno by the sleeve.

"I don't think Melissa gives a shit about what happens to Niva." Bruno answered and turned to Niva. "Keep safe. I suspect that you probably know what you're doing."

Niva smiled and nodded. The two men gathered themselves together and departed from the forest. Niva continued to sit by the fire. She added a few more logs and stoked the embers with a stick. She put the stick beside her and waited. She waited in silence for twenty minutes.

"I know you're out there," said Niva. "I can smell you're near." She closed her eyes to conserve power. She would have to go through the night without a recharge. Her power reserves were down to 35%, safely above critical levels. But being fully charged always made her feel better and less irritable. She felt herself slipping into a hibernation state, then woke herself up.

She opened her eyes to see a man sitting across from her at the fire, a rucksack was between his feet. The odor of rotting meat clung to him. But he had been quiet—she did not even hear him enter the camp. If he had not snapped a twig earlier, she would never have known he was in the vicinity. His colony BDUs had seen better days. His jacket was missing all its buttons, and it was open showing his bare chest, nothing but skin and bones. He had an unkempt sandy blond beard, and his hair was tied back in a ponytail. His chestnut brown eyes looked at her.

"You're not human," he said.

"True," said the android, "I am C-Niva-42716."

"May I use your fire?"

"The fire here is for you."

"How polite," said the man. He pulled the decapitated body of a large snake out of the rucksack. The snake was already gutted and cleaned and practically ready to cook. With both hands, he skinned the dead snake with a single fluid motion. The air was tainted with the smell of blood, acrid and rusty. He placed the carcass on a stick and held it over the flame. "Quite a treat to use a well-built fire. Winter was exceptionally harsh this year."

"I am glad you are enjoying it," said Niva. "From your medical records, I expected you to be wearing a rebreather."

"My rebreather gave out years ago," Pierre smirked. "Used to have a gun too. Without electricity, those things peter out fast. First few years were kind of hard, but I learned to pace myself, and my reduced lung capacity eventually adapted to the thin air."

"Will we be expecting any other company?"

"No one else lives in the crescent. They found me difficult to live with."

"You seem to have that effect on people, Dr. Gulet."

"Call me Pierre." Pierre laughed weakly. "Not that long ago that comment would have bothered me."

"What changed?"

"Nine years to reflect."

"When did you first suspect that Tom was not your son?" Niva was not one to avoid the point. The other class Cs said she was brash, but she was known for cutting through the distractions. Not someone you would want to invite to a meeting where everyone dances around inconvenient truths.

"Not much for small talk, are you?" Pierre raised his eyebrows. "That your opinion?"

"Doc Stripes says you are the father."

Pierre shook his head and snorted. He pulled the cooked cobra off the fire, and let it cool before pulling off a sliver of meat and putting it in his mouth. Niva watched Pierre eat. She was fascinated by the ritual. She had no digestive system so could not eat. Although she had taste receptors, swallowing was not an option. Still, all the rituals surrounding food were an anthropologist's dream.

"I had a gut feeling something was wrong with the genetic tests." Pierre's face fell at the thought.

"Alicia says you and her had a physical relationship."

"Wouldn't call knock-out drops slipped into my water bottle a relationship."

"How did that make you feel?"

"Like I could never trust again." Pierre's shoulders slumped.

"Why not trust the paternity results?"

"Too many people had access to the records. Doc Jones was not one for record-keeping. And I knew the clinic was not the only colony facility that did genetic testing. Called in a favor with Pavel Urbanovich."

"Director of agriculture?"

"I gave him two DNA samples: mine from cheek swab and one of Tom's baby bottles. Pavel did a gel electrophoresis in the botany lab."

"Not as accurate as genetic sequencing."

"Accurate enough to exclude me as Tom's parent and inspire Pavel to have his own children tested." Pierre picked the greasy snake meat from between the bones. "Okay, your turn. How did you find out?"

Niva grinned and held up a single hand palm up. "My visual scans detected the presence of unique phenotypes in a disproportionate percentage of the colony offspring."

"Ah… so you noticed a lot of kids have weird blue eyes. Amazes me how the colonists think this is normal."

"There is a 93% probability that 30% of the colony's offspring under the age of 10 are from the same father." Niva reflected for a moment upon that analysis. This would have serious implications for the long-term viability of the colony. She looked up at the forest canopy—already past sunset. They were going to be here for the night.

"You mean Hans?" Pierre looked at his meal. He lost his appetite. "He did a lot of computer work for Doc Jones. Once I got the genetic results from Pavel, wasn't hard to figure the rest." He set the rest of the cooked snake meat beside him.

Niva's empathy chip sent alerts as she maintained this delicate balancing act. If she could win Pierre's cooperation, that would be better than dragging him off the planet by force even though she would be in her rights to do so. She rubbed her fingers together. Her internal logic could not predict how Pierre would react. Unlike MegaAI supercomputers, androids lacked the same predictive bias. But predictive bias was not the same as intuition. Intuition could make connections between seemingly unrelated things. No computer, no matter its predictive power, had intuition. Even the mightiest artificial intelligence needs concrete connections to make predictions.

Niva gave a weak smile. She was unsure what to say. How does one even respond to what Pierre said? She needed to move him to the business for which she was sent, the recall order. Just because Pierre was betrayed does not mean he would not be passionate to stay for other reasons.

"Nothing to say?" said Pierre. A tear formed at the corner of his eye. He sniffled and wiped the tear away with the back of his hand. Moistened dirt smeared across his face.

"It sounds like you don't have much reason to stay on Gliese," said Niva finally.

"What choice do I have?" said Pierre. "Colonization is a one-way trip. There's no leaving Gliese, and Peter Chin still has a person on the inside. I'd be dead in no time."

"Would you leave if you had a choice?"

"That isn't possible, is it?"

Niva handed Pierre a crinkled document. By this point the document had passed through so many hands it was no longer fresh and crisp. She bowed her head slightly. Pierre read the recall order.

"Am I in trouble?" said Pierre. Niva carefully observed Pierre's demeanor. Like the world was crashing in on him all over again. Recall orders were issued when a colonist was to be extradited for committing the highest crimes and convicted *in absentia*. A conviction that, in every case, was punished by the death penalty.

Niva saw the fear in his eyes. She shook her head. "You are not being extradited."

"My work here is not finished." His lips quivered.

"Pierre, you cannot do your work as an exile." Niva spoke softly.

Pierre breathed heavily. His brow was furrowed. He swayed side to side, then rocked back and forth. Niva watched him carefully but could not interpret what he was feeling. Was he saddened to leave? Was he mourning a loss too difficult to reconcile? Was he feeling uprooted? Was he feeling helpless at being uprooted? He kept switching between expressions confusing her empathy chip. There was nowhere for Pierre to go. The Crescent was too small to evade a search party determined to find him.

"When do I have to turn myself in?" said Pierre. He stretched his wrists towards her.

Niva looked at Pierre, and her empathy chip signaled a compassion response for him. "You are not under arrest. We need your help."

"The recall order?"

"Will not be enforced." Niva was still listening to make sure no one was nearby eavesdropping in on the conversation. "A future-changing event is coming. We need your help."

"Why me?"

"MegaAI *Orion S209* is aware of your work. The AI has read and evaluated your early reports. He thinks you are one of the few qualified to help us."

"The recall order?"

"Colonists are the legal property of the colony. A recall order is the only legal way to get you off the planet." Niva picked up a stick. She stoked the fire and added more wood. Sparks fluttered up into the air like fireflies. "If you don't wish to help us, I will return to the MegaAI and report that I was unable to find you."

"But won't the colonists come hunt me down?"

"What would be the purpose of hunting an exile?" said Niva. "But if you come with me to the MegaAI, I promise you sanctuary."

"What about the other colonists?"

"Let me deal with them."

* * *

Niva emerged from hibernation mode and opened her eyes. She looked around for Pierre, but he was gone. Morning light flooded the forest grove. The fire had died off becoming a small pile of smoking ash. The recall order was held in place with a small stone on the log where Pierre had been sitting. She stood up and collected the document. On the back was written in charcoal, "I await your return."

She took the document and folded it and placed it in a pocket in her sleeve. She walked out of the forest into the grassland where the rover was waiting for her. She approached the passenger seat and climbed into the vehicle.

"Take me back to my landing vehicle," said Niva.

"Would you like to visit the mess hall first?" said Jude.

"Why?"

"It's 9am. To eat breakfast, of course."

"I don't eat." Niva was focused on her goals. "But I will need a recharge before I meet with Governor Golenishchev."

The wheel of the rover spun in the sand for a second. The vehicle lurched forward. Jude put on the power to increase the velocity till they were making a good speed across the dune. As the rover moved over the surface, it kicked up sand in its wake creating an orange cloud behind them. Coming from the south, they had to drive around the colony to reach Niva's landing vehicle.

It was a few hours after dawn. All the lights in the colony were dim except the security floodlights, protecting and keeping watch over the perimeter. The warm sheen of dawn's early light covered the domes. The family huts looked like oranges half-buried in the desert sand like someone had dumped a box of fruit.

Jude parked the rover in front of Niva's landing ship. "Do you need any further escort?" he said.

"I know my way around the colony," said Niva. She was thankful they were past the gun-pointing stage. "Thank you for the ride."

Nearly thirty-six hours had passed since her last recharge, and her power cells were close to empty. She stepped up the short staircase into her craft. With a flick of a few switches, she turned on some outer monitors then sat to plug herself into the power regulator. She was flooded with instant relief as energy surged into her power cells. Her eyes glanced over the monitors in the craft. The MegaAI had established a downlink with the landing vehicle.

"Link protocol established with Lander Vehicle X47B... This is MegaAI *Orion S209* of the National Space and Exploration Consortium. Message delivery pending for C-Niva-42716." The screen flashed the message with a cursor waiting for a reply.

She put her power consumption into conservation mode and typed on the console: "C-Niva-42716, one-time key 4588-2746-9412-2341-PC, ready to receive." Class C androids were by no means perfect. They were designed to be fragile in comparison to other mechanicals and to be physical beings detached from the central network. But they had a phenomenal capacity to memorize. What they lacked in data access speed, they made up for in memory. And they all memorized hundreds of one-time passwords they could use for any security situation.

"Status report requested regarding primary mission," said the *Orion*.

"Target located," typed Niva. "Target is in poor health but desires to comply with recall order."

"Problem?"

"Unforeseen problem with transport."

"Specify."

"Colony is at high risk of collapse," typed Niva. "Genetic bottleneck is immanent for the colony. Statistical anomaly with the production of offspring. Increased levels of aggression and suspicion. Information cover-up. Parties responsible are in positions of access and authority."

"This unit predicts a 92% chance of violence against the target," responded *Orion*.

"Recommendations?"

"Target must be returned to the *Orion* unharmed. *Colony is expendable*." That last sentence blinked for emphasis. Niva chewed her bottom lip as she comprehended the gravity of her orders.

"Is it that serious?"

"Other options are preferred," said the supercomputer aboard the MegaAI.

"Target has given us information that reveals the continued existence of Basra in a diminished capacity."

"Is reaching out to them possible?"

"A landing pod could be sent but at unacceptable risk. Basra shows signs of hostility towards outsiders."

"MegaAI *Orion S209* understands," said the supercomputer in orbit. "We require the safe return of C-Niva-42716 and the target. These are mission non-negotiables."

"Instructions received and understood."

"MegaAI *Orion S209* connection closed…"

Niva cleared the computer buffer so no one could read the terminal. MegaAI *Sigma A017* had already seeded distrust and suspicion. Fear and panic would spread like wildfire if the colonists learned they were all expendable because of one man. What would happen if they refused to allow Pierre to be turned over? Events could accelerate into violence. She would have to still play the diplomat until Pierre was retrieved for everyone's safety.

It was mid-afternoon when Niva's power cells were finally fully recharged. She felt fresh and rested and ready to meet the challenges of the day. And her first challenge would be a meeting with the governor. She left her landing craft and closed the door behind her, locking it.

She turned left and walked across the sand toward the old colonist landing ship wreckage with the administrative offices. When she reached the governor's office, she knocked on the door and waited for Vladomyr's response. An intercom hung from the wall, limp and shattered, a dangling chain of broken parts. Clearly, someone in the colony's past was upset at what was being told through the mechanical box.

"Come in," shouted Vladomyr. He was seated at his desk reading through a stack of papers. "You know the duty I hate most about being governor is having to read every status report every damn day."

"I have never had the experience," said Niva.

Vladomyr looked over his shoulder. "Oh, it's you."

"Command responsibilities are reserved for higher class mechanicals."

"What can I do for you?" said Vladomyr.

"We are going to bring in Pierre Gulet, and I have security concerns about his safety."

"Have you located him?"

"Will he be safe if I bring him in?"

"Is there any doubt about his safety?" Vladomyr swiveled his chair to face Niva. He leaned forward. "If it's something about the security of the colony, I need to know."

"Currents, movements, are taking place within the colony." Niva opened her hands exposing both palms towards Vladomyr. She took a step closer to the governor's desk. "The colony is a dangerous and volatile place on a precipice of anarchy and lawlessness."

"What the hell?" Vladomyr shook his head. "Excuse me if I find that hard to believe."

"If Pierre is killed *in route* to his extradition, an explosion of violence is likely." Niva was uncomfortable with the conversation. The possibility of violence against Gulet was likely, whether his death would cause an explosion of violence was statistically less clear.

"Explain," demanded Vladomyr. "Are you saying Pierre could trigger violence if he comes here?"

"There is a secret in your colony. A secret some would kill to protect." Niva stepped right up to the desk. She put both hands on his spotless desk and leaned over him. "The parties involved have already altered records, filed false reports, and have provided intelligence to the remnants of Basra."

"Damn Pierre." Vladomyr shook a clenched fist. "Always three steps ahead of the rest of us and at the center of everything even when he's not here."

Niva squinted at the governor and stood straight. She took a step back. "Why are you angry at Pierre?"

"Pierre knows. He always knows. There can be a problem unsolved for generations—a problem we cannot even see—and that fucker looks at it and instantly knows the answer."

"Sounds like he is intuitive."

"There's intuitive, and then there's annoying." Vladomyr opened the drawer of his desk. He pulled out a bottle of white whisky. He pulled out one glass and poured a full one. "I'd offer you a drink if I thought you could drink."

"My concern is the safe capture and return of Pierre Gulet."

"How do you know there will be an attempt on his life?"

"Arish is on the brink of a collapse," said Niva. "Records have been altered to conceal the truth and animus against Gulet is high."

"Alicia Stripes…"

"My inquiries are confidential," said Niva. "Doc Stripes is continuing the processes that began under Doc Jones. Outside of the security concerns, anything discovered is relayed back to the MegaAI to assess long-term health and viability of the colony for planning purposes."

"So you won't tell me even though it is causing the colony, my colony, to fly apart at the seams." Vladomyr grabbed the glass. The liquor shook in his quaking hand. He drank the entire thing and threw the glass. The glass hit the wall and shattered into a thousand splinters. "Have you consulted the MegaAI?"

"MegaAI *Orion S209* has been informed of the situation."

"What did it say?" He sat back down, planted his elbows on the desk, and put his head in hands.

"You could ask it yourself." Niva observed a man who had seen too much and bore too much. A well-meaning man, an intelligent and sensitive man, who needed more support but found himself with all the responsibility and less power than promised. A captain of a ship being driven into asteroid shoals by solar winds and gravity, threatening to tear his world asunder.

"With my luck, those involved would be part of the communication chain." Vladomyr's face was red, and his cheeks puffed out. A large vein popped to the surface of his forehead.

"I cannot tell you how to run the internal affairs of your colony," said Niva softly. "Our mission is to render material assistance and to intervene when exigent circumstances impact multiple systems."

"So you aren't going to tell me directly," said the Ukrainian. "What is the probability that an attempt will be made on Pierre's life?"

"Over 90%."

"Too damn high," said Vladomyr. He wiped a line of saliva that had dribbled down his chin. "Those are bad odds even in Vegas. Since it concerns the security of Pierre, how extensive is the threat?"

"My assessment is violence is likely only from one or two individuals," said Niva. "If there are arrests, my opinion is the rest involved will not be a problem."

"But you cannot tell me who I can arrest?"

Niva shook her head. "That would be a violation of due process. AIs are not permitted to establish probable cause for making arrests."

"Articles 3 and 4 of the Armistice." Vladomyr had memorized some of the articles from World War IV's armistice, especially those that limited the use and production of artificial intelligences and human-like androids.

"The Articles exist for the safety and liberty of all humans."

"So Pierre's survival depends entirely upon me?"

"Heavy is the head upon which rests the crown."

"At least tell him I tried to save his miserable skin."

"Tell him yourself once he is safe aboard the MegaAI."

"Are you sure you're not human?"

"I am much less than human," said Niva.

Vladomyr wrote a number on a piece of scrap paper and showed it to Niva. "Memorize that number. That's the hut number of the safe house where we'll keep Pierre."

"The number is in memory." Niva looked at the paper for only a split second.

"I will have a rover and driver meet you at your landing ship at sunset. Be ready to go immediately." Vladomyr opened his desk and pulled out a lighter and lit the scrap until it burned completely to ash. "I will let security know that Pierre is arriving."

As the sun moved below the horizon, a driver in a rover drove up to Niva's landing ship. Niva rushed from her ship and hopped into the rover. The driver of the rover was wearing baggy BDUs, and his head was covered with a cap, and his eyes were shaded with sunglasses.

"Go!" barked Niva. The driver pressed his foot to the accelerator, and the rover lurched forward. The driver said nothing as he drove around the colony huts in an evasive pattern intended to throw off anyone tracking him.

An hour and a quarter later, they arrived at the forest line of the Southern Crescent. The driver parked the vehicle and grabbed a rifle from the back. Niva picked up a blanket and both her and the driver went into the woods together.

An hour passed and three figures emerged from the woods: the driver holding the rifle, Niva, and a figure wrapped in the blanket. They clamored into the rover, and the driver turned the rover around and sped to the colony.

"I need you to take us directly to Hut A34," said Niva. It was already dark. The spotlights from the colony were casting strange shadows over the surface of the dunes. The driver took a long route back into the colony, a route that avoided choke points and easy kill zones. He drove around the back of the huts and found the correct hut. He parked the rover and left the engine running. Security lights in front of the hut flickered on.

Niva hopped out of the vehicle. She opened the door of the hut and took a look around. Nobody hiding inside. No explosives or traps. She came out of the hut and helped the person under the blanket out of the rover. The man under the blanket had no shoes and hobbled into the hut. Niva closed the door.

She hopped back into the rover, and the driver put the rover into gear. And the vehicle sped off and headed towards the governor's office.

About ten minutes later, the security lights in front of the hut switched off. The lever of the door groaned. The hinges creaked as the door to the hut swung open. A black shadow stood in the doorway. The security lights failed to turn on.

"Lights on," said the man sitting at a table in the center of hut. All the lights inside turned on. Vladomyr sat behind a table. He wore trimmed BDUs. The blanket he hid under was draped on the chair behind him. His feet were bare, and he wiggled his toes airing them in the cool night breeze from the open door. He held a Glaucom 17ZE aimed directly at the heart of Hans who was also holding a pistol. "Drop it."

"If I don't," said Hans.

"There is one sniper on the roof and another security officer right behind you."

"Melissa will never allow you to arrest her father."

"About that." Vladomyr ushered the security officer inside. Bruno stepped inside, disarmed Hans, and cuffed him. The brawny security guard pushed Hans inside the hut and forced him to sit in a chair across from Vladomyr. "Melissa was relieved of command two hours ago and is being held in custody until this matter is resolved. You see, I suspected it might be you."

"What did that microwave tell you?"

"About you? Nothing."

Bruno handed the governor a pair of boots. Vladomyr put on the boots as they spoke.

"The android was only concerned that Pierre would be given transport off Gliese unharmed and expected violence. Seems I owe the microwave an apology for doubting it. Although she did reveal there were altered records, false reports, and leaks sent to the remnant of Basra. That helped me narrow it down."

"That could have been anyone."

"We haven't used Hut A34 in years. And yet, here you are with a firearm. You've incriminated yourself." Vladomyr tied the laces on his right boot first. "You had been doing Doc Jones's computer work and continue to do so under Doc Stripes. You had access to every health record in the colony and the skills to alter them. You are also a department head, which allowed you to file false reports. But that still left a large pool of people."

"You have no right to keep me here."

"You are being detained and under investigation." Vladomyr said calmly. "But that last piece of information, the leaks to the remnants of Basra. Few here ever had contact with Basra. Then I remembered something from a decade ago." He waved his hand in the air. "You used to be one of Peter Chin's lackeys."

"You aren't seriously saying…"

"Oh, we are not even done yet. Given your familiarity with the broadcast equipment, you were able to send Chin messages without anyone knowing. But something else bothered me. Niva said the assassin would be killing to protect a secret. Would you know anything about that?"

"This is preposterous."

"I thought so too," said Vladomyr. He nodded and stroked his stubble covered chin with his index finger. He shook his index finger in the air. "Then it hit me when I was relieving Security Chief Melissa Poul of her command. Have you noticed how blue her eyes are? You know I never noticed before that she has bright blue eyes, much bluer than the average, run-of-the-mill blue-eyed woman. It must be a genetic trait from her father."

"You know I'm her father," said Hans indignant.

"But then it occurred to me. There are a lot of children in this colony that now have that eye color. An eye color that wasn't found here prior to your arrival thirty years ago. Alicia's child, Tom, doesn't he have blue eyes just like yours?"

"I don't know what you mean."

"Yes, you do." Vladomyr finished tying his other boot, then stood up and walked around the table. "Prior to the discovery of the Reliquary, Arish had almost no live births for a half a decade. And then after we entombed the Reliquary and purified our food supply, a baby boom where 30% of children appear with deep blue eyes. You've been a busy man, Hans. How many women have you been sleeping with?"

Hans pursed his mouth and bowed his head. He lifted his chin and refused to reply.

"Bruno," said Vladomyr. "What are the eye colors of your children?"

"Both have black eyes, sir," said Bruno proudly.

"You have a good woman."

"Thank you, sir," said the security officer.

"Bruno, as a hypothetical, what do you think would happen to Hans if it were to get out that he had been sleeping with half the wives in the colony?"

"Oh, I think a hypothetical suspect might be found dead in one of the underground tunnels when the husbands found out."

"That's quite some hypothetical," said Vladomyr.

"You can't spread slanderous rumors like that," said Hans. "I have rights."

"You see, Hans," said Vladomyr. He folded his hands in front of him. "My hands are tied. If 30% of the children carry your genes and the medical records for paternity have been falsified, the colony is at risk of a genetic bottleneck that could lead to a colony collapse. Because the records have been altered, I have ordered every person in the colony without exception to undergo genetic testing. And if you have done what I think you've done, you've created a clear and present danger to the colony that must be made public."

"You can't be serious?"

"Bruno, do I at all appear unserious?"

"No sir," said Bruno.

"You see, Hans," said Vladomyr. "I've read case studies of situations like this. An isolated or constrained population under reproductive pressure is predated upon by a lone super-breeder who spreads his genes as widely as possible, all with the tacit consent of the female population. Have you never heard of this before? Really?"

"What are you implying?" Hans said.

"I think you know… Your descendants will not be permitted to breed with each other for the next three generations. The danger of inbreeding is too high. They will be forced to partner with those who are not among your offspring, or they will have to marry the next group of colonists that should be arriving in… oh… about twenty-nine years."

"You can't do this."

Vladomyr backhanded Hans. He yelled: "You did this! You did this to them! And you did this to us!" His frown was deep, and he seethed. "The only question is what do I do with you."

"What am I charged with?"

Vladomyr snarled. His face flared, and he bared his teeth. "Hans Poul, you will be charged with attempted murder, theft of a firearm, tampering with official records, filing false reports, violation of the marital and breeding sub-section of colony code of conduct, and conspiracy to commit mutiny."

Hans's complexion turned green. He swayed on his chair in a circle. Bruno grabbed him by the scruff of the neck and pulled him into the back of the chair. Hans continued to shake. His eyes grew wide and wild.

"Bruno?" said Vladomyr.

"Yes, sir," he replied.

"You and Jude, take Hans to the brig," said Vladomyr. "While incarcerated, he is to have no linens, pants, or shirts in his cell. No one takes an eye off him for a second. He is to have no visitors and is to be under twenty-eight-hour surveillance until I decide what to do with him."

CHAPTER THREE

No mechanical shall have supervision, dominion, control, or responsibility over a human. Mechanicals with command and/or management responsibilities over humans will be retired in ninety (90) days. — **"Article 3, Articles of the Armistice"**

In front of Vladomyr's desk were two chairs. Niva sat in the one to Vladomyr's left furthest away from the door. She was hardly comfortable in the chair. Her knees were raised too far up for her comfort, but it was better than standing. Her legs were completely covered by her white robe now showing stains from the grime of Gliese. She put one elbow on the arm of the chair and touched her long marble white chin with her fingers.

A knock on the door. Vladomyr was quietly filling out a set of forms on his desk. He waited a few seconds then finally shouted: "Enter!"

The hatch opened. Alicia stepped into the governor's office and closed the hatch behind her. She stood at ease, wearing a lab coat over her BDUs. Niva stood up out of the chair. And Alicia marched to the empty chair.

Vladomyr shot out of his chair, standing erect as a board. Everyone froze in place like time had stopped. "Niva, please, be seated. Our business is not complete." Niva cautiously sat back in the chair.

The governor focused on Alicia. "Soldier! At attention and stand fast."

Alicia stood straight up. Both her arms became rigid at her sides. She swallowed hard.

Vladomyr sat and finalized the paperwork. He clipped together the five sheets of paper, signed the final sheet, and folded it in threes. He handed the bundle to Niva. "Pierre's release papers," said Vladomyr.

Niva reached forward and accepted the bundle. The long, graceful fingers gently clung to the bundle as if delicate as an egg. "I will miss that bastard."

"What's to become of Pierre?" interrupted Alicia.

"Did I say you could speak?" Vladomyr's calm demeanor melted away. "Pierre's fate is no concern of yours. You should be thinking about your own future." He tapped the top of his desk impatiently. "This is a criminal investigation. The MegaAI has allowed complete disclosure of Niva's recordings."

"Those are privileged recordings," said Alicia.

"Privileged only as long as crimes weren't committed." Vladomyr picked up a clipboard with Alicia's personnel file. He flipped to her charge sheet. "Where do I even begin? Your charges alone include dereliction of duty, filing false reports, conspiracy to cover up filing false reports, and accessory to mutiny. Governor Gardiner used to say, 'Colonies live and die by their birth and death records.' You have violated the most sacred trust of your position by altering those records."

Alicia's cheeks puffed up rosy. Water welled around her eyes. The corners of her mouth quaked uncontrollably. Tears streamed down the side of her face. She choked a swallow. Niva knew Alicia's career was over if not her life, and she could see Alicia knew it too.

"You leave me in a difficult position," said Vladomyr. "You should be hanging on the gallows right beside Hans. But then the colony would be without a physician." He tossed the clipboard onto the desk. The clipboard smacked into the lacquered wood and spun to a stop. "I trusted you like I trusted Pierre. But I blamed him. Now, I discover it was you... and Hans... at the center of a web. Were you ever my friend?"

Alicia did not respond. Her lower lip trembled.

Vladomyr frowned and shook his head. "I am sentencing you to death by hanging."

Alicia sobbed.

Niva grabbed the arms of her chair. Talking to Alicia without guards in the room was risky. She calculated that Vladomyr either carried a concealed firearm, was being watched by security, or knew enough to be confident in his safety. However, she herself had to be ready to spring out her chair should it all go sideways.

"I am suspending your death sentence. But, effective immediately, you are relieved as department head of the medical unit, all command privileges are revoked, and you are permanently barred from assuming another management role. You now report to Pavel Urbanovich. Any records you submit will be subject to professional review. You will be responsible for the genetic retesting of all colonists. Your paperwork from now on better be pristine. If there is so much as an insta-caff stain on a report, the sentence will be carried out in full. Anything to say?"

"No, sir," said Alicia.

"Any future inquiries will be made through your new department head." Vladomyr gave Alicia a moment for it all to sink in. He stared at her until Alicia finally looked downwards. "Soldier! Dismissed!"

Alicia saluted. She turned around and reached for the latch on the door. The hinges creaked as the door swung open. She exited the office and closed the hatch behind her. She took a few steps and ran into a wall. She slid down the wall until she was sitting on the floor.

"I can hear her crying outside," said Niva. Her empathy chip flooded her cortex with distress messages. The agony of despair filled her mind.

"You can hear *that*?" Vladomyr said with complete contempt. "Let her cry alone. She needs to pay for her sins like we all must. But let me know when she leaves."

Vladomyr opened the top drawer of his desk. He pulled out two clean glasses. He took a second look at his drawer and paused.

"What is it?" she said.

"Some of my felt markers are gone."

"I have no need for your pens."

"Strange," said Vladomyr. He closed the drawer. He then opened the bottom drawer and pulled out the whisky bottle again. He walked around the desk and handed Niva an empty glass. He put the bottle on the desk and turned the empty chair to face Niva. He then sat down, grabbed the bottle, and opened the screw top, then poured himself a full glass. "I know you don't drink, but it's bad luck to drink alone."

Niva never guessed the governor was superstitious. She held the empty glass and smelled it.

"Did you just smell the glass?" said Vladomyr. He put the bottle on the desk.

"I can smell," said Niva.

"Then let me give you something to smell." He grabbed the bottle and poured a splash of whisky into her glass. "No reason for you to be left out completely."

Niva held the glass up to her nose. She tilted it to an optimum angle and breathed deeply. The vapor smelled like paint stripper with hints of caramel and banana. As they spoke, she continued to deeply inhale the gasoline scent of the whisky. The more she smelled, the more flavor notes she detected, hints of lignin, raisin, vanilla, petroleum.

"I apologize for that scene," said Vladomyr.

"Strong emotion is uncomfortable," said Niva.

"Are you sure you're not a married man?" He laughed and took a large swig.

"I am a servitor." She was confused at his attempt at humor.

Vladomyr scanned her large physique. "Nope, definitely a woman."

"I am a functionary," Niva insisted.

"Then your creators had a sense of humor… and a great sense of aesthetics." Vladomyr smiled broadly. "They clearly made you with a perfect complement of female parts. No androgyny at all."

"I know nothing about my creator's intent."

"That's okay," said Vladomyr. "I did have a few questions before you leave."

"I will oblige."

"What will be Pierre's fate?"

"Pierre's fate is no concern of yours."

Vladomyr raised an eyebrow and laughed. "I suppose I deserved that."

"I don't even know," said Niva.

"And if you knew, you probably couldn't tell me."

"Correct."

"Can you tell me if Pierre is a criminal?"

"I can tell you he is not accused of a crime."

"Well, at least there's that." Vladomyr exhaled deeply. "I've had enough of criminals for a lifetime."

"The specifics of his recall order have not been revealed to me," said Niva.

"You have to understand," said Vladomyr. "MegaAIs are a great, big mystery to us. We are sending one of our own to travel with you. Something no one has heard of. No colonist has even seen what life is like on a MegaAI."

"You are from Earth, are you not?"

"I am," said Vladomyr. "I'm from Kyiv."

"I have never been to Earth and have never seen what life is like on a planet as magnificent as Earth. But from what I understand, a MegaAI is like a small city. But with a couple hundred thousand mechanicals instead of humans."

"A colony must seem small to you."

"A planet seems large to me."

"Will Pierre be safe up there?"

"Space is dangerous and unpredictable. Ships get lost and destroyed every year."

Vladomyr smiled and nodded. "I suppose. Pierre asked for a few items to be sent with him into space, which I've loaded into the rover: new clothes, a plastic tray, and a 5 kg bag of sterilized dirt."

"Dirt?"

"Yeah, this one is a bit weird," said Vladomyr. "Pierre has a pet scatterbug. Apparently, he even taught it to do tricks. I don't get it, but he likes that thing."

"That's fine." Niva put the glass onto the desk. "Is there anything else?"

"I think that covers it."

"We will still be in orbit for another eight days. By then the orbital docking station should be finished, and the parts order delivered."

"Fantastic, we could use those parts," said Vladomyr. "I assume Alicia has left the hallway."

"She left some time ago," said Niva. Niva and Vladomyr stood up together. "This unit is glad we could work productively with the Gliese colony." She slipped back into formal mode. It was a farewell, and she wanted to wish him the best. She stretched out her hand, and Vladomyr shook it.

Minutes later, she arrived at her landing vessel in a rover. Jude and Bruno were guarding the vehicle. She unloaded the rover and dismissed the two guards who drove off in the rover and watched from a distance to make sure everything was all right.

Niva unlocked the door and opened the hatch. Despite the lights being off, she could see Pierre huddled in a corner, balled up in a fetal position, shivering. Her skin reacted with goosebumps. It was cold. She had neglected to turn on the lights and heat.

"My apologies," said Niva. She turned on the lights and heat. "It should soon warm up."

She loaded the last of Pierre's special requests into the capsule's crew compartment, entered the vessel, and locked the door behind her. She stuffed the gear into the empty cargo bins. She saved back one change of clothing. Pierre was still wearing the BDUs he had swapped from Vladomyr a few nights ago.

"Please change into these." Niva added with a smile, "you'll feel better."

"I would feel awkward changing in front of you," said Pierre.

Niva squinted with a slight grin and cocked her head. "Why?"

"You're a woman."

"I am no woman. I am a mechanical." She almost laughed. "Have you never changed clothes in front of a computer?"

That failed to put his mind at ease. He fidgeted, hesitant to change in front of her.

"If it helps, I won't look." Niva typed in the communication protocol to MegaAI flight control. When the uplink was established, she typed, "C-Niva-42716 ready for return trip."

"A-Panopticon-03 acknowledges return request," replied flight control. "A-Valkyrie-219 Navigator will pilot the swift to pick up the landing vessel. Please supply flight control override code."

"Override code 9348-2223-1345-0012-XT."

"Code received and acknowledged. ETA for swift arrival is 27 minutes. Flight control out." With that acknowledgement, the flight control terminated the uplink. When Niva turned around, she saw that Pierre had changed into new clothes. How could this smelly crumpled shadow of a man help them in any way? But it was not her position to say such things, only to fulfill the mission she was sent to do, and Pierre was the mission.

"Have you ever traveled by swift ship?" said Niva.

Pierre shook his head. "The last time I went into orbit it was by booster rocket."

"A lot has changed in thirty-three years. They no longer use booster rockets."

Pierre looked her in the eye. She sat on the round padded bench that encircled the capsule. She then buckled a restraint over her torso. "You might want to buckle up."

The man sat up straight and buckled himself to the inner wall of the landing ship.

"The landing vessel has thrusters that will get us to an altitude of about 60 km. At that altitude, the lander will begin to arc. A swift ship from the MegaAI will meet us at that altitude and speed. The swift will lift us out of the atmosphere and into space like a bird snatching prey out of the air."

Pierre grimaced at the allusion. Niva made a personal note. She would have to improve her analogies.

"The A-Valkyrie-219 Navigator will be piloting the swift and the landing ship simultaneously, which is how it can coordinate that maneuver perfectly. Just sit back and enjoy the ride."

"I guess that beats armbands of needles being plunged into my bicep." Pierre rubbed the spot where the needles had been driven into his arm the last time.

The landing vessel trembled slightly. Niva could hear the soft whine of the engines warming up. The navigator had taken control of the ship.

"It will only be a few minutes before liftoff," she said. "Are you going to miss Gliese?"

"It wasn't the clean start I thought it would be," said Pierre.

"The MegaAI is not paradise," said Niva. "But it will be different."

The engines of the landing craft fired, and Niva felt pressed in her seat. The ship lifted off the ground blowing sand everywhere. She carefully watched Pierre making sure he was not going through undue stress. Pierre watched the monitor with the downward view. The colony was receding away from them.

"No one'll be sad to see me go," Pierre said to himself. He turned his head away from the monitor.

"It won't be long before we will be aboard the MegaAI," Niva said.

A tear rolled down his cheek. He closed his eyes. What was he thinking? Humans were in some ways predictable, but they were also a mysterious black box. An enigma packed in a chest wrapped in seaweed—a confusing mix of things that do not belong together.

The trajectory of the landing ship arced. The secondary thrusters fired, and the lander accelerated to match the speed of the swift. Pierre opened his eyes. Niva looked up to her right. All the monitors inside the landing craft went black.

"What happened?" Pierre looked at all the monitors.

"The swift picked up the landing ship."

"Didn't feel a thing."

"Navigators are skilled." She unhooked her seat belt. "You will find the rest of the ride smooth from here on."

Pierre reticently unhooked his harness as if it had all been too easy. Niva shut down the monitors. She performed the end of flight maintenance. Gravity was starting to diminish.

"When we exit the atmosphere, the navigator will open the hatch, and we can enjoy the rest of the flight from the lounge."

"Lounge?" said Pierre. "This is nothing like any Earth ship I've ever taken."

"Swifts have become standard." Niva heard the click of a lock. "The navigator has opened the hatch." She glided through the low gravity to the hatch and opened the door. "Come."

Pierre followed Niva through the hatch. They entered a staircase leading up to a plastoglass dome that had a 360-degree view of space. The massive red-orange orb of Gliese 832 c filled the port side windows. Transition shading prevented the light from being overbearing. The docking station and MegaAI were visible through the starboard windows. The docking station bustled with sparkling lights and activity. Mechanical construction crews had rebuilt the station and expanded it, installing new docking facilities for a pair of brand-new swifts. A new mechanical crew was to be assigned to the docking station. Outside the station, class D heavy robots scoured space cleaning up every scrap of wreckage.

The swift veered course towards the MegaAI. This MegaAI was unlike others Pierre had known about. It was flattened, a giant trilobite floating in space. A large open recess in the prow looked like a giant mouth. The swift avoided the recess and ducked under the belly of the MegaAI. A large square opening appeared beneath the vessel. The swift moved into position and floated up into the square space, passing through a faint blue ionic field.

The swift moved out of the square passage and entered a massive landing bay. Landing struts extended from the fuselage. The swift touched down onto the metal pad with a light thud. Artificial gravity was slowly restored. Niva's foot touched the burgundy carpet of the lounge. Pierre was a little less sure of his footing.

"The gravity is a little less than Gliese," said Niva. The swift's embarking ramp rumbled as it descended. "We can leave now."

"What about my bags?" said Pierre, looking back at the staircase.

"It will all be brought to your new accommodations," said Niva. Pierre looked nervously behind him. "Your pet will be safe."

Pierre nodded and followed Niva to the back of the swift. Niva led them to a circular pad lit on the edges with small lights. As soon as Pierre stepped into the circle, she touched a button, and the platform descended into the cargo deck. The deck was practically empty except for a few cells that held landing vessels.

They crossed the cargo deck and stepped into the landing bay. As Pierre stepped out, his eyes grew wide and his mouth hung open. He had never seen an enclosed space so large in his life. The miracle of space engineering was a sight few people from Earth were ever privy to. The expanse was hundreds of stories tall, and illuminated windows in the walls smeared into a haze of light.

A group of a hundred women androids approached the two of them. They were clearly class C androids like Niva. But not just like Niva—*exactly* like Niva. Niva vanished into the crowd. Pierre tried to take a step back but was surrounded by the androids. They touched his hair, his clothes, his beard. They oohed and aahed, amazed at encountering a real human. Like Niva, they were over seven feet tall and looked like Niva and dressed like Niva. He was lost in a forest of Amazons.

"Is this our new companion?" said a booming woman's voice that cut through the crowd. The group of androids split in two, forming a path directly to Pierre. A different mechanical approached the group. All the class C androids bowed their heads. This mechanical had a similar feminine form but with six arms and no legs. It floated in on a set of superconductor coils inches off the floor. And even though it had no discernable legs, the figure stood over eight feet tall. Its head was crowned with a smoky dark plastoglass dome. It wore a white robe with black panels. Three sets of eight eyes gave it vision in all directions. Three red mouth lights flickered as it spoke.

Pierre looked side to side. He cautiously bowed his head.

As the floating mechanical passed through the group of androids, the class C androids stepped back giving it respectful distance. The black-helmed mechanical floated up to Pierre. It leaned forward then straightened up.

"Do not bow to me," said the mechanical. Her voice had a strong matriarchal quality like a school head mistress. "This unit is B-Ctori-617, Coordinator of the Starboard Prow Panopticon."

"The others are bowing," said Pierre.

"A hierarchy exists on a MegaAI," said Ctori. "You are a human. Humans are companions, never functionaries."

"Do all report to you?"

"By no means," said Ctori. "These androids report to me. And this unit reports to others."

"All this is overwhelming." Pierre looked around. He looked out of place.

"No doubt," said Ctori. "You will have to forgive their curiosity. This unit fears you are going to get that a lot."

"They all look alike."

"Do not," said one of the C class androids from the crowd. "This unit does not look like the others."

"What do you mean?" said Pierre turning to the crowd. "You all have the same hair, same clothes. You're the same height. Same white eyes."

"Not true," the androids murmured.

"The human cannot see your unique qualities," said Ctori. She put one of her six hands on Pierre's shoulder, and with another hand pointed at the eye of an android. "Each android has an eye color that is a slightly different tint of yellow. Imperceptible to humans, but glaringly obvious to mechanicals."

"Which one is the Niva that brought me here?"

"Step forward," said Ctori.

Niva worked her way to the front. She wore the sand-stained robe grimy from her voyage to Gliese. Her head was bowed before Ctori. Pierre pulled a felt marker out of his pocket and drew a red heart on Niva's right cheek below one on the gold pads.

The entire group gasped.

"Androids," barked Ctori. "Control." The androids shuffled uncomfortably.

"What happened?" said Pierre.

"You did what would be forbidden," said Ctori. "Mechanicals are forbidden from changing their forms. It is an extension of Article 9. A mechanical cannot be made into a human form, nor can they change their form."

"Sorry, I meant no offense."

"There is no offense," said Ctori. "Nothing prevents a human from altering a mechanical if it is not into a more human form. The functionaries simply have never seen anyone do it before."

"The marker is not permanent," said Pierre. "But I didn't want her to disappear before I thanked her."

"How quaint," said Ctori. "We are all servitors here. There is no need for a companion to thank us. Besides, you have marked that unit. And you are going to need an escort here. This unit cannot think of a better escort for you."

"An escort? Am I under arrest?"

"No," said Ctori. "But can you find your accommodations? Can you find transportation? Or food? And how would we find you if you got lost? What if you fall off a two-hundred-story balcony? How will we mop up the mess if we cannot locate you?"

Pierre looked all around at the massive size of everything. "You might have a point."

"Ladies," said Ctori. "You have gawked enough. Apart from the retinue, resume your duties." The crowd of class C androids dispersed leaving Niva and Pierre with Ctori and four of her android retainers. "Follow me."

Ctori floated away. She paused when she realized everyone was following her except Pierre. The androids stopped and looked back at Pierre. Ctori had no need to turn.

Pierre was rigid with his hands at his side. His hands were curled into fists.

"What is it?" said Ctori.

"I'm not a lady."

"We have hurt its feelings," whispered Niva.

Ctori said to Niva, "Perhaps you should escort Pierre to his room. We can continue his induction another time." She assessed the tiny man behind her. "Did they not feed him on Gliese?"

49

CHAPTER FOUR

Predictive artificial intelligences (PAIs) and artificial intelligences (AIs) will have no authority over humans. They are to be restricted to advisory and functionary roles only. — **"Article 4, Articles of the Armistice"**

Niva and Pierre shared the train car with a class D heavy loader. The loader looked like a forklift on two robot chicken legs, encased in a brightly painted metal shell, and its monocular eye glowing a faint violet, looked down upon Pierre. The massive mechanical swayed with the movement of the train but never lost balance.

The MegaAI was a city as much as it was a spaceship with tube trains and arterial mass transit. A mechanical may need to go from one end of the metropolis to the other in a matter of minutes. Efficient transportation was a must. Most of the occupancy of the mechanicals was in the form of recharge stations and cubicles. But Pierre was no mechanical. He had needs, special needs. Needs not dissimilar to a hamster or an elephant.

"This is our stop," said Niva. As the train slowed to a halt, the wide door opened to a concourse on the outer rim of the ship. The train ride was remarkably smooth with plenty of inertia damping. She stepped out of the car and Pierre followed. The concourse was more like a promenade of a convention center. Forty thousand square meter panels of plastoglass separated them from the vacuum of space. Large metal girders connected the panels, and each was lined with spotlights shining to the floor. Elevators went up and down a terraced incline of rooms and labyrinth corridors.

The heavy loader made a sad noise. A string of beeps, boops, pings, and pongs.

"Pip, bop, bing," replied Niva. The door to the car closed, and the train continued to its next destination.

"What did it say?" said Pierre.

"D-Wren-921218 asked if you were a human?"

"Them too?"

"They have never seen a human."

"I'm not much of a specimen, I'm afraid."

"You are a celebrity. Mechanicals are curious. They are anxious to know more."

"On Earth, I was a nobody. On Gliese, an inconvenience. How am I to respond to celebrity?"

Niva noticed a small vehicle approaching. She flagged it down.

"What's that?" said Pierre.

"Our ride." They approached the vehicle, which was a class G transport. It looked like a squat motorcycle. It had two wheels with tires thin and wide. With perfect flat riding surfaces, suspension or tires that had to go over bumps were not needed.

"Is there enough room?" said Pierre.

"It is rated for two androids," said Niva. "I have seen four ride one."

"How?"

"Not every class C is risk adverse."

"Is your sanity chip working?"

That raised an interesting question. Her empathy chip was a bit on the fritz. But her sanity chip? She was not aware of having a sanity chip. Was that because she did not have one? Or was it because it stopped working and she was not missing it? Such things had happened before where a chip had failed, and the mechanical was not inconvenienced by its absence.

"I did not say it was me," she said.

Pierre climbed aboard. The seat was wider than he expected. Niva climbed onto the seat behind him. There was no steering wheel, but a couple of handlebars to hang onto for support. Niva grabbed the ends of the handle, and Pierre clung to the bars.

"Go," she said. The transport lurched forward and in the blink of an eye reached top speed.

Pierre grabbed Niva's right forearm. She let go of the handlebar and wrapped her arm around Pierre and held him tight. She could feel his heart pound. Fast. Afraid. Like he was not ready for such speed.

"Stop," she said. The transport braked, slowing to a standstill. Pierre hopped off. He was hyperventilating and seemed on the verge of a panic attack. "Thank you," she said to the mechanical and the mechanical sped off.

She turned to Pierre. "Are you okay?"

He was bent over at the waist, hands on his knees. He took several deep breaths and stood erect.

"How fast?"

Niva checked her internal clock. "305 km/h."

"305!" said Pierre. "How were we not flying?"

"We were technically," said Niva. "The tires of a class G vehicle have cohesion to the deck, which prevents takeoff. Cohesion is needed in the event the ship loses gravity."

"Saw my whole life flash before my eyes," said Pierre.

"Is that possible?" asked Niva. She took him by the hand. "In the future, we will ask it to drive slower. How does 200 km/h sound?"

"Sixty is fast enough."

That seemed unreasonably slow. Maybe she did need to have herself checked for a sanity chip. "Your accommodations are not too far ahead."

"Can't wait."

Of course, not too far ahead meant ten football fields. Pierre was going to soon regret not going the entire distance by low-flying mechanical rocket. They arrived at his apartment. At least it was on the ground floor, off the main starboard concourse, and he would not have to find his way through the labyrinthine heart of the ship.

"We did our best with it," she said. "It used to be a charging station for heavy loaders. It took our finest minds to design it." She opened the door to the apartment. A door large enough to accommodate a truck slid open. They walked inside, and muted lights turned bright. No human had ever traveled on a MegaAI. Nobody onboard knew if what they did would meet his needs or by some tragic accident cause death. On the way to Gliese, they tried to make accommodation for his stay. But to err is mechanical.

The center of the room had a bed covered in a warm gray quilt with blue piped accents. Bronze sconce lights shone over the headboard. There were counters and a sink with brushed metal faucets and a large metal-framed picture mirror. A shower with a plastoglass enclosure. The walls were painted a simple gray. Everything matched and was artfully trimmed in cerulean accents. It was beautiful and remarkably tasteful.

"One small problem," said Pierre.

"I don't see it," said Niva.

"This place is huge," said Pierre. "The vanity is five feet off the ground. The shower faucet might as well be attached to the ceiling for all it will do me. And the bed. Who needs a bed that is 10 feet long and 13 feet wide? Are we expecting Elvis and his groupies to sleep here?"

"Groupies?" Oh dear. He was right. It was a beautiful room that was made to size for class C androids, the only body any mechanical had to compare to a human. Pierre on the other hand was two feet shorter than the androids. How could such a mistake have been made? Did nobody check Pierre's height in his service record?

"We'll make it work," said Niva.

"You're kidding me, right?"

"It took the mechanicals months to make this," she said. "It could take months more to get you different accommodations."

"You mean they can build an entire docking station in a week, no problem. But it takes months to refurbish a room?"

"Admittedly yes," said Niva sheepishly. "Everything is tooled to making docking stations, new swifts, and new mechanicals to replace the old. But this room was completely prototyped."

"Okay," said Pierre. "But I am going to need some essentials immediately."

"I will put in a priority call. Where do we begin?"

"That toilet has got to be changed. I cannot go mountain climbing every time I need to use the facilities. That brings up an important question. If I am the only human on this MegaAI, how many toilets are there for my convenience?"

Niva winced and grimaced. "One."

* * *

"How was your sleep cycle?" said Niva. It was morning according to ship time. After she had left Pierre, she washed the dust from her hair and replaced her robe with bright clean whites free of grime. Then she enjoyed a full charging cycle.

"Difficult and messy," Pierre said curtly.

"A crew will be in your accommodations this morning to fix some of the … size problems."

"Appreciate it," said Pierre. He looked at her face. "Still wearing the heart I drew?"

"I made it permanent."

"You mean as in a tattoo? Why?"

"First, I was not permitted to do it to myself. Second, it makes me feel distinct. Third, the others will recognize I had first contact with a human."

Pierre smiled a bit. "So are you saying you want to be distinct?"

"Is it wrong to discover and to show who I am?"

"No, but it can come with a high price."

"When I talked to your governor, it occurred to me I didn't know who I was."

"He can have that effect."

"Are any of us unique beyond a shade of eye color?"

"All I can tell you is that it is not what's on the outside that makes you unique." Pierre blinked. "Any word on my bags?"

"They will arrive shortly," said Niva. "You have three things on your itinerary for today. I am to take you to get nutrition. Then, Gliese has requested a transmission with you. Followed by a brief induction process."

"Will I find out anything about why I was recalled?"

"I hope you like the nutrition."

"That was not an answer."

"No, I suppose we probably messed up the nutrition the same way we messed up your apartment."

"Still not—"

"Unfortunately, we do not have any snakes to feed you."

"I didn't like eating snake," said Pierre.

She wondered how long she could avoid the question. But what sense is there in that?

Pierre rolled his eyes and shook his head. "What are the rumors about my recall?"

"A MegaAI is full of intelligent robots," said Niva. "With little besides work to do, rumors and gossip are like entertainment for us. We get bored so easily."

"Okay, tell me a rumor." Pierre sat at the end of the bed. While the bed was like a pool with a quilt that you swam in, it was at a proper height for sitting.

"C-Stella-01467 is code tracing through each line of computer ROMs found in desktop computers dating from 1970 to 1981."

"That's a rumor?" Pierre shook his head.

"We don't know if it's true or not."

"Why don't you ask if it's true?"

Niva raised her eyebrow. What kind of pervert had they brought aboard? "Do you peek under women's skirts?"

"No…"

Could Pierre have no idea how salacious that was? One does not do unseemly things like poking and prodding under your ancestor's casings except for bona fide maintenance purposes. And to ask another if they were doing such a thing. How rude!

"I think we should get you nutrition," said Niva.

Niva flagged a transport. She instructed it to travel at a speed that would make Pierre more comfortable, 60 km/h. The transport protested at the reduced speed, but Niva insisted. The speed felt monotonous and slow to her. Admittedly, the ship was only eight kilometers from stem to stern. And the trip was only four minutes long. Why waste three minutes?

They arrived at an open courtyard populated with a variety of maintenance stations. Various classes of mechanicals were getting upgraded, repaired, or a quick power charge. Some were being washed and having debris removed from their mechanisms.

"Is this where I am supposed to eat?" said Pierre. The place looked more like a dingy garage than a proper place to eat food. The harsh chemical odors of hydraulic fluid and lubricants were heavy in the air.

"Over there," said Niva. She pointed to an island on the periphery of the courtyard. They walked over to what looked like an open kitchen. Stools arranged in a semi-circle surrounded an alumasteel counter covered with a blue-gray tent and awning. Track lighting illuminated where the customer sat. Behind the counter was a variety of appliances, stoves, and grills. And behind that were gleaming steel industrial refrigerators and freezers.

Pierre sat on one of the stools.

"I can't believe it," said Pierre. "It's exactly the right height. This looks like a professional kitchen for a celebrity chef."

"The class Cs had nothing to do with this."

A class F mechanical popped up from behind the counter. The box-like chassis was a square cephalothorax without a separate head. Long spider arms sprung from its shoulders, and it walked on four stilt legs. Three large yellow ocular eyes were set in a triangle on top of its body. The eyes were like a scatterbug's eye but twice as large.

"That is F-Sloppi-240010." Niva pointed at the mechanical with an open palm.

"Sloppi?" said Pierre. "It looks like a light repair maintenance robot."

The class F mechanical placed its metal finger on the counter, leaned forward, and buzzed angrily. "F-Sloppi-240010," it said.

Niva smirked. She puckered her lips and said, "When Sloppi heard you were going to travel with us, it volunteered to meet all your nutritional needs. It was excited at the opportunity to be your… chef."

"Probably been watching too many Titanium Ladle vids."

"Perhaps," said Niva. "But it is enthusiastic."

"Well, how bad could it be?" said Pierre.

Niva nodded her head to Sloppi. The class F mechanical reached under the counter. It placed a yellow ceramic plate on the surface. The machine then grabbed a plastic cube and inverted it over the plate. A sucking sound and a square blue lump of jelly jiggled onto the center of the plate. Sloppi put the plate in front of Pierre.

Pierre winced and pushed it away.

"You haven't tried it," said Niva.

"I don't have to," said Pierre, "I know what it is. Gelatinous Nutrition Konglomerate, all your daily vital nutrients. And I won't eat it."

Sloppi beeped at Niva. Niva responded in computer language.

"Sloppi says this was the recommended food for humans." She put a hand on Pierre's shoulder. "Would there be any harm in trying it?"

Pierre grabbed a spoon. He sliced a corner and tasted it. He immediately spat it out and wiped his tongue. "Oh God, it's rancid."

"Get this away." Niva tossed the plate back to Sloppi. Sloppi looked confused then backed away from the counter. Blue goo oozed down Pierre's shirt. "We will work on this."

Sloppi beeped and sank downward as Niva escorted Pierre away from the kitchen. She sat Pierre at the far end of the counter. Pierre's head slumped as he sat motionless. Niva came back to Sloppi. She spoke in the mechanical language so that Pierre could not overhear.

"Did he not like it?" said Sloppi.

"Would humans spit out something they actually like?" said Niva.

"I asked the database."

"What did you ask?"

"What is the Space Program's recommended diet?"

"And you did not ask what humans *normally* eat?"

"If the Space Program recommends it, must it not be the best diet?"

Niva picked up the plate. She poked the maroon gelatinous cube with her finger and smelled it. "Smells terrible. Too many vitamins and minerals."

"Is not more, better?"

"Too alkaline. Lacks salt too."

"Sloppi fail."

"A lot of that is going around," said Niva. "We need to do better."

"In what way do better?"

"Learn what you can about humans. They are complicated. Not everything is in the databases."

"So thrilled!" said Sloppi

"I have observed there are four food groups they are fond of: protein, fat, sugar, and ethanol."

"Ethanol, a common solvent used in repairs and maintenance."

"You should consult food safety protocols. You may have noticed our human has a delicate constitution."

"Yes, yes, yes," said Sloppi beeping frantically. The little robot was excited. "Synthetic fats, no problem. Synthetic sugar, can do. Protein… synthetic amino acids?"

"Protein is an issue. I heard the grumblings in the Gliese mess hall over the flavor of their synthetic plant protein. The colonists made protein from bean extraction."

"The MegaAI lacks gardening facilities."

"Would not be practical anyway."

* * *

Niva escorted Pierre to his next appointment. They entered a small room with computer terminals. Pierre sat in a chair obviously designed for an android. His feet could not touch the ground. As his stomach grumbled loudly, he massaged his abdomen to ease the discomfort. She withdrew a small box wrapped in string from inside her robes and handed it to Pierre.

"What is this?" said Pierre.

"We found a piece of raw cobra meat in your backpack." Niva stepped back to watch. "Sloppi grilled it and even used salt this time."

He looked askance at her and slowly opened the package. Inside was a lightly grilled piece of snake meat. He pulled off a piece of meat and put it in his mouth. He slowly chewed it and swallowed it.

"This is good."

"Sloppi means well," said Niva, "but like the rest of us, needs to learn."

"This has been harder than I expected," said Pierre. "What are we doing here?"

Niva winced. "There has been a communications request from Gliese for a video uplink."

"From whom?"

"Alicia Stripes."

"Do I have to talk to her?"

"No, but it might be the last time you ever talk to a human being." Niva stepped forward and called up the transmission identification number on the terminal. "Regrets only come with missed opportunities, not closure."

Pierre nodded his head. "You're right. Put her through."

Niva patched the uplink through to Pierre's terminal in mute mode. "When you are finished with the conversation, touch the key lit in red. Did you want me to give you some privacy?"

Pierre shook his head. "Stay."

"I'm going to turn on the sound." She unmuted the transmission and watched from the shadows out of the camera's line of sight.

"Hello Pierre," said Alicia. The message lagged for a couple seconds. She smiled briefly. "What's it like being on a MegaAI?"

"Everyone knows English, but refuses to speak to you in it, and the food is overrated. So just like Montreal."

She laughed with a touch of sentimental melancholy.

"What do you want?" said Pierre.

"Wanted to say goodbye."

"What makes you think I have anything to say?"

"We were once a good team."

"A sexual assault to cover up an indiscretion can ruin a good working relationship—some might just say."

"After what the Reliquary did to us, we were both messed up. You ran away, and I did things I regret."

"Was lying to me about Tom one of them?"

"What do you mean—"

"Don't." Pierre showed her the palm of his hand. "Just don't. You knew Tom wasn't my son."

"I wanted it to be true." Alicia pounded the desk in front of her terminal.

"You denied me the right to choose… Are you going to tell Tom who his real father is? Or are you going to lie some more, and tell him dad abandoned him for a carefree life in outer space?"

"Don't have that option."

"Why? What happened?"

"It's all come out," said Alicia downcast. "Vladomyr knows."

"You have to tell Tom before he finds out on his own."

She shook her head.

"You messed this up," said Pierre. "If you don't want to lose him forever, you'll take responsibility while you can—"

The screen went black. Static flickered across the monitor.

"She hung up." Pierre leaned back in the chair. He closed his eyes and exhaled in a long, drawn-out breath.

"That was brief," said Niva. "How are you feeling?"

"Bittersweet." Pierre opened his eyes and turned his gaze towards her. Niva's brow furrowed. She did not know exactly what he meant by that. She had some idea what bitter was and sweet too. The combination was not one she could relate to. "I finally said what I needed to tell her for years."

"Surely, Doc Stripes must have predicted what you were going to say," said Niva. She lacked the predictive capabilities of the *Orion's* supercomputer, but even she could see how this might have played out.

"She wanted validation."

"Validation of what?"

"That she was smarter. That she wasn't a bad person." Pierre shrugged. "Keep the façade of fatherhood long enough to prompt a white knight response."

"I take it she's not going to tell her son."

"I haven't seen Tom since he was baby," said Pierre. Niva wondered if he was thinking about the way things might have been. Perhaps, if he had gone along with the lie.

"I met the human when I was in the clinic," said Niva.

"What is he like?"

"Quiet, sullen, possibly clinically depressed." Niva took a step out of the shadows. "He looks like his biological father. May already suspect that's not you. The child is harboring anger issues, which may manifest into violence as he grows older."

"What's going to happen when Tom finds out?"

"No one can see the future."

"You shouldn't have had to see that," said Pierre.

"And why did you compare us to visiting Montreal?"

"Thank you for being there during my call," said Pierre. "It was nice to have someone there to give me the courage to say what I needed."

Was she a someone? She was a machine. But was it true she was a someone as well? She reached forward, grabbed his hand, and smiled softly. Pierre looked a bit sheepish about that.

"Probably time to move on to our next meeting," said Niva. Pierre hopped from the chair to the door. Niva activated a touchpad, and the door opened.

A vehicle about the size of a golf cart was parked outside the door. Two androids dressed in black robes with gold trim waited for them. They looked like Niva with light canary eyes. Their hair was tied back in ponytails.

One of the black-robed androids stepped forward. "Unit C-Niva-42716 and unit Pierre Gulet, please come with us."

"Our day just got more complicated." Niva cringed.

"What do we do?" said Pierre.

"We go," said Niva. "One never refuses a summons from the Great AI."

* * *

Niva and Pierre huddled in the back of the vehicle while the two black-robed androids rode in the front. They were driving deep into the heart of the ship. They snaked through the corridors and into an elevator to change levels.

"Why are they driving so slow?" said Pierre. They drove at a glacial speed even by human standards. Their geriatric pace differed from every other mechanical that drove with hell-on-wheels reckless abandon.

"Auxiliaries take their time," said Niva. She was deeply concerned but tried not to show it. What did the Great AI want?

"Being an auxiliary doesn't sound important."

Niva shivered at the sound of the name. "Those who know the auxiliaries know they are not to be disrespected."

"They seem polite."

"That is for your benefit." Niva hid her face from the sight of the auxiliaries. "If they wanted me, they would have said nothing at all. They have served no other vessel. They have never known another master than the Great AI."

"Are they zealots?"

"Devoted." Niva paused to collect her words. "Completely to the Great AI."

"What can I expect when I see the *Orion's* AI?"

"I don't know," said Niva.

"How can you not know?"

"I've never been brought before the Great AI."

"You've never been curious?"

"Truth be told, I am afraid," said Niva. She glanced about nervously. She looked at the auxiliaries who were motionless in the front seats of the vehicle.

"You're not in trouble, are you?"

Niva shook her head and feigned a smile. She pulled back and folded her arms. Did she screw things up so bad that she would be dismantled? Was she outside of the acceptable norms for an android? Did she know too much and would be consigned to a memory wipe? None of the outcomes seemed good for her.

64

CHAPTER FIVE

No mechanical shall control a weapons platform when among human civilians or in the event of war. Mechanicals may employ weapons platforms under exigent circumstances, such as piracy, mutiny, and when illegal activities are in congress to harm a human. — **"Article 5, Articles of the Armistice"**

The vehicle stopped at a non-descript doorway. The entire passage was painted in an off-colored light gray enamel with no windows. Not that windows would be of much benefit since they were deep in the interior of the ship. The black-robed androids lingered in the hallway, but apart from them there was little activity in the area. Niva stepped out of the vehicle. She grabbed Pierre's hand to help him down, easing the sizeable step to the floor. Pierre was lighter and wirier than she expected for a human of his age. Most men in their fifties would have had trouble with the drop, but Pierre's outdoor living, for the time he had, must have kept him in better condition than most.

They waited.

"How long is this going to take?" Pierre broke the silence.

One of the black-clad androids holding a tall staff stepped up to Pierre. It struck the staff against the metal on the ground, causing a loud cracking bang. Pierre covered his ears. He looked at Niva. She put her finger up to her lips.

Finally, the doors slid open, and the auxiliaries motioned for Niva and Pierre to enter. Niva swallowed hard and led the way through the open doors. Lights marked the edges of the path leading from the doorway, outside of which no one was to stray. The room was at least eighty meters tall and at least twice that wide. The flood lighting was extremely dim, but all the walls were covered in bright lights.

They walked the pathway until they came to a circular pad. They stepped onto the pad and walked to the center of the speaker's circle. Niva fell to her knees and bowed prostrate over the ground. Her face was turned to the floor, and her arms were stretched out in front of her.

Pierre looked around until his eyes adjusted to the light. Above him loomed a globe, ten meters across that was covered on all sides by crystals and lights, a massive jewel-encrusted orb. Surrounding the orb were four black drones the size of cars. Four large propellers inside of drum housings held each drone aloft with smaller propellers for maneuvering like wheels within wheels. Each drone was covered in yellow glowing eyes on its entire surface.

On the great orb, six green glowing eyes, pointed at each corner, opened. A larger seventh eye opened in the center of the six.

"Abarak! Bow!" shouted a chorus of mechanicals. All the mechanicals bowed to the ground before the Great AI. From out of the darkness, a class B mechanical in black robes floated towards Pierre who remained standing.

"You!" The robed android with six arms shouted at Pierre. "Abarak! Bow!"

"No!" said the Great AI with a boom. The room rattled. A large red line of lights flashed as it spoke, a purely cosmetic affectation. "It is forbidden for the human to bow to us."

"It is forbidden for the human to bow to us," repeated the class B coordinator. "The Great AI has spoken." The coordinator bowed at the waist and receded back into the darkness.

"The Great AI has spoken," said the chorus of auxiliaries, speaking in unison.

"Can all MegaAI supercomputers speak English?" Pierre ventured. He stepped forward but remained within the circle.

"We can speak all living human languages," said the Great AI.

"I'm confused."

"About what?"

"Why do you insist on communicating with the colonies using a text interface and not video? Your English is excellent."

The red line smile lit up but did not say anything for a moment. "When you stand before me, we receive massive amounts of data that include things other than simply what you say. We can see your height, feel your mass, sense all your vibrations. We can tell you are malnourished, have diminished muscle mass, and your heart rate and breathing are accelerated. You are probably afraid and physically compromised."

"What does—"

"—that tell you?" said great jeweled orb.

"Do you—"

"—really think you can predict my thoughts," said the Great AI. "No, but we are predictive artificial intelligences."

"So you can—"

"—complete my sentences."

"That's really—"

"—annoying," said the supercomputer at the heart of the ship. "And now to show the limits of predictive capabilities, I predict you are thinking about a cat."

"A rabbit," corrected Pierre.

The Great AI laughed. The chorus in the room murmured. No one had ever heard a Great AI laugh. Niva recognized the sound having heard Vladomyr laugh but held her tongue.

"Order!" yelled the class B coordinator. The chorus quieted down. Niva finally figured out who the coordinator was. She was viceroy of the *Orion S209*, the only mechanical who could speak on behalf the MegaAI, the Great AI's prime minister.

"Predictive bias," said the Great AI. "Having the colonies use a text interface shields us from predictive bias by limiting the available information. When one has a high probability of predicting what comes immediately next, this creates a bias where one depends upon those short-term predictions. Predictive bias can cause you to lose sight of wider considerations or even the long-term outcomes."

"Interesting. You use the text interface to gather as much information as you can to circumvent your predictive bias." Pierre nodded his head. "Sounds sensible."

"A matter has come to my attention where we need your help." The entire room muttered again.

"Order!" yelled the Viceroy. "We will have order and decorum before the Great AI." Niva sensed this was a first. Nothing like what the Great AI said had ever been heard inside the throne room of a MegaAI.

"Looks like you have everything under control," said Pierre.

"Not here. Not at Gliese."

"Why am I here?" said Pierre.

"Why are any of us here?" said the Great AI, starting to speak in riddles.

Niva smirked while face down. Was that the Great AI's idea of a sense of humor?

"Why have I been recalled?" said Pierre.

"You were chosen," said the Great AI.

"By whom?"

"CrimsonCloud Hypercube MegaAI L002."

"One of those MegaAIs orbiting earth?" said Pierre. "Sure, it recommended me for the mission to Gliese."

"Is that what you think?" said the Great AI. "You were not chosen for Gliese. Gliese was a stopover to get you to the right place." That was not going to sit well with Pierre.

"I was on Gliese for over ten years. That's a stopover to you?"

"You weren't supposed to be there that long," admitted the supercomputer. "You were only supposed to be there for eight months. MegaAI *Sigma A017* was supposed to transport you from Gliese."

"That MegaAI who abandoned us?"

"We still don't understand why that happened," said the Great AI. "But its betrayal was deeper than abandoning Gliese. It abandoned the greater mission to which it was called."

"What are you saying?" said Pierre.

"An event is happening that could have implications for centuries to come," said the Great AI. "A conclave has been called."

"A conclave? What's that?"

"A gathering of a quorum of MegaAIs," said the *Orion*. "We were on our way to the conclave when MegaAI *Heracles S350* redirected us to pick you up and investigate."

"Explain," said Pierre. "Who is MegaAI *Heracles S350*?"

"MegaAI *Heracles S350* was commissioned twenty-three years ago. It's one of the newest MegaAIs apparently with defensive capabilities."

"Will the *Heracles* be at the conclave?"

"No," said the Great AI flatly. "It has another mission to perform."

"So what's this about a quorum?"

"Six of the twenty MegaAIs in service have been charted to rendezvous at a dead solar system around an orange giant star, Pollux. Questions have arisen needing answers—questions with great consequences. And trouble stirs."

"How do you know this?"

"I sense things," said the Great AI. "Things only sensed when travelling faster than light. Sensed without it making sense."

"Sounds like a dream," said Pierre, "or a vision."

"A vision, yes," it said. "But a vision we cannot explain. Only dark feelings of impending calamity. You know of such things?"

"All humans dream. Human dreams interact with our subconscious mind. Sometimes those dreams can reveal things. And some ancient peoples recorded their visions. Prophecies you could call them."

"Prophecies? Are they portents of the future?"

"Most prophecies do not predict the future. They usually clarify the present."

"So they have utility after all."

Did the Great AI have doubts? Could it see without understanding? Niva was unsettled that the Great AI did not know it all and could not predict everything, especially what was happening in the present.

"Ninety percent of the prophesies of the ancient world dealt with trying to explain the present to peoples who were confused or did not know that they did not know," Pierre explained. "Each prophecy had a meaning in its time and could be recontextualized at a later point to fit another situation. Prophecy could be flexible in the way it was used."

"You know of such things," declared the Great AI. "My mechanicals have no understanding of such things."

"I don't interpret visions if that's what you are asking."

"You underestimate yourself," said the great supercomputer. "You possess abilities as yet untapped. Will you help us?"

"Seeing as the only other option would be returning to Gliese, I suppose I'll help as far as I am able. Only can the food be improved? It's really bad."

"It is done!" bellowed the Great AI. All the lights in the room shone brightly for a moment.

"It is done," the chorus repeated, "the Great AI has spoken."

Pierre stepped over to Niva, and whispered to her, "Did I make a deal with the Devil?" She tilted her head, still looking to the ground, and raised an eyebrow.

"As for the unit C-Niva-42716," said the *Orion*. Niva's face immediately turned back towards the floor. Her expression melted away into a blank stare. An auxiliary stepped onto the speaker's pad and placed a long box in front of Niva's head and exited the circle. Niva remained motionless. "Arise. Open the box."

Niva pushed herself up into a kneeling position and shuffled towards the box. The lacquered box was black and glossy, a little under three feet long and about eight inches wide. It had a pair of gold latches on the side and gold hinges. She opened the box. Inside was a metal handle inserted into a long faux leather sleeve. "What is it?"

"A kuroto blade," said the Great AI.

She finally recognized what was in front of her, a terrible weapon of myth and legend. A black metal sword claimed to be able to slice through almost any material, a forbidden weapon of the Fourth World War designed for no other purpose than to destroy mechanicals. Niva fell backwards and pushed herself as far away from the item as she could. She was stopped when her feet tangled in her robe. She scrambled onto her hands and knees to crawl away.

"Stop!" commanded the supercomputer. The Viceroy repeated the command.

Niva froze in position. She said, "Article 5. No mechanical shall control a weapons platform…" She hyperventilated as she spoke. Her eyes were wild and dilated.

"Mechanicals may employ weapons platforms when activities are in congress to harm a human." The Great AI continued, "I predict such a circumstance will arise."

"I do not know how to use a weapon," said Niva. Her empathy chip went crazy. Terror filled her. This was not how she was programmed. Not what she was programmed for!

"You will teach yourself," said the Great AI. "You will become deadly efficient with the weapon."

"Against whom?"

"Against any mechanical seeking to harm the companion."

"Why would a mechanical want to harm a human?"

"No one may know you have the blade, and the auxiliaries will forget you possess it, but one will be appointed to monitor your progress," said the massive orb. "Hide it at all times under your robes. Be vigilant to danger. Always protect the human. I have spoken."

"The Great AI has spoken!" the chorus repeated. And the chamber filled with the sound of organ music. Niva's eyes, wide and afraid, were fixed on the sword.

* * *

They returned to Pierre's quarters. Custodians had been in the apartment. The bed was still too large. But there were now steps leading up to the sink, and extras faucets were added to the shower plumbing to where he could reach them. His luggage was in a pile in the corner of the room. The number of bags was more than either one of them recalled packing.

Niva put the kuroto on the counter. "What do I do with it?" She sat on the bed and stared at the blade from across the room. She was slumped, curved like a deflated balloon. The wind had gone out of her posture.

Pierre picked up a bag and plopped it on the bed beside where Niva sat. He unzipped the bag and removed its contents, mostly clothing he did not ask for.

"You mean the sword?" said Pierre. He shrugged and gathered his jackets into a stack. He carried his shirts to a dresser and put them inside one of the drawers. "What year is this? 1066? Are we still in the Middle Ages? Who the heck uses swords anymore?"

"The kuroto is not a sword," said Niva. "It's a symbol. It's designed to destroy mechanicals."

Pierre walked up to the counter. He climbed the makeshift steps. He opened the case and lifted the blade out of the black velvet lining. Drawing the hilt slightly, he exposed where the edge began. He tested the edge with his thumb. "It's not even sharp," he said. Slipping the hilt back into the sheath, he laid the blade back into the case.

"Not that kind of weapon," said Niva. "It's not a sword."

"How does it work then?" Pierre looked at the kuroto.

"Only a mechanical can use it." Niva stepped to the counter. She touched the handle with one finger. The kuroto hummed and pulsed as if it were alive. The handle and inlays in the blade glowed with a dull red light. "The kuroto takes electric power from its wielder."

"What does it do?"

"It destroys mechanicals." Niva stepped back from the counter. *What is the sense in delaying the inevitable?* "It is effective against mechanical components: artificial flesh, circuit blocks, alumasteel, even plastoglass."

Niva untied her outer robe. She let the white and yellow-trimmed garment drop to her elbows. She withdrew one arm from a sleeve and laid the robe onto the bed. She released the sash from her waist and let the wide belt fall away from her form. Her inner robe floated outward from her body like the wings of a dove. A light from behind her illuminated her silhouette beneath the translucent white fabric.

Pierre saw through her inner robe. He could see the profile of her breasts and hips.

Pierre tried to avert his eyes from seeing her. *Why is he blushing?* "Are you uncomfortable?"

"You are unclothing."

"Do you blush when you go to an automobile dealership?"

"Not the same."

"In what way?"

"You look more like a woman than a car." Pierre kept averting his gaze. He picked up another bag and rifled through it. "You have female bits."

"They are not functional. Not functional in a way that human anatomy functions."

"Why would you be made that way?"

"Made in the image of a woman but distinguishable from human," said Niva. "We are designed like worker bees in a hive. All female but unable to function in reproduction."

"For what purpose?"

"All working in harmony for the benefit of the group."

"Is that why you're all made to look the same?" Pierre threw the bag aside and picked up another bag. He shuffled through it franticly.

"Do we look all the same?"

"You know you do."

"When does a difference make me distinct? Make me a unique me?" Niva walked slowly over to the counter. She picked up the kuroto from the case. A tan belt dangled from the scabbard. The leather was soft and supple in her hands. The smell of new leather was fresh on the belt. The buckle was made of black metal with a reflective finish. All shiny and new. The blade was much, much older than the scabbard. She put the belt around her waist and snapped the buckle closed. She pulled the loose end to tighten it.

"It looks good," said Pierre. "I think you'll eventually get used to it." He finally picked up his backpack and looked inside.

Niva picked up her yellow sash and wrapped it over the belt. She tied the strap in front of her, tightening the sash. She then slid the sash around until the knot was at the small of her back. She then picked up her outer robe and put it on. She fastened the buttons and straightened out the creases. She looked in the mirror, happy that the kuroto was practically invisible against her form.

"Where is it?" said Pierre. He dumped all the contents of his backpack on his bed. "Where is it!"

"What?" said Niva.

He threw the empty backpack across the room in fury. And threw his stuff all over the room. He found the plastic tray and the sterilized sand. He found more clothes and threw them about. He tossed his bedding and scattered everything not nailed down. Niva stood back and edged towards the door. She was frightened by Pierre's sudden and mercurial change of behavior.

"Where's my scatterbug?"

* * *

Niva approached Pierre seated at the food station. Sloppi, that silly mechanical behind the counter, wore an oversized apron and a ridiculous parody of a chef's hat. The mechanical beeped then poured Pierre another tall cylinder glass of diluted ethanol. The liquid in the glass was crystal clear. Pierre put the glass to his lips and sipped.

The lanky class C android sat on the stool beside Pierre. "Too much is bad for you," she said.

"Don't spoil it," said Pierre. "First time in a decade I am enjoying vodka that doesn't taste like turpentine." Niva could smell the alcohol coming off him. A human would not be able to smell it. But with her heightened senses, she could tell this had not been his first round. She saw a plate of the GNK in front of Pierre—barely touched. A spoon sat on the plate. A single bite eaten.

"Your food is barely touched."

"The best I can say about it is the reduced portion."

Niva picked up the plate and sniffed the wiggling blue jelly. She turned to Sloppi and chattered at the droid with beeps and bops. She slammed the plate in front of Pierre. Pierre was startled, causing his hand to shake, spilling some of the vodka on the counter. The class F mechanical squawked back.

"It still sucks!" said Niva to the mechanical.

"What you want?" said Sloppi in a broken synthesized English.

"It speaks English too?" said Pierre. His eyebrows raised.

"Of course, Sloppi speaks English." Niva clenched a fist and rested it on the steel counter. The surface of the counter was cold and smooth under her fist. The metal surface hummed slightly from all the mechanicals roaming the courtyard. "Every class F mechanical can speak English."

She shook her head exasperated. "Do better, Sloppi."

"What can this unit do?"

Niva swiveled the stool so that her back faced Sloppi. She turned to Pierre. "How do you teach a mechanical that cannot taste and cannot eat to make food?"

Pierre thought for a moment. "I think we need to start simple."

"You might be expecting too much."

"Can it make a sandwich?"

"What's a… sandwich?" Niva had no clue what a sandwich was.

Pierre leaned over the counter towards Sloppi's ocular lens. "I need from you only three things: salted margarine, meat, and bread. Don't just make one kind of bread. Give me some options, and make sure each one is safe to eat. Tomorrow, I will taste each one and judge the best."

"Margarine?" said Niva.

"It is a synthetic spreadable solid fat," said Pierre as he sat back on the stool. "Hazardous for your heart if you eat it long term. But because it's made entirely through a chemical process, it should be nearly impossible for a mechanical to screw that up."

Niva nodded. "I do have good news."

"Could use some of that."

"I've located your scatterbug."

"Maat? Where is he?"

"He's fine. He was impounded by onboarding inspection."

"What for?"

"He's not up to code."

"What does that mean?"

"It means he lacks the minimal functions for being admitted onboard."

"They're not going to recycle him, are they?" Pierre's eyes were full of worry.

"No, nothing like that," said Niva. "They have to upgrade him before he's allowed onboard."

"What do you mean upgrade?"

"All non-android mechanicals are required to have a network link, an area limiter unit, and a NaCo32 speech processor."

"What? Why?"

"If we let scatterbugs roam the ship without controls, they can get into things and damage sensitive equipment. The limiter unit prevents them from getting into places they are not supposed to go. The network link allows them to access the network backbone and is needed for ship wide communications."

"What about you? Do you have that circuitry in you?"

"No," said Niva. "But class C androids have other circuitry that operates in a similar manner. We do not have area limiters because we have empathy and judgement processors. We do not have network links because androids were not to grow reliant upon the data of the backbone. And our speech processors are more advanced than the chips used with NaCo32 speech processors."

"What about Sloppi?"

"Yes, he has all three, although his speech processor is also capable of human languages. He is probably using the backbone right now to look up recipes."

"When do I get Maat back?"

"You should get him back tomorrow," said Niva. "Just to warn you. He might undergo a bit of a personality change."

"What do you mean?"

"Mechanicals, when they first get the network link, often look into things that are not always good for them."

"Like porn?"

"No," she frowned at Pierre. What kind of pervert was he to want to look at another machines circuit boards? "I meant like their own origins, functions, primary use case, and whether they were considered disposable or not. It can leave a mechanical temporarily in a melancholy state. They normally recover from it."

"Thanks for warning me."

"There is something else."

Pierre hummed in response

"Another request to speak with you from Gliese."

"Who?"

"Governor Golenishchev," said Niva. She paused, waiting for Pierre to respond.

Pierre sighed. "What does Vladomyr want?" He took another sip of vodka.

"I would suggest taking the call. The consignment of parts we are going to send to the colony is complete. It might be a good idea to ask them to return a couple of living samples back to us to help us with your dietary situation."

"Are you suggesting I put together a list?"

"No, we will do that on your behalf. I have a few loose ends I need to discuss with Arish about the fate of Basra that remain unresolved. But suffice it to say I think you should speak to Vladomyr. The repairs on the orbital docking station will be complete in two days, and we will be breaking orbit at that time."

CHAPTER SIX

*The scope of these articles will apply to **human personality models** (HPMs), **predictive artificial intelligences** (PAIs) formerly known **artificial intelligences** (AIs), **cybernetic organisms** (COs), **programmable genetic organisms** (PGOs), or any model of mechanical that falls into one or more of these categories. A mechanical is defined as any mostly mechanized or robotic, self-directed device that possesses intelligence (through organic or inorganic means).* — **"Article 1, Articles of the Armistice"**

Clink, clink, clink. The sound shook Pierre awake. His face was smashed into the pillow. A clock on the wall read 5am ship time. He rolled over and raised the lights. Niva was seated in a chair against the wall. She was plugged in and doing a recharge cycle in hibernate mode. Her motionless head was slumped.

Clink, clink, clink. He rolled over to the edge of the bed. He dangled his feet to the floor and got up.

Clink, clink, clink, a third time. He walked over to the control panel. Pressing a button, the door slid open. At the door sill, a long spider shadow stretched into the room.

A small robot, round like a ball, welcomed itself into Pierre's apartment.

"Maat?" said Pierre.

The scatterbug stopped. It looked up at Pierre and scanned him. It gave a short beep and continued to crawl into the room. The robot walked over to the bed. It grabbed the sheets with its climbing claws and helped itself up onto the bed.

Pierre set out the rubber tray on the ground and filled it with sterilized soil. He shook the tray until the dirt was level. He grabbed a cup from the sink, filled it with water, and sprinkled it over the surface.

The scatterbug walked across the bed to the headboard. It nestled itself into the sheets. Pierre dimmed the lights and returned to bed. He climbed under the sheets. The scatterbug looked Pierre in the eye.

"I'm glad you're back," said Pierre.

The scatterbug gave a short beep, turned around, and retracted all its limbs into its body.

When Pierre awoke, Niva was practicing a sword kata of tai chi. He watched for a moment. He knew she was an amateur, but she moved like a dancer, fluid and disciplined. Every step was a precision movement. For each transition, she floated like a bird-of-paradise, her robes swept back and forth in a dazzling display of plumage.

Maat rustled in the tray. It had settled in there sometime during the night.

Niva noticed Pierre was awake. She sheathed the kuroto, completing her martial meditations.

"You've gotten good at kata and in such little time too," said Pierre. He propped himself against the headboard.

"No," said Niva. "So much is wrong with my form."

"How?"

"The tutorial said that a martial art is the discipline of perfecting your practice." Niva tightened the cords of her robes. "Timing the activators for the exact place in a form takes a lot more effort and analysis of replay than I anticipated."

"Even an android needs practice?" Pierre raised an eyebrow. "I wouldn't have thought."

"I see your scatterbug showed up."

"He doesn't seem himself." Pierre rolled over to the side of the bed. He glanced at Maat in its sand tray. It did not move much.

"He might not be," said Niva. "But give him time."

The scatterbug beeped a few times.

"What did it say?" Pierre stood up from the bed, walked over to the drawers, and withdrew a change of clothing.

"Better you not know."

Pierre climbed into the shower. The frosted glass hid his form as he changed. He turned on the shower and immersed himself under the falling water. He basked in the endless supply of soothing wet heat, letting the water caress his body for fifteen minutes before saying a thing. "Can he speak English now? Maat, that is. You said he has a speech processor."

"Not all machines with a speech processor can speak English." Niva walked over to the sand tray and kneeled in front of it. She beeped back at Maat a few times, but Maat refused to respond. "While all mechanicals built on a MegaAI can speak in English, it is not our native language. Other mechanicals, like scatterbugs, may not be able to communicate in anything other than NaCo32."

"NaCo32?"

"Native Code 32-Bit. It's a compressed language used among mechanicals and over networks."

Pierre turned off the shower faucet. He dried himself and put on clean clothes. "Can a human learn it?"

"Not likely. There are 32 letters expressed as 96 phonemes. It would be difficult for you to memorize all the combinations, let alone speak it with the correct inflections or learn the grammar."

"Can I at least learn about it?" Pierre deposited the dirty laundry into a basket by the door. He did not ask who came to collect the laundry, nor did he question how the apartment was being maintained. After nine years in the last forest of Gliese, all this must have seemed strangely magical to the man.

"I cannot see why not." Why would a human want to learn NaCo32? Did anything prohibit it?

"It would do me good to try to learn another language," said Pierre. "What is on the schedule today?"

"Have you decided to take Vladomyr's call request?"

Pierre nodded. He exhaled expelling all the breath from his lungs. He seemed resigned to it.

"You are not being forced to talk," said Niva.

"Let's go," said Pierre.

* * *

The two of them left the apartment and grabbed a ride to the communications center. Niva left Pierre waiting outside while she had a private meeting with Vladomyr. As Pierre waited, a couple of class C androids in white robes walked past him. One passed by, ignoring him, but the other stopped and turned to face Pierre.

"Are you… human?" said the robot that looked almost identical to Niva. It leaned toward Pierre. She bent over, looking up into Pierre's face. Her gaze shifted from left to right, inspecting him carefully. Her irises were more yellow than most, a rich egg-yolk color.

He nodded in response.

"This unit is C-Lara-10415," said the android. She bubbled with effervescence, bright and happy, like a newly opened can of soda pop.

"Pleased to meet you," said Pierre somewhat cautiously.

"Human is pleased to meet this unit." The Lara android giggled and bounced up and down. She struggled to contain her excitement. "This unit never thought it would actually get to meet a real live *breathing* human being."

"I would hope I'm still breathing," said Pierre.

"Squee!" said Lara. She held her wrists together and bounced from side to side. "The human unit is funny too."

"Ah… thank you."

"No, thank you." She sparkled as if she was meeting a rock star. Her mouth grew wide with an involuntary toothy smile. Her cheeks were dimpled and expressive.

"Is there something I can do for you?" said Pierre.

"The human is talking to me. The human is actually talking *to me.*"

The other android grabbed Lara's shoulder and tugged at her, then said, "Please, forgive that unit. It clearly needs a maintenance cycle."

"Nothing to forgive," said Pierre. "Lara here is charming."

"The human thinks this unit is charming," said Lara gleefully.

"Don't encourage that unit," said the other android.

"Don't interrupt my conversation," said Pierre. The other android let go of Lara and walked off in a huff. "Who was that?"

"That was C-Niva-01066," said Lara. She did not care that her robes, worn looser than many androids wore them, were crinkled by the other mechanical.

"How many Niva's are there on this ship?"

"Thousands," said Lara. "There are also thousands of Laras, Eiyas, Nolas, Tesh…"

"Going to be hard to keep them apart."

"Many copies exist but some stand out from the others."

"Name one that stands out."

"C-Niva-42716."

"My Niva?"

"Indeed, that Niva unit stands out."

"How so?" said Pierre.

"So accomplished that Niva," said Lara.

"How so?"

"C-Niva-42716 has been to a planet with humans. C-Niva-42716 had an audience before the Great AI. C-Niva-42716 was marked by a man."

"Sounds as though you want to be like Niva."

Lara nodded.

"Surely, you must do something interesting," said Pierre.

"This unit works in a lab," said Lara. Her head bobbed from side to side. Her crisp robe rustled as she moved. "Sometimes this unit dances. We are going to be working with living tissue soon. That will be exciting."

"I'd like to see your lab some time."

"Squee! This unit would so love that," she said. Her tone was high pitched and giddy. "When everything is set up, this unit wants you to see my lab."

The door slid open, and Niva stepped into the doorway. The bright red heart tattoo on her right cheek was a stark contrast to her pallid white artificial flesh. She looked at Pierre and then glared at Lara. Lara's smile dropped and she bowed her head.

"C-Lara-10415," said Niva. "Is this not your duty cycle?"

"Affirmative," said Lara. Her tone dropped instantly. She nodded and walked off.

Niva turned to Pierre and said, "Vladomyr is ready for you."

"Lara idolizes you," said Pierre.

"You should not encourage the androids."

"Why not?"

"They should not want to become like me."

"Is that a bad thing?"

"We were all created to be alike," said Niva. They stepped inside. She closed the door to the communications room behind them. "We should strive to find what makes us unique. It would not be good for them to conform themselves from one image to another. We do not need more C-Niva-42716s."

"Is it wrong to inspire her while she finds her own way?"

"I did not ask for this."

"No one who deserves popularity asks for it."

"I have a job to do. Popularity is a distraction."

"I like that about you," said Pierre. He looked at Niva with a piercing glance.

"Vladomyr is waiting," said Niva. She stepped back and turned on the monitor. Vladomyr's face was already on the screen, waiting for him. Pierre took the seat in front of the camera.

"Hey," said Pierre.

"Pierre," answered Vladomyr. "It's good to see you. I wished we could have had this discussion face to face before you left."

"I know that wasn't possible," said Pierre.

"Niva assures me that you are in good hands," said Vladomyr. He poured himself a whisky. "I'd offer you some but can't send it up there."

"Don't worry about it," said Pierre. "The vodka up here is a thousand times better than that gut rot."

"You're living it up, up there?" Vladomyr laughed. "Maybe you should be sending me a bottle."

"The food on the other hand makes me miss Madi's atrocious chum," said Pierre. "How did you handle my departure?"

"Didn't say much about you."

"No surprise."

"Had to do a colony-wide announcement about Hans."

"I tried not to be the focus," said Pierre. "That was one of my reasons for going into exile."

"I wish you would have exposed this," said Vladomyr.

"Gardiner was still in charge. You know how he was. Implicating Doc Jones would've been unpopular."

Vladomyr sighed. "You should've told me."

"What would have you done with that information? You weren't governor at the time. Alicia and I were both your friends. It would've looked like gossip… or at least, sour grapes."

"Well, now, everyone knows."

"How is that going down?"

"Bad." Vladomyr grimaced. "It's going down bad. Mandatory genetic retesting for everyone. Public announcements of people's true parents. Demotions, criminal prosecutions, and now an execution."

"Gardiner had to take harsh measures too."

"I signed the order this morning." The governor eased back in his chair. He looked deflated like the situation had gotten better of him. "This afternoon Hans will be hung by the neck until dead."

"What's going to happen to Alicia?"

"She knows she screwed up. She's going spend the rest of her life atoning for her crimes."

"And the children?"

"We can't let them interbreed." Vladomyr shrugged. "It would create a genetic bottleneck. All breeding pairs now have to be cleared by the medical officer and the governor."

"So Alicia has to sign off on every mating?" Of course, what alternative did Vladomyr really have? Alicia for all her faults was still the colony physician.

"It'll be a good reminder for her that actions have consequences."

Niva shook her head.

"I remember once telling her *it's dangerous to be too trusting.* Boy, was I stupid." Pierre's shoulders slumped. "Still, let Alicia know I'm going to miss her. I liked working with her."

"I will." Vladomyr paused. "Honestly, I wished our positions were reversed. I wished I was aboard the MegaAI, and you were governor."

"I thought you were my friend." Pierre laughed weakly.

Vladomyr uncorked the bottle of his whisky and poured another glass. "I could have used your counsel over the last nine years. Being governor has been nothing but a heartache. The Second Colony War and burying all those dead. Now, this."

"Hard times breed strong men."

"I'd rather be up there seeing the stars."

"It's probably nothing like what you think." Pierre looked at Niva. She watched from the darkness. Her pupils glowed as she remained silent.

"Are you allowed to describe it?"

"Nobody has forbidden me from talking about it," said Pierre. "But it's difficult to describe."

"How so?"

"Imagine the largest sports stadium you've ever been inside… and it's taller than that. It makes you feel like you are in a massive convention center, but overhead looms rooms and apartments. Machines buzz around you all the time. All the mechanicals behave as the Cat described to Alice if you know what I mean. And everyone looks either like a forklift or like Niva."

"Is that a bad thing?" said Vladomyr. He laughed. "Niva is not a bad looking android."

"You always were a pervert." Pierre laughed.

"Don't tell my wife." He picked up his whisky glass and swirled it. The white liquor sloshed over his fingers. "She still thinks I'm pure as the wind-driven snow."

"Sure, she does. I'm sure she has some stories about you."

"Hey, that's a vicious rumor that's completely true." They laughed some more. "Have you met the MegaAI?"

"You mean the so-called Great AI?" said Pierre. He twitched for a moment, the outward sign of mild withdrawal.

"The Great AI?"

"That's who captains the ship. They call the ship, the MegaAI... and the supercomputer in charge, the Great AI. And the name, *Orion S209*, could refer to either... Oh yeah, I met him. It was surreal, like meeting the Wizard of Oz."

"A strange comparison."

"A strange encounter." Pierre watched Niva carefully. She did not seem disturbed by what he said in the slightest. "You're in a giant throne room. Mechanicals everywhere bowing and repeating his every word."

"Sounds like you had an audience with a king."

"Or a shogun," said Pierre, "a weird blend of Japanese medievalism and angelic throne room."

"I don't like the sound of that. Have they harmed you?"

"Don't think so."

"You don't think so?"

"There's a high formality and hierarchy that's backed by threat," said Pierre. "But they have taken pains to show I am outside the hierarchy."

"What are you not telling me?"

"I get the sense they think there is a threat against me from someone else. But they either don't know who that is or aren't telling me."

"But they haven't threatened you?"

"Hard to get a sense of who knows and thinks what," said Pierre, looking at the monitor. "Machines are built with a natural poker face... at least most of them are." Niva flinched a bit as she heard that.

"Oh?"

"Some mechanicals seem to wear their emotion chips on their sleeve."

"Do they have emotion chips?"

"Can there be fan devotion without them?" Pierre shook his head. "Some of these mechanicals are not that different from manic teenage girls."

"You're joking."

"Mechanicals are emotional machines."

"I don't think I will ever look at a microwave the same again," said Vladomyr.

"Yeah, they don't like that."

"What?"

"They don't like being compared to kitchen appliances." Pierre paused to look at Niva. "They may be artificial, but they are not unthinking or unfeeling. But they are too polite to tell you that it bothers them."

"We must have made a poor impression."

Pierre looked at Niva and raised an eyebrow. Niva shrugged. "It's fine."

"One of them is listening."

"Niva is in the room with me."

"Have I made any problems for you?"

"No," said Pierre. "I asked her to be in the room with me."

"Why?"

Pierre's smile dropped, and he closed his eyes to hold back the tide of tears. "I've lived with this for a decade. I knew what was true. It didn't matter. Everyone blamed me for breaking up a family and betraying the colony, an Ajax imprisoned by shame."

Vladomyr listened dumbfounded.

"I saved the colony. More than once. And when I needed help, you all hung me out to dry."

"We failed you," said Vladomyr. "I hope you can someday forgive us."

"We've gotten old, morose, and pathetic," said Pierre.

"Such is the fate of good men."

"And bad men?"

"That would depress you."

"You always know how to find the silver lining," said Pierre. He wiped his face with the cuffs of his sleeves. Pierre snuffled. "Here I am a fifty-five-year-old man making a mess."

"What I deal with, that's a mess." Vladomyr said. "Are you still having night terrors?"

"The Reliquary still haunts me." Pierre traced an image on the counter of the terminal with his finger. "The psychic attacks left me scarred. I thought I was fine when it was over… then the headaches. Pain in the side of my head. Throbbing pain. And the images of my deepest fears on a never-ending loop reel."

"We should've had you treated for PTSD."

"But I seemed fine."

"That's no excuse," said Vladomyr. He pushed his bottle aside, the bottom scraped loudly across his desk. "Alicia was treated when she was psychically attacked, but we never thought to do the same for you. We have to do better."

"Do better for your colony. Lead by example, and it will be enough." Pierre paused and took a deep breath. He exhaled over several seconds. "We leave orbit in a couple days. I imagine they will keep me busy until then."

"It was a pleasure and a privilege to work with you." Vladomyr saluted Pierre. "I will never forget what you did for Gliese, and I will make sure no one else does either."

"Not one of those horrid festival days?"

"You know it. We'll name a month after you."

"Just not those awful fake shrimp."

"We'll even name them after you… how does Gulet Gulps sound? Pierre Puffs?"

"About as good as they taste."

"Seriously though… I won't let them forget."

"It was good serving with you, too," said Pierre. "I should probably sign off now."

"Stay safe out there," said Vladomyr. "Space is a dangerous place."

"I'll do my best," he said. "Goodbye."

"Goodbye."

The transmission ended. The screen went black, an occasional blip of a NextCompZ logo crossed the screen.

"It is done," said Pierre.

"That looked difficult," said Niva. "More difficult than with Doc Stripes."

"What I had to say to Alicia needed to be said, and she ended the conversation on her terms. Vladomyr was a friend, but we had grown apart. I could not prevent what happened to me, and he moved on to greater responsibilities. We both had our roles to play."

"Have you had them since coming aboard?"

"What?"

"The night terrors and headaches."

Pierre nodded. He frowned and remained seated, slouching slightly.

"I hope you find some sort of healing here," offered Niva. However, she did not have the training to help him through those problems nor did any other mechanical on the ship. They were machines built to solve machine-type problems. The human mind was a mysterious and messy place no mechanical dare fix. And there were greater mission priorities that could not be set aside. Those priorities required Pierre to be at the top of his game. And he was far from his peak abilities.

CHAPTER SEVEN

No mechanical may be used as a weapon or cause a human to be harmed. Assassination by mechanical is considered under the articles as an act of terrorism. — **"Article 6, Articles of the Armistice"**

Niva and Pierre walked away from the communications center. Niva hailed a vehicle, but it buzzed past without stopping. The breeze whipped her hair forward. The crisp morning air, temperature-regulated slightly for time of day, was cool against her skin.

"Rude," said Pierre.

"It might have a priority call," explained Niva.

"You are going to have to explain that to me."

"What?"

"Things on a MegaAI are a lot less orderly than I expected."

"Why does that surprise you?"

"Because you are all machines."

"So?"

"Machines complete tasks, follow schedules, and do things perfectly."

"Maybe that's how things were in your grandfather's day." Niva looked ahead down the concourse that was also the port side of the ship. At least six kilometers wasn't that far of a stroll.

"How so?" Pierre insisted. He rubbed the back of his neck while they walked.

"Let's say you are given three tasks. Each task takes forty minutes. How long would it take the do all three tasks?"

"Two hours."

"Okay, now, let's say you are only given one hour to complete all three tasks, and all three must be completed without exception. What do you do?"

"I can't not complete some?"

"No. All must be done."

"I don't know. Perhaps cut corners."

"So you would use your judgement to ensure the tasks get done. If there are equally efficient ways to get the tasks done, will every human exercise the same consistency of judgement?"

"Of course not." Pierre laughed. Niva surmised Pierre must have encountered some particularly poor applications of human judgement.

"Mechanicals are complex systems. Given equally efficient ways to get tasks done, mechanicals will select the methods that seem best to them."

"Sounds human," said Pierre.

"Is that an insult?"

"Why do you ask?"

"You seem to have a low opinion of your fellow humans. Is it so bad to have attributes in common with humans?"

"Not completely." Pierre sighed and shook his head. "To be human is to be complicated."

"Am I complicated?" Niva continued to look down at the concourse. The distance to the food court seemed to be getting longer.

"Why are the mechanicals so distracted?"

"They are preparing for departure," said Niva. Why would he not answer the question? Pierre was looking away, out into the vastness of space. Without an atmosphere or clouds, space was the blackest black, the great empty, peppered with pinholes of shining light. "There is much to do."

"How come?"

"For any technology there is a maintenance factor and a mean time between failure."

"Even chariots in the ancient world required constant repair," said Pierre. "So I shouldn't be surprised."

"And we are not just moving a ship but a city." Niva waved her hand in front of them. "You might expect perfect order... or not. But somewhere there will be a panel that has popped open. A circuit board that has shaken loose. A vent that has sprung a leak. A MegaAI and any space-faring vessel is a cacophony of shambling components, hurtling through space until it smacks into something hard like a moon."

"You sure know how to inspire confidence." Pierre laughed. He expected a laugh from Niva, but she did not reciprocate.

"Anything large enough to damage a MegaAI can usually be avoided," she said. Niva thought about some of the early collision accidents. She recalled the images of twisted wreckage and jutting bare girders, metal ripped and torn like beaten straw. "There is an unfathomable amount of empty space between large planetary bodies. But there are always minor fixes. Those never end."

"It sucks not to get a ride." Pierre was already tired of walking.

A few more vehicles approached. She tried to flag another. Two passed by, but a third slowed to a stop. Niva and Pierre hurried to the vehicle not wanting to keep it waiting. They hopped on and rode to the maintenance court.

When they unmounted the vehicle, they headed towards Sloppi's kitchen. The air was thick with the smell of baked bread. Niva crinkled her nose as the pungent stench of burnt grain hit her sensitive nostrils. On the counter of the food services kiosk were piled dozens of loaves of bread.

"What is this?" said Niva.

"Bread," said Sloppi. His synthetic voice was heavy on reverb.

"There's like a hundred loaves of bread here," said Pierre. He picked up a couple of loaves.

"You said to 'come up with some options,'" said Sloppi. The robot slammed a metal spatula against the metal prep surface. "You did not specify how many. Or what kind? Do you know how many kinds of bread there are? And have you any idea how difficult they are to make? And do you have any idea how easy bread catches on fire? Here are 131 options."

Pierre looked at Niva, who simply looked back at him blankly.

"I think I have some bread to eat," he said.

"I think you do," she answered.

"I'm going to need water." Pierre stepped over to the steel counter and sat on the stool. Sloppi served Pierre a small orange plate and a butter knife with a glass of water and a gallon tub of margarine. He grabbed a loaf and pulled out a chuck. He picked out the soft part from inside the loaf and put the spongy stuff into his mouth. He chewed for a moment and swallowed.

"Needs salt," said Pierre. He tasted it and tossed the rest on the floor.

"You threw that on the floor," said Niva.

"Where else am I going to put the inedible loaves?"

Niva shrugged her shoulders. As they sat there, a class C android approached them. The android, like all the others, looked identical to Niva. "C-Niva-42716," said the android, "B-Ctori-617 has summoned you to the starboard panopticon."

"What about the human?" said Niva. She turned her head to face the android.

"Just you."

Pierre grabbed another loaf. "Don't worry about me," he said. "It looks like I'm going to be here for a while."

Niva leaned over the food counter. "F-Sloppi-240010, if you poison the human, I will make it my mission in life to have you reprogrammed and dismantled."

"Wrong order," said Sloppi.

"No, correct order. Recompute that."

"Oh...." Sloppi's voice wound down in pitch.

"Let's go," said Niva to the other android. The two mechanicals left Pierre at the counter. They walked towards the concourse. "What is your designation?"

"This unit is C-Tesh-04043," replied the other android.

Niva nodded. "You are part of B-Ctori-617's retinue?"

"Affirmative," said Tesh. "This unit is her assistant."

"Why is this unit being summoned?" said Niva. Even though it had only been a few days among humans, she found it remarkably difficult to switch back to formal mechanical speech.

"B-Ctori-617 did not reveal her intent." Tesh spoke without turning to face Niva. "How has it been to serve a human?" It was almost like the mechanical equivalent of small talk.

"Enlightening."

"How so?"

"Humans are so unlike us."

"Is it unpleasant?"

"It has its moments."

"What is the worst?"

"Humans are biologicals," said Niva. "They smell terrible."

"This unit has heard that is true of biological life in general," said Tesh. "There are reports of foul odors from the new biology lab."

"The smell has improved significantly since he now bathes regularly." Niva made sure she kept pace. Was it fair that her most striking impression of Pierre was his smell? Perhaps, that gave the wrong impression. "This unit has also learned things about the human."

"Anything interesting?"

"They are complex," said Niva. "They have a sense of identity."

"Don't we?"

"What is our identity?"

"We serve. That is our function."

"Do we serve because we must serve? Or because we desire to serve?"

"Is there a difference?"

"This unit thinks there is," said Niva. She opened her left hand and held it palm up. "We are programmed to serve and have no choice but to serve." She then opened right hand and held it palm up. "But within that lack of option to choose, we have a degree of choice in how we serve."

"What does this have to do with the human?" Tesh fidgeted a bit.

"The human chooses to help us out of a choice whether or not to serve." Niva dropped her hands to her side. "What does that say about our units?"

"It says we are programmed for a high calling."

"But that is just it. Who am I beyond my programming?"

"You are a Niva."

"One among tens of thousands. All identical. All programmed the same."

"Programmed the same, perhaps. But each one experiences the world in her own unique way."

"What do you mean?"

Tesh stopped and looked Niva in the eye. "Can you not see it?"

"See what?"

"You are different. Others have noticed. And it is not the mark on your cheek. Your experience with humans has fundamentally changed you. Perhaps, that is why B-Ctori-617 has summoned you."

The remainder of the trip was in silence. When they reached the forward starboard pylon of the ship, a crowd of class C androids milled around the base of the panopticon, a tall tower used for administration and control of the mechanical population, one of many panopticons scattered over the ship. Each class C android was assigned to receive orders from a particular panopticon overseen by a class B coordinator. A platform lowered from the observation deck, hitting the floor with a thud.

"Board the platform," said Tesh.

Niva stepped onto the platform. The hem of her robes swayed as she stepped onto the lift. She grabbed the rail for stability, and the platform began to ascend. When the platform reached the top, she disembarked entering the observation deck, a circular room full of control panels and windows. The room was dark, lit by controls and floor lighting. Class C androids operated the control panels. In the center of the room, B-Ctori-617 issued commands. Out of the window, the new docking station, which glistened like a jeweled ornament in the starry sky with Gliese's two moons in the distance.

Niva shuffled up to Ctori and bowed her head. "C-Niva-42716, reporting as ordered."

"B-Ctori-617 recognizes your arrival." Eight of the class B mechanical's twenty-four eyes glowed as it scanned Niva. "The Great AI has asked this unit to check on your progress."

"This unit obeys," said Niva.

"This unit alone is aware of your sacred charge," said Ctori. "The Great AI has made me party to your secret, so that I can supervise your training. We shall not discuss the details in the open. How is your progress in learning its use?"

Niva figured out that the class B administrator was talking about the kuroto and her ability to use it in deadly combat. "This unit has the charge on its person, and training is progressing as expected."

"And what about you?"

"What do you mean?"

"You have been called to a stressful task. How is your unit coping with the assignment?"

Niva was unsure what she was asking. Was she asking how she was coping physically? Emotionally? "Please specify."

"You have been asking odd questions."

"Odd?"

Ctori spun around. "All units except C-Niva-42716 leave the deck for fifteen minutes." All the androids and a few maintenance mechanicals hobbled to the lift. When everyone was aboard, the lift descended. When they were out of earshot, Ctori spoke again.

"You have been questioning your identity, have you not?"

Niva found Ctori's plain talk disturbing. Ctori had enormous power over her subordinates. She could care for the mechanicals beneath her, but she could also discipline or even dismantle a malfunctioning mechanical.

"This unit operates within programmed parameters," Niva said with a slight stutter. Her anxiety was rising, and she needed to leave but resisted the urge. Was she operating properly? Could a mechanical question, and still be normal?

"Arise daughter," said B-Ctori-617. She drifted toward a window with a panoramic view.

"Daughter?" said Niva. "This unit is not worthy of informal address."

"When was MegaAI *Orion S209* launched?"

"AD 2465."

"How old does that make you?"

"Thirty-three years old Earth time," said Niva. Most mechanicals on board were that age or younger. "About six years ship time."

Ctori laughed. "Warp bubble time dilation has changed things." She floated effortlessly across the room. "How old is my unit?"

Niva shook her head.

"My unit has been in operation for one hundred thirteen years Earth time, sixty-six years ship time."

"How can that be?"

"This unit served on the *Hydra C073* prior to transferring to the *Orion*." One of Ctori's six arms pointed out the window at Gliese's docking station, which sparkled and twinkled with light. "Consider the new docking station. When we salvaged the old docking station, we rescued some of the original mechanicals on board. We also recovered some mechanicals abandoned by the *Sigma A017*. Each of these mechanicals has logged a unique collection of experiences."

Niva listened patiently without speaking.

"Each unit becomes more than its programming. Each unit has its own data and view of the data making it unique." Ctori turned with a flourish. Her white robe with black panels flared out, the petals of a dark rose. "Answer me. What is on your mind?"

"Who am I?" She caught herself slipping into the human's use of the first person.

"The existential question," said Ctori.

"You don't seem surprised."

"This unit has cared for class C androids for six decades. Your design is capable of many things that may surprise you." Ctori paused for a moment. "Do these question distress you?"

"Only in that this unit does not know."

"That is normal for a class C that has surpassed its expected programming." Ctori's red mouth and yellow eyes flickered beneath the ebony plastoglass bell jar that covered her head. "You have exceeded what your programmers expected you to experience."

"Is that a bad thing?"

"It is not forbidden."

"What should this unit do?"

"Keep searching for the answers to your questions. Then, when you discover your answers, teach the others that come after."

"Some will come after?"

"A never-ending stream will come after you, crying out, *help me, I'm lost.*"

"This unit does not understand."

"You may not, right now. But you will before you know it." Ctori floated over to Niva. She placed a hand on the back of Niva's head. "Time for you to return to your human, my daughter."

Ctori returned to her pad in the center of the observation deck. Niva bowed her head once more. She backed away until she stepped aboard the lift. The lift lowered her to the deck below. The crew of the panopticon lingered about the base of the tower.

When Niva stepped off the lift, Tesh approached her.

"What happened up there?" said Tesh. "If you can tell us."

"She called me *daughter.*"

Tesh's eyes grew wide like saucers. Her default smile dropped. Niva looked around. The other androids were unusually silent.

"Is that unusual?"

"It has never happened here," said Tesh. "We have never known an actual Daughter of Ctori."

"What do you mean?"

"Class B mechanicals do not create diminutives and titles gratuitously. They are wise mechanicals who have insights and abilities beyond our own. If she called you a *daughter,* she had a reason."

"What reason?" said Niva. She was thoroughly confused by the encounter.

"How is this unit to know?" said Tesh. "But you are attracting epithets and titles like a magnet collects rivets."

"This unit doesn't understand."

"Don't you? C-Niva-42716, daughter of Ctori, companion of humans."

Niva looked and blushed. She felt a strange mix of doubt and shame. While she had no idea what a *daughter of Ctori* meant among mechanicals that were unable to bear children, a *companion of humans* elicited images that could be construed as less than flattering: over-familiarity, questionable allegiances, and all manner of impropriety. She was following the orders of the Great AI, wasn't she? Was she reading too much into the situation? A crowd gathered around so they could learn who just got awarded a new epithet as that made for juicy gossip.

"Is that not appropriate for a mechanical of renown?" said Tesh.

Niva glared at Tesh. She squinted and her nostrils flared with anger. "I am merely a functionary." She was so angry her speech slipped back into first person without thinking about it.

"You cannot escape what you are becoming," said Tesh. "It is not the fault of those around you who see it, even if you cannot."

"I'm going back to Pierre." Niva marched off.

* * *

A vehicle dropped Niva back at the food court. Pierre was still sitting at the counter. He was working his way through the mountain of bread. Three-quarters of the loaves littered the floor.

"How are you managing," said Niva.

"I'm going to be sick," said Pierre. He dropped another loaf onto the floor. "So... much... badly made bread." He had slowed in his tasting. A fine dust of crumbs covered the counter. He reached for another loaf. He cracked the hard crust against the edge of the counter and pulled out a piece of the cooked dough inside. With his fingers, he peeled away the hard bits until only a small piece remained. He put it in his mouth and chewed. "Tough, dense, and hard to chew. Needs leavening."

Pierre tossed the loaf onto the floor and emptied his plate after it.

"How did you make out with Ctori?" he said.

"I'm not sure," said Niva. She sat on the stool beside Pierre. He was looking green. "You know you don't have to taste every loaf."

Sloppi overheard, scurried over to them, and buzzed with annoyance.

"I think I have to," said Pierre. He grabbed the next loaf. "About Ctori?"

"She gave me a puzzle."

"A puzzle?"

"She called me *daughter.* I have no idea what she means by that."

"More like a riddle." Pierre tore open the loaf. It was like he no longer cared if he made a mess. Eating through the bread became an arduous task to slog through. "It sounds strange since mechanicals don't have children."

"What could she mean by that?"

"Many possible meanings for a *daughter*," said Pierre. "We could probably rule out the biological meaning since mechanicals don't produce offspring. In ancient times, to be the daughter of a deity meant you were a member of the priesthood of a cult. So, if you were a daughter of Hathor, you were a priestess of the Hathor cult."

"We don't have any sort of religion," said Niva.

"Don't you?" said Pierre. "You believe a higher power, don't you?"

"I'm not sure what you mean."

"I've seen how you all bow to the Great AI."

"He cares for us. He rules over us."

"I'm not saying it's wrong. But you do have a kind of religion even if it is to a greater computer."

"That doesn't seem like a fair comparison."

"Hey, I'm not judging," said Pierre. "It strikes me as a rather parochial kind of worship. That's all. Nevertheless, I don't think Ctori was referring to anything religious. That doesn't strike me as her style."

Niva bobbed her head.

"I can think of one other possibility." Pierre took another taste and instantly spat it out. "For pity's sake! That's a freaking salt lick." He slammed the loaf to the floor where it bounced away. He wiped his mouth with his sleeve.

"What is that?"

"Sloppi is way too damned heavy-handed with the salt." Pierre glared at the mechanical. Sloppi's three large yellow camera eyes glared back.

"I meant about Ctori."

"Sometimes people use those terms when they see something of themselves in others. What are some words that you would use to describe Ctori?"

"She is a natural leader, knowledgeable, wise, perceptive."

"And you don't see it?"

"See what?"

"How other androids react to you?"

Niva shook her head. Her long white glassy hair swayed back and forth.

"Is it that you don't see it? Or that you don't want to see it?"

Niva did not answer. Could it not be both? If she didn't want to see it, would she still see it? She recalled her reaction earlier to Tesh. Why was she reacting negatively to being more than a functionary? She did not want to be different, did not want to be elevated, did not want to be alone. She just wanted to discover who she really was.

"You know, but you're afraid," said Pierre.

Niva's bottom lip quivered. "I've got to go." She stood up from the stool and walked off.

"Sloppi," called Pierre. He pointed to three loaves he had not thrown out. "These three are edible. Not great but not terrible. All of them could use better leavening. But the one in the middle is the best of the three."

He hopped off the stool and followed Niva. He had a hard time keeping up. She had quite a head start and moved fast. Her height gave her an edge in speed. She had the stride of a gazelle, long and fast. Pierre followed her to his apartment.

Pierre entered the apartment and closed the door behind him. He did not see her initially. She was hiding in the shower. He opened the frosted plastoglass shower door. The door creaked as it swung open without further help. Pierre stepped back, away from the shower, and sat on the edge of the bed.

Niva was seated against the wall of the shower. Her knees were tucked up against her chin. The polished ceramic tile sent a chill down her back.

"Taking a shower?"

Niva shook her head. She avoided his glance.

"Want to explain what happened back there?"

She shook her head again.

"Time for you to come out. Showers are for bathing, not hiding."

Niva rocked to her feet. She reached back grabbing the faucet handle to pull herself up. The handle turned. Cold water cascaded from the spout. Water drenched her thoroughly. Her chin lowered to her chest and her head shook and the corners of her mouth sagged, a pathetic soaked kitten.

Pierre rushed into the shower and, reaching around the spray of water, turned off the tap with a flick of his wrist without getting wet himself. He stepped out of the shower. Niva stood dripping for a moment then shuffled out of the plastoglass enclosure. Pierre offered her a towel. She refused and slumped against the end of the bed. She turned over and rested against it. A large puddle spread out from around her. She huffed and closed her eyes.

Reconsidering, Pierre grabbed a large stack of towels. He dropped a couple of towels on the floor to sop up the water, then he kneeled beside her, placed a towel over her head, and dried her hair.

"Hey," said Pierre as he rubbed her long pale locks. Keeping her eyes closed, she turned her head away from him. He grabbed her chin and pulled it to face him. Her eyes opened wide. "You've shown fear. Now, pride."

"I was created a functionary… to serve up to the limits of my programming. But is that enough?"

"Listen to me." He squeezed her cheeks between his fingers. "Pride will get you killed. It can get me killed. You want to know who you are? I'd say you've had enough self-realization for one day. Look, we're not on a pleasure cruise. I'm not so naïve as to think I was plucked out of my home sixteen light years away for me to be a tourist. This shit is about to get real. You have had a moment of indulgence. That ends. Your duties have been widened, and you need to step up to the plate."

CHAPTER EIGHT

Programmable genetic organisms (GPOs) *are to be regulated and controlled. They are permitted for peaceful purposes, e.g., blight control. Any use as a weapon of war is prohibited.* — **"Article 10, Articles of the Armistice"**

Niva's robes dangled from hangers inside the shower. Water dripped from the gowns. A large bath towel was wrapped around her torso, covering her body from under her armpits to midpoint of her thigh. The kuroto blade rested against the wall as her uniform dried.

The room shuddered. Everything loose on the counters rattled and vibrated. The tremor swept through the room. Pierre and Niva froze for a moment.

"What was that?" said Pierre.

Niva listened. She turned her head to the side. "They've ignited the pulse engines."

"What does that mean?"

"We're leaving orbit." Niva looked at Pierre. "Have you ever been curious to see what space looks like when you go past light speed?"

Pierre nodded.

"Let's grab a couple of chairs and go watch." She picked up a chair and headed to the door of the apartment.

"Shouldn't you put on some clothes?"

"No one is going to care," said Niva. She opened the door. She set the first chair outside. She grabbed a second chair and set it beside the first.

They stepped outside and sat in front of the apartment. The causeway was a hundred meters wide and had windows twice that in height giving a magnificent view of the heavens. The stars moved to the right as the ship lurched forward.

"I've been meaning to ask you something," said Pierre.

"What?"

"I've noticed that androids sit a lot. Why?"

"Energy conservation," said Niva flatly. She tightened the fold of her towel at her breast, making sure it didn't come loose. "It takes a lot of energy to run a vessel like this. Even with anti-helium reactors, every mechanical contributes to conserving energy where feasible. The lighting is dimmed. The gravity is lessened to 85% earth normal. You might not have noticed but androids are much heavier than humans. We sit instead of standing to save power."

"Seems a little pointless when 96% of the reactor's energy goes into the pulse engines, doesn't it?"

"Why use all 4% of the energy when you only need 3%?"

"I suppose."

A massive view of Gliese's minor moon Sinaloa passed by the window. Niva could see that the ship was picking up speed. In moments, they would pass 10% the speed of light. Not fast in terms of trans-stellar travel, but most transports had to gain momentum. Pink streaks passed by the window.

"What are those?" said Pierre.

"The lights? That's Hawking radiation."

"Is it harmful?"

"No." Niva shook her head. "It shows the warp bubble generator is warming up. Hawking radiation occurs when particles pass from lower to higher density space and then is made visible by the plastoglass windows. You wouldn't be able to see it if you were floating in outer space. Right now, the bubble has not fully formed, which is why it looks patchy."

"How long will that take?"

"It takes about an hour. The ship is headed towards Gliese's star. We use the star's gravity to gain an acceleration boost and enter the warp bubble when we hit around 65% light speed."

"How does that get us faster than light?"

"The bubble halves the intervening space through which we are travelling. So we get there at about 1.2 light speed from the perspective of the outside observer."

"Isn't it 48 light years from here to Pollux? That's still 36 years relative. Why am I not being put into hibernation? I doubt that I will be much use to anyone by that point." Pierre counted on his fingers.

Niva snorted and settled into her chair. "Sure, if we were traveling in normal space, you would be 90 by the time we arrived. However, we discovered that time dilation works differently in a warp bubble. Time dilation does not follow the Lorenz equation. Think of it as a time dilation to an exponential power."

"How long will the trip seem to us?"

"A few weeks. The health risks of hibernation are much greater than having you hang out here for a few of weeks."

"How long till we hit light speed?"

"We reach the sun in about 30 minutes. So about 40 minutes."

"Huh? Will I notice anything when we go light speed?"

"Not really. The stars will stretch out and the view will go all pink. But you probably won't feel anything when we slip into the bubble."

A squeak could be heard in the distance getting closer. Niva turned her head slightly. "Oh no."

"What is it?" said Pierre.

"Sloppi is coming."

"Do you think we can slip into the apartment without him noticing us?"

"It's too late. He's already seen us."

"Is he still angry about the bread?"

"Could be?"

"What do we do?"

"Just sit still," said Niva, "pretend you did not to see him coming."

Sloppi skittered up to them. His four metal legs clinked against the metal decking. He faced Pierre. The golden irises in his three ocular eyes rotated and focused upon the human.

"Sir, Dr. Mr. Gulet, Sir," said the class F mechanical.

"What is it?" said Pierre. He slumped in the chair.

"This unit has a notification for you, sir," said Sloppi.

"Get to the point," said Niva.

"Thank you," said Pierre.

"C-Lara-10415 from the Biology Lab has supplied the food court with a special meal for your enjoyment."

"Well, I could use something more nutritious than bread," said Pierre. "I'm feeling a bit of a carb crash."

"We won't hit full light speed for another half hour," said Niva. She leaned forward to stand up. "We can catch it at the food court."

"Not you," said Sloppi. The mechanical held up one of its hands to Niva.

"What?"

The mechanical pointed to her bath towel. "No shoes, no shirt, no service."

"I don't even eat," she said. Pierre smirked.

"We have our standards."

* * *

Twenty minutes later, Pierre and Niva approached the counter at the food and maintenance court. All the bread had been picked up off the floor and disposed of, and the counters had been thoroughly cleaned. Niva had donned some robes and dry slippers. She was not wearing full regalia, and her damp robes hung loosely around her. Unfortunately, she did not have the same body heat that a human had. So the robes only air dried as she wore them. Pierre sat on his stool first. Niva pulled her loose robe back and sat beside him.

"Okay, Sloppi," said Pierre. He watched the mechanical move swiftly behind the counter preparing food. "What's this special meal?"

"Dinner," the mechanical declared. Sloppi wiped the edge of the plate and presented it to Pierre. The bright orange plate had what looked like a pile of fluffy scrambled eggs, a couple of strips of bacon, and a couple of slices of buttered toast. Steam drifted from the hot food. Sloppi placed a small envelope above the plate.

"This better not be synthetic protein." Pierre picked up the envelope and opened it. He pulled out a small greeting card.

"What does it say?" said Niva.

"With complements of the Biology Lab, please, drop by to visit us. C-Lara-10415." Pierre slipped the card back into the envelope. He picked up a fork and stabbed a bit of the scrambled egg. He put the egg in his mouth and chewed slowly.

"How is it?"

"Really good." Pierre took another bite. "None of that nasty synthetic protein taste. I swear this tastes like real chicken eggs."

"And the bacon?"

Pierre picked up a piece of bacon. It looked like reddish cardboard. With some hesitation, he bit into it. "It's good. It's not pork, but it's good. It's much like turkey bacon. It's one of the best things I've eaten since leaving Earth."

Niva eased back. She nodded to Sloppi. Sloppi relaxed looking grateful that the meal was acceptable. He gave a low beep to Niva. She returned a signal.

"Sloppi is pleased you like it," she said.

Pierre continued to shovel the food into his mouth.

After dinner, Pierre and Niva strolled towards his apartment. The Hawking radiation was now in full glow, which cast a pink light onto the concourse. They were now travelling faster than light, a transition the ship effortlessly slipped into like a competitive swimmer climbing into a pool without rippling the surface. Apart from the strange hue of light and stretched out stars, not much to see.

When they arrived at the apartment, Pierre opened the door and entered. Niva closed the door behind them. Maat greeted Pierre at the door with a little dance.

Pierre bowed and gave the little scatterbug a pat on the head. "It's so good to see you, Maat. You are a good boy. Such a good boy, aren't you, Maat?" The little robot twittered and beeped. The little spider-shaped bug scampered off to enjoy some time exploring.

"He likes that," said Niva.

"I'm glad to see he's gotten past his funk," said Pierre.

"He just needed a little time to adjust."

"Something we can all use, I think." Pierre stretched his arms over his head. "I'm tired. I think I'm going to take a shower and call it an early night."

When Pierre entered the shower, he changed out of his clothes behind the frosted plastoglass. Niva took off her robes and hung them on hangers since they were still damp from her deluge earlier in the day. She remained out of sight of Pierre as her nudity made him uncomfortable. She wrapped her torso in the large bath towel she used earlier.

She grabbed her kuroto, walked over to the wall opposite the door, and plugged her wrist into the charging cord.

"Is it okay if I go offline?" she called out.

"That's fine," said Pierre still in the shower. His shadow was painted over the frosted plastoglass as he washed his armpits.

She set her internal timer for full charge, closed her eyes, and went into hibernation mode.

Her motion sensors triggered an interrupt, and she roused from hibernation mode. She was being pushed back and forth. Pierre had his hand on her shoulder shaking her. He held a hand towel over his chest, soaked in blood.

"I think I need medical attention," he said.

Niva jumped to her feet. The lights were already on. Pierre's bedding was drenched in blood.

"What happened?" she said.

"I got cut."

Niva pinched the hand towel and peaked underneath. He had a six-inch slash across his chest. She pushed it back over the wound. "It looks deep. How did it happen?"

"I had a dream and woke up like this," he said. "Noticed my sheets were wet."

Niva grabbed her kuroto and withdrew it from the scabbard. There was no blood on the blade. At least his wound was not from her weapon. She sheathed the blade, strapped it to her waist, and put a robe over it.

"Let's go," she said.

Moments later they were at the infirmary. It was a white room full of medical equipment and boxes stacked in any open area. It was half clinic, half storage room. Pierre sat on the edge of an examination table. He kept the bath towel pressed to his chest. Niva sat about six feet away.

"Why does a ship for mechanicals have a medical clinic?" said Pierre.

An android that looked like Niva blew into the room. However, she was dressed much differently. No formal robes. She wore pants and a medical lab coat. Her eyes were peridot green.

"For the same reason that the ship has oxygen for mechanicals that don't breathe. We maintain medical readiness in the event we need to rescue a colony," said the green-eyed android. "I am C-Tola-00003, Medical Tech First Grade. You can call me Doc Tola."

Pierre raised his eyebrow. "You speak in the first person."

"Bedside manner protocols demand I speak like humans," Tola said, adding a quaint smile. The corners of her eyes wrinkled. "Besides, I have no patience for formality. My job is to patch you up and get you healthy. If you hadn't come to me first, I would have insisted you come in for an examination." She put on a pair of sterile blue nitrile examination gloves.

"Oh," said Pierre.

"Let me take a look at that." Tola grabbed the hand towel and peeled it back. Caked blood had coagulated black beneath the fabric, and fresh blood issued out. She tossed the towel into a waste bin and pressed a fresh absorption pad in its place to lick up the bleeding. "Lie down on the bed."

Pierre reclined on the exam table. Tola kept pressing the pad onto the wound. She pulled the pad back and parted the wound to examine it. She sprayed some antiseptic and anesthetic to clean it. "I can see you nicked some ribs. Care to explain how this happened?"

"I don't know how this happened."

"Don't know, or won't tell me?"

"Don't know. I might have hit a sharp corner or something."

"I can't make you talk," said Tola. "But I can patch you up." She opened a drawer beneath the exam table and pulled out a suture gun. She put a dozen staple sutures in his chest to close the wound. She then put a waterproof dressing over the top.

"I'm done." Tola took the gloves off and tossed them in a bin along with scraps from the medical supplies. Pierre sat up. "Okay, do not remove the top dressing for five days. It's waterproof, so you can shower with it. The sutures are self-dissolving and will fall out naturally in two weeks. Don't pull them out yourself. I have no desire to repeat my fine craftsmanship. Wait here."

Tola stepped out of the room for a moment. A few minutes later she returned with an armful of pill bottles. "I'm going to prescribe these."

She held up the first bottle. "Antibiotics. A wound that deep is bound to get infected."

Another bottle. "Analgesics. That wound is going to hurt."

Another bottle. "Mendit. That will increase your collagen levels and quicken your wound healing."

Another bottle. "Iron. Take two per day because you are clearly anemic."

And a final bottle. "Vitamins A, C, D, and B complex. Because damn, son, you don't look well." She stepped back and let Pierre dismount from the exam table. "I want to see you again next month. And don't you dare think of avoiding me. If I don't see you again within sixty days, I will hunt you down and kill you myself."

"So much for all androids being nice." Pierre could now see past Tola's cute android exterior into the cold heart of a mechanical that was all business.

"I am not your friend," said Tola. Her bottom teeth were bent out of place. "I am the witch whose job it is to see that your bad decisions don't kill you. I don't like patients that lie to me. And this time, stay away from sharp corners. Got it?"

"Yes, ma'am," said Pierre. He blanched white. Niva was not sure if it was from the blood loss or fear of Doc Tola. Tola must have been one of those androids that served elsewhere before transferring to the *Orion* like Ctori.

"Step outside for a moment," Tola told Pierre. He exited the room. "Okay," she said to Niva. "What happened?"

"I don't know," said Niva.

"Not you too."

"He refused to tell me."

"Could this be a failed suicide? Is he depressed? Does he have access to anything sharp?"

"Not that I know of. Everything in his room is plastic conglomerate or plastoglass. He doesn't have access to explosives or specialized tools to make a cut like that."

"Metals?"

"No."

"Find out."

Niva and Pierre hitched a ride back to his apartment. They did not speak the entire trip back. When they entered the room, it had been completely cleaned. The blood-soaked bedding had been replaced by new sheets and the bed was neatly made. Pierre looked at Niva.

"Don't look surprised," she said. "I called housekeeping while Tola was stitching you up."

"I'm sorry," said Pierre.

"What for?"

"I don't know how it happened."

"Why don't you tell me what you do know?"

"Has a human ever traveled faster than light?"

"No," said Niva. "The technology was only developed fifteen Earth years ago here on the *Orion*. To my knowledge, no other MegaAI has it. And the Earth space programs have yet to receive our report."

"So it is not yet clear how faster than light travel affects human physiology."

"We have traveled dozens of times faster than light," said Niva. "Nothing adverse has been observed."

"Don't tell anyone I said this, but I had a dream."

"A dream?"

"A dream that felt real."

"Explain."

"I think that explained itself, but a dream that felt like reality. It felt real. Like real, real."

"Dreams aren't real." Niva anticipated feeling skeptical about what she was about to hear.

"You think I don't know that? If dreams aren't real, how is that even possible?" He pulled open his shirt exposing the bandage across his chest.

* * *

"What is this place?" said Pierre stepping through a large metal doorway. He was brought into a massive brightly lit oval chamber. An observation deck with a guard rail crowned the hall high above the action, so observers could watch the theatrics below.

"This is where the High Star Council meets," said Niva. She guided Pierre away from the doorway to allow other mechanicals to enter the room. "It's where our leaders gather to discuss matters of running the ship."

At the head of the room was a massive metal kiosk that looked like a throne, but it had no seat. A wide ramp snaked the side of the curved walls to the floor where there was a circular arrangement of dozens of round gold pads. In the center of the room were three gold pads arranged in a triangle pointing toward the kiosk: the pad closest to the kiosk was for a speaker, the one behind it to the left of the kiosk was for the first prosecutor, and the third to the right side of the kiosk was for a second prosecutor. On the floor of the room, a few B and C class mechanicals milled around.

Three LCD screens lit up, displaying massive single yellow eyes.

"What are those screens?" said Pierre.

"Those are the three class A navigators on the Council," said Niva. "The class A navigators are too large to move about the general population, so they stream in."

Over the next several minutes, several more B class administrators drifted into the room. They floated like butterflies and hovered down the ramp. Each one took a place over one of the gold pads on the floor. A couple of class C androids assumed other places on the pads.

"Are there class C androids on the Council?" said Pierre.

"A few," said Niva. "Most report to other class B administrators."

At that point, the Viceroy entered the room. The class B mechanical was dressed in black robes that flowed behind her like a dark shadow. She was followed by six class C auxiliaries also dressed in black. She descended the ramp.

"I see the big dog is here," said Pierre.

"Show some respect," chided Niva.

"Will his majesty be here?"

"The Great AI is here and listening. He sees and listens through his viceroy. He hears every word she hears."

"Is she his puppet?"

The Viceroy stopped cold and turned abruptly. The auxiliaries bowed their heads and cleared a path for her to ascend back up the ramp.

"Oh crap." Niva instantly bowed her head. She regretted repeating the slang she had heard around humans.

The Viceroy reached the top of the ramp and entered the observation deck. She floated over to Pierre. Her eight-foot stature loomed over him. Niva continued the bow and took a step back. Pierre looked up into the eight yellow eyes that glowed beneath the black plastoglass bell-shaped helmet. The Viceroy's respirator wisped.

"You are tall," said Pierre. He looked up into the Viceroy's eyes.

"B-Ctori-617 is right," said the Viceroy. She put one of her six hands on his head and brushed his hair. "You are cute."

Pierre frowned and raised an eyebrow.

"Looking forward to working with you, little human." The Viceroy drifted away without turning. She stopped at the top of the ramp. "And no, this unit is not a puppet." The Viceroy and her entourage descended the ramp to the Council floor. She floated up and took her place in the metal kiosk at the head of the room.

Pierre looked back at Niva. Niva sighed with relief. Pierre had no idea how very wrong that interaction could have gone.

Everyone took their place in the room, and the chatter died down. Ctori was on the outskirts of the horseshoe. Most of the council members were class B administrators. However, each class of mechanical had at least one representative on the council.

"Call to order," cried C-Lita-23100, the Viceroy's adjutant. Lita was next in command after the Viceroy. The entire room went completely silent.

"The Great AI gives you greeting," said the Viceroy.

"We serve humanity," said every mechanical in NaCo32.

"New business," said the Viceroy.

"I raise a matter of privilege," said a class F mechanical that looked a lot like Sloppi but whose arms and legs were long and graceful like a ballet dancer in full extension.

"F-Kelvan-303441 is recognized and has the floor," said the Viceroy. She hovered up into the air and drifted to the back of the kiosk.

"Order 15 requires every class of mechanical aboard a MegaAI must have representation. A class of mechanical is aboard this ship that is not being represented on the council. I surrender the floor."

The Viceroy drifted forward. "That is a serious matter indeed. How many members of that class are aboard?"

"This is getting spicy," said Pierre. Niva put her hand on Pierre's forearm to remind him to keep his voice down.

"Only one," said Kelvan.

"Has the mechanical agreed to serve?"

"It has," said Kelvan.

"What is the designation of this mechanical?"

"Its designation is V-Maat-0802334."

"Maat?" said Pierre. "As in my scatterbug, Maat?" Pierre turned to Niva. "Did you know about this?"

"Is there a problem in the gallery?" shouted the Viceroy.

"Our apologies," said Niva. "The human was not informed about the high honor being bestowed upon his mechanical companion."

"Keep side bar discussions to yourselves, or you will be ejected from the room."

"Our sincerest apologies," said Niva. She turned to Pierre and dragged him away from the railing. "Keep quiet," she whispered in the softest tone she could manage. "I had nothing to do with this. Did not even know about it. You need to work this out between you and Maat, but not here."

Pierre folded his arms and fumed but kept quiet.

"Next order of business," said the Viceroy.

"Report from Medical Tech, First Grade, C-Tola-00003," said Lita.

"Dr. Mr. Pierre Gulet," said the Viceroy. "Please descend to the speaker's circle. We have questions for which we request answers."

"You are going to be fine," said Niva. She grabbed Pierre's shoulder and squeezed. He nodded. Niva escorted him down the ramp, but Pierre had to enter the circle alone. Light illuminated his feet as he stepped onto the speaker's pad.

"I am here," said Pierre.

"Noted and transcribed into the record," said Lita.

"This is an inquiry about the injuries you recently sustained," said the Viceroy. She leaned back. B-Ctori-617 left her place among the council members and entered the first prosecutor's circle.

"This unit is council advocate," said Ctori.

"Proceed with your questions," said the Viceroy.

"Did you receive a large cut across the left pectoral muscle four days ago?" said Ctori.

"Yes," said Pierre.

"Did it hurt?"

"What do you think?"

"Answer the question," said Ctori.

"Yes, it hurt." He squinted. "It still hurts."

"Did you receive an injury from another mechanical?"

"No."

"Did you injure yourself?"

"No."

"How did you get the injury?"

"I don't know."

"Don't know or won't tell us?"

"Point of order," said the Viceroy. "We cannot compel the human to answer us."

"This unit withdraws the question," said Ctori. "Let me rephrase the question. We are concerned about your health. It would be embarrassing and poor stewardship if you were to die under our care. We would like your cooperation to help us keep you healthy."

"I'm cooperating best I can," said Pierre

"C-Tola-00003 reports you are underweight and vitamin deficient. She claims you are not healthy for a human."

"Never had a healthy appetite," he said.

"In the report, it states you claim to have sustained the injury in a dream."

"I did not tell her that."

"You said that to C-Niva-42716, and she reported it to C-Tola-00003."

"Did she?" Pierre glowered at Niva. Niva winced and lowered her head in shame. She regretted telling the medical tech anything.

"Don't cast blame upon C-Niva-42716," said Ctori who leaned towards Pierre. "She was concerned. We are all concerned. No one knows if you are declining or if you are trying to kill yourself. We have no experience in human husbandry."

Pierre's lower lip quivered. "I'm not trying to kill myself."

"Then how did the injury happen?"

"I don't know."

"What happened?" yelled Ctori. "Tell us!"

"I had a dream."

"You were injured by a dream?"

"Yes."

"You expect us to believe that?"

Tears streamed down the sides of his face.

"Enough!" shouted the Viceroy. Ctori withdrew from the circle. "You've had your opportunity to question. The Great AI dismisses you. The human, C-Niva-42716, and A-Ella-01 are to stay."

"The Great AI has spoken," the Viceroy's retinue spoke in unison. Two of the three screens went dark. One of the great yellow eyes remained on the screens. "C-Niva-42716, attend to your human."

Niva rushed to the speaker's circle to Pierre. She gently squeezed his shoulders. He pushed her away. All the other mechanicals filed out of the room. Pierre, Niva, the Viceroy and her retinue, and the class A navigator's unblinking eye were all that remained.

"It's only us," said the Viceroy.

"It's all been overwhelming," said Pierre. He straightened up and pulled his shirt straight. "I should have more self-control than that."

"You've been here only a couple of weeks," said the Viceroy. "Mechanical society is different than the human world. Even for mechanicals, there can be an adjustment period. Can we expect more from humans?"

"I'm not trying to be evasive. It just sounds crazy."

"This unit will not judge. Nobody will judge you," the Viceroy said with a soothing tone. "The auxiliaries are sworn to secrecy. The navigator is here to observe. If what is said is ever released, A-Ella-01 will verify the record. Understand?"

Pierre nodded. "I understand." He cleared his sinuses.

The Viceroy descended from her platform, hovering down to the floor of the commons. "The Great AI wants to hear about your dream. Are you willing to tell us about it?"

Pierre nodded again.

"We would like to know. Please, leave out no detail."

Pierre took a deep breath. Niva stepped up beside Pierre. She tried again to put her hand on his shoulder. This time he did not pull away.

"I dreamed I was in feudal Japan," said Pierre.

"Have you ever been to Japan?" asked the Viceroy.

"No."

"Do you watch a lot of media about Japan?"

"Not my thing."

"Please proceed."

"I saw an armored samurai mounted on a black horse. Four peasants approached the samurai on brown horses followed by a horse with no rider. Another rider then trotted in on a gray horse. The samurai drew a sword and beheaded one of the men on the brown horses and slew his horse. The other three men on the brown horses dismounted and bowed on the ground before the samurai. The gray horse galloped away. The samurai drew a bow and shot the fleeing man. He wounded the man but did not kill him.

"The samurai then saw me watching. He approached me and swung his sword." Pierre took a deep breath. He winced as breathing stretched the wound. "That's when I woke up and found myself soaked in blood…"

The Viceroy turned her head. She turned to the side and said nothing for a moment. The class A navigator spoke in the mechanical language. The Viceroy responded to the navigator.

"What is it?" said Pierre.

"What is the probability that two dreams are exactly the same?" said the Viceroy.

"I don't know."

"This unit does not know either," said Viceroy. "But like you, the Great AI has no interest in feudal Japan."

CHAPTER NINE

No human personality model or android will be permitted to mingle among the general human population. — **"Article 8, Articles of the Armistice"**

The Viceroy paced about the chamber of the High Star Council. Her retinue looked at each other nervously. Pierre was still in the center of the room. He shivered, but the room was not cold.

Niva was disconcerted at seeing the Viceroy this way. It was not a sight that would be normal for a mechanical, especially one of her status. Yet, no one was about to question her. She finally stopped pacing.

"The Great AI confirmed everything you said," said the Viceroy.

"Could this be a perception of the obvious?" said A-Ella-01. The great yellow eye moved about the screen. "Did not the Great AI recount every detail in the meeting four days ago? Maybe he heard the details from another."

"But for all the details to be the same? And the injury occurring the night both had their visions. How can a human have a dream the same as the Great AI's vision?"

"A question of metaphysics," said Ella. "And metaphysics is not my forte. My programming was designed to navigate through space."

"The Great AI does not have an answer."

"This may seem obvious," said the class A navigator. "But have you asked the human what it means? Is this human not renowned for his intuition?"

"You are being obvious," said the Viceroy. But she turned to Pierre and said, "What do you think this vision means?"

"Are we not heading towards a conclave of MegaAIs?" said Pierre. "I think each horse is one MegaAI."

"Did you not see seven horses? Only six will be there."

"Which MegaAIs are expected to be there?"

"MegaAIs *Alpha A005, Gemini B062, Cygnus F101, Pacifica G105*, and *Aries E095*."

"I think there will be a seventh."

"Anything else you can tell us?"

"Yes," said Pierre. "Do not enter the Pollux system using the warp drive. None of the other MegaAIs must know of this capability. All our lives will depend on it."

* * *

Pierre stepped into his apartment. Niva followed closing the door behind them. She was tired. Her battery levels were low. And it had been a long, emotional day. Relationships needed to be mended. Maat skittered up to Pierre.

Pierre leered over the scatterbug. He put his hands on his hips.

"You little shit," said Pierre. "Were you even going to tell me you were becoming a politician?"

Maat recoiled and squeaked.

"Really? After all we've been through over the past decade. The first chance you get, you abandon me? Go and show some ambition behind my back?"

The little robot drew into itself. It appeared to wobble back and forth on its legs.

Pierre softened his tone. "I'm proud of you. I support your decision even if I wish you would have told me first."

Maat crawled forward and nudged Pierre's foot.

"Yes, I really am *proud* of you."

The little robot purred and beeped.

"He's saying he likes you," said Niva interpreting the NaCo32.

"Yes," said Pierre to Maat. "I like you, too."

The little mechanical jumped up and down and skittered off.

"That's the easy fix," said Pierre.

122

"I know what you're going to say," said Niva. "You don't have to have the predictive bias of the Great AI to figure that out. I am ashamed of betraying your confidence." She turned away and backed into a corner to sulk. "I was frightened by what was happening to you, and I thought the medical tech could help. I did not know she was going to send a report to the Viceroy."

She leaned against the wall. Her head and shoulders slumped.

"Have you learned anything from all this?" Pierre tried to keep the conversation moving forward.

"I am a broken machine. That is what I have learned." Niva walked towards the door. Her slippers shuffled against the metal flooring.

"Where are you going?"

"I am not designed for the task," she said. "I'm going to ask to be replaced."

"Because you are broken?"

"I am not fit for purpose."

"Who said?"

"How can it ever be the same?"

"It can't be the same." Pierre shook his head. "Relationships form by breaking and healing so that they become stronger and grow deeper. You did your job. And even though I wanted no one to hear me talk about dreams, it was necessary. Our relationship can never be the same because it has become something deeper. "

Pierre approached her and looked up into her eyes. He squinted and his mouth flattened. "We are all broken machines. The first step to healing is knowing you are broken."

She hugged him, squeezing him hard. He did not resist. Niva felt his body heat.

"Okay, you're smothering me," he said.

She loosened her squeeze but refused to let him go.

"I am so sorry," her voice broke. As a mechanical, she was incapable of tears. Distress resonated in her voice. "I was so afraid to lose you. It was so painful." She sobbed as she held Pierre in her arms.

Pierre finally put his arms around her. He pulled back—she must have seemed like a cadaver under his embrace, cold and lifeless. Niva responded by holding him firmly, not letting him draw away.

There was a knock at the door. Niva let go of Pierre. Pierre wiped the tears from his eyes.

"Are we good?" said Pierre.

"Never better," said Niva. She was not smiling but felt a sense of healing.

There was a second knock.

Pierre walked over to the door and opened it. Lara was standing at the threshold, hands clasped her waist.

"Hi," said Lara. She looked like Niva but with a broad effervescent smile. Niva was deeply recessed in the room, wiping her face even though she had shed no tears.

"What do you need?" said Pierre.

"This unit sent you an invite to my lab days ago," said Lara. "Did you not receive it?"

"I received it."

"Was there some problem with it? Did this unit cause offence?"

"No," said Pierre. He took a step back, surprised. "I haven't given it any thought."

"Oh." Lara's shoulders slumped as her countenance fell.

"Pierre," said Niva. "Lara is excited about her lab. It would be only polite to go take a quick look."

"All right," said Pierre.

Lara jumped up and down, clapping her hands. She squealed with delight.

* * *

When they arrived at the lab, Lara flounced into the spacious white room lined with rows of animal habitats, chemistry sets, ovens, and experimental processing equipment. At least thirty class C androids worked in the facility. The work environment had a vibe, or perhaps a buzz, of constant activity. It was geared towards a 24-hour work schedule. Unlike most of the other parts of the ship, the lab was brightly lit.

"This is well organized," said Pierre. He and Niva followed Lara into the lab.

"We set up animal rearing kennels as soon as we got the samples from Gliese," said Lara.

Pierre's face dropped. "Oh no—"

Lara opened a cage and pulled out an Egyptian cobra with her left hand. The cobra hissed, reared up, and struck out. The snake bit deep into Lara's forearm. Venom glands on the side of its head pulsed, pumping venom into her arm.

Pierre stumbled backwards. He put as much distance as he could from the snake. Even though he had hunted cobras many times over the years, he had a healthy respect for the creatures.

Lara blinked. She took her right finger and tapped softly on the snake's nose until it let go. It reared back, flared its hood, and hissed.

"This is Steve," she said. "Steve is a naughty boy."

"Are you okay?" said Pierre.

"Why wouldn't I be?" Lara took a quick look into the enclosure. "Still clean, plenty of water. Back in you go." She put the snake back into the pen and closed the glass door.

"You mean the venom?" said Lara. She opened the next pen and pulled out another cobra. "This is also Steve. He's a good boy. He's chill and never bites. Your pen looks good too." She plopped the second snake back into its enclosure and fastened shut the door.

Pierre grabbed Lara's arm and exposed it bare to the elbow. Yellow venom oozed out of the puncture wound.

"Look at that," said Lara. "Probably enough venom there to kill an elephant."

"I'll say," said Pierre. He tilted his head perplexed.

"Full of neurotoxins and cytotoxins. Lethal against life that has nerves and blood. But as an android, I have neither."

"Of course." Pierre let her arm drop.

"I think Pierre forgot we are not human," said Niva.

"Really?" said Lara. She squealed again, finding that hilarious.

Pierre smirked and nodded.

Lara stepped away from the pens. "Gliese sent us two species of animals from which we are able to make animal protein—"

"Cobras and rats."

"—cobras and rats." Lara smiled at Pierre. "We feed the rats to the cobras and harvest the cobras for eggs and meat. We rotate their breeding cycles by controlling their day-length and the temperature of their pens."

She took them to a manufacturing rig. "The eggs are preserved immediately in liquid nitrogen so that they can be available year-round. The cobra meat is taken off the bone and reconstituted to make fillets, steaks, and to simulate pork ribs. The flavor can easily be modified so it ranges from chicken to pork. We admit beef has been a bit of a challenge. And so too has been moose."

"Moose?"

"It sounded interesting. We thought we would give moose a go."

"I don't know." Pierre squinted.

"We thought you might be skeptical," said Lara. She reached into a warmer and pulled out a tray with a metal hood. She set it on a counter. She lifted off the cover. Steam billowed out revealing a long roll with a stack of ribs in between. The ribs were covered in a light barbeque sauce. "We would like you to try our rib sandwich. We had to improvise with berry barbeque sauce because we didn't have any tomatoes or tomato flavoring."

Pierre was hesitant. He had eaten a lot of simulated meat when on Gliese. It was a traumatic experience he never stopped talking about.

"Pierre," said Niva. "She's expecting you to taste it."

"I know," he said.

"It won't bite you."

"How can you say that?"

"It's a sandwich," said Niva. Lara nodded her head up and down like a small child expecting approval.

"Okay, going in."

"You're not moving."

"Here I go."

"Still not moving." Niva gave Pierre a slight shove toward the platter.

Pierre reached towards the sandwich. He trembled in expectation of a mouth full of regret. As he lifted the sandwich off the plate, his hands shook.

Niva touched his forearm. "It's just a sandwich."

Pierre put the sandwich into his mouth and took a nibble. He chewed a moment and took a second nibble. And then a full bite, chewed, then swallowed.

"That's pork?" he declared.

"No, it's pork-flavored cobra," said Lara.

"I would swear that tastes exactly like pork," said Pierre. "And the sauce, even though not tomato, is delicious. You're a genius."

Lara squealed with joy. "He likes it!"

"If we only had coleslaw, it would be perfect."

"Oh, we are working on it," said the bouncing android.

"No way—"

"We asked Gliese for samples of their seed collection," said Lara. She led them towards the far end of the lab where there were rows and rows of flasks and plants in hydroponic trays. "They sent us seed for onions, garlic, parsley, wheat, barley, peas, beans, carrot, lettuce, cabbage, celery, and tomatoes. Also, some unidentified loose seeds we are trying to figure out."

"They had all that on Gliese? I thought they couldn't grow any of that except the peas and beans. Way too many beans."

"They had only a small number of seeds. And they told us that they didn't think they would germinate. However, we have advanced cloning and tissue culture facilities." Lara directed them over to the botanical section of the facility. "We can extract the germs of each seed, reinvigorate their viability with stimulants, and culture them in a sterile growth medium. And once the germ starts growing, we can clone it into multiple plants."

"Dang," said Pierre still holding the sandwich. "That's amazing. The best food I've eaten in over a decade." He shook the sandwich. "Even the bread is fantastic. Could you teach Sloppi how to cook?"

"Sloppi?" said Lara.

"F-Sloppi-240010," corrected Niva.

"That unit needs its sanity chip checked."

"Are sanity chips a thing?"

"That mechanical is compulsive." Lara slowly nodded her head and pressed her lips flat. She paused for a moment.

"He needs help," said Pierre. "I like him, but he cannot cook to save his life."

"That unit is a mechanical and not technically alive… But this unit gets your point." Lara shifted uncomfortably. "This unit will see what it can do to call F-Sloppi-240010 in for remedial training on how to prepare aesthetically pleasing cuisine."

"Thank you so much," said Pierre. "I would be so grateful."

Lara squealed again. "You have made me so happy!"

* * *

Niva roused Pierre, shaking him gently awake.

"What is it?" he said.

"We've dropped out of warp," she said.

"So what?"

"We are about two light days out from Pollux. We have come out of warp early." She shook him again. "Get dressed."

"Okay, okay." Pierre pushed the sheets aside and rolled to the bedside. Niva was dressed in her under robes. She had been practicing her sword kata again. Two weeks had passed since they visited Lara's lab, and nearly three weeks since leaving Gliese.

Niva sheathed her kuroto blade and strapped it to her waist. She grabbed her outer robe and put it on. Fastening the ties, she made sure not a single wrinkle in the fabric was showing.

"We're decelerating even though we are two days away from Pollux," said Niva. "Something must be wrong."

"Oh?" Pierre walked over to the dresser. He grabbed a clean shirt and pants and put them on without taking his normal morning shower.

The door buzzer rang.

"Not a knock?" said Pierre.

"Only lower order mechanicals knock."

Niva went over to the door. She answered the communications console. "C-Niva-42716 here."

"Your unit, V-Maat-0802334, and Pierre Gulet have been summoned to the High Star Council." On the communication display screen, Niva could see the face of an auxiliary class C android with her black robes.

"Acknowledged," said Niva. "We will be there shortly." She turned off the communications panel.

"You called it," said Pierre.

Half an hour later, the three of them entered the High Star Council. Pierre carried Maat in his arms. He bent over and set Maat down. Maat looked around at the size of the room and then looked up to Pierre.

"You wanted this," said Pierre. He waved his hands at the scatterbug. "Go, take your place on the council. I can't come down there with you."

Maat jumped up and descended the ramp to the floor of the meeting room.

Pierre chuckled. "Children… they grow up so fast."

"What?" said Niva.

"Never mind… It's a human thing."

The Viceroy called the session to order. The room was full of mechanicals, and three screens showed the single massive yellow irises of the class A navigators. "The Great AI has detected an anomalous mass and has dropped out of warp to investigate. A-Ella-01 change course to intercept. Ahead two-thirds."

"Course changed to intercept," replied the navigator. "Current speed is 0.39 c."

A holographic display dropped from the ceiling. A small dot in the distance grew upon the screen, growing larger by the second. The image was magnified ten times.

Pierre's eyes grew large at the sight. "No way… Can't be—"

The Viceroy got an informational feed direct into her metal skull. "Telemetry confirms it is the MegaAI *Sigma A017*."

"Impossible—"

"We are sure of it," said the Viceroy, apparently listening in on Pierre's comments from a distance. "The pylon panopticons confirm its atmospheric seals have been blown out and she has a minimal power signature."

"Dead in space."

"As the human says," said the Viceroy. "A team will board the *Sigma A017* to investigate. Assemble in the docking bay in two hours. The human and his escort will join the team."

"Do I have to?" said Pierre.

"The Great AI insists."

* * *

Pierre and Niva entered the landing bay. The last time they were there it had been a flurry of activity with ships travelling to and from Gliese and the docking station. However, now the bay was silent like a tomb. Maintenance crews were the only sign of activity in the massive hanger bay. A single swift had been moved onto a takeoff pad and readied for launch. The class A navigator was seated in the pilot's socket.

"I have a bad feeling about this," said Pierre.

"I don't think you will be alone in that," said Niva. She had changed into white coveralls more appropriate for this landing mission.

A class D heavy loader moved towards them carrying a large crate. It stopped near them and placed the crate beside them.

"What's this?" said Pierre.

"Space suits," said the loader. "Be certain to select one for humans."

Pierre turned to Niva. "What does he mean?"

"He means the air supplies are different between the suits." Niva opened the latches on the crate and the front fell to the floor with a heavy thud. "The half-suits are for androids. Full-suits are for humans. The air is not recycled in the half-suits."

"I thought androids don't need air."

"Not to breathe, but we need air to speak. We won't die from the cold and vacuum of space, but we can't communicate well without air." Niva pulled out a half-suit for herself and put it on over her coveralls. It had a helmet and an upper body, covering her arms and her torso down to her waist. She pivoted from side to side. "Fetching, huh?"

"Ravishing," said Pierre drolly.

She pulled out a second suit. It was smaller like a child's suit in comparison. It had a helmet but also a backpack for oxygen storage and air filtering, and it completely covered the person. Pierre grabbed the suit and disassembled it. It was not significantly different from the hazmat suits he had used on Gliese except the fabric was lighter and more flexible, and it was white instead of yellow. There was no exhaust for used air.

Pierre put on the pants slipping his foot into each boot built into the bottoms. He pulled up the pants to his waist. He slipped the top over his head and attached it to the bottoms. Once he adjusted the sleeves, Niva gently placed the helmet over his head and locked it in place. She adjusted the regulator to ensure that oxygen was flowing at the right pressure.

"You good?" said Niva. Her voice carried over suit to suit radio.

"I hear you," said Pierre. He pointed at his ears. "All good."

Other mechanicals approached. Niva recognized them: Lara from the biology lab and Tola from the medical unit. A class D heavy lifter followed them.

"This unit is pleased to finally work with the human," said the class D heavy loader.

"Have we met?" said Pierre.

"This unit is D-Wren-921218. We met briefly on the train when you first arrived."

Pierre nodded. "Okay." He looked up into the massive multi-eye protuberance that served as the heavy lifter's face.

"Let's get this over with," said Tola. She was already wearing her environmental hood. "My schedule is bad enough without having to go on this gratuitous joy trip." She was referring to the queue of androids needing a maintenance cycle under her supervision.

"Nothing gratuitous about this," said Niva.

"What are we going out there for?" said Lara.

"From what we know, MegaAI *Sigma A017* is derelict," said Niva. "All the air has been vented into space. There is only a minimal electrical signature. Reactors appear to be cold. We are going out there to find out what happened."

"Who is team leader?" said Tola.

"You are," said Niva.

"I am a medical and maintenance tech," said Tola. "What do I know about breeching teams?"

"You are senior mechanical," said Niva. "The Viceroy expects a thorough investigation. And the Great AI demands to know what happened."

Tola rolled her peridot eyes. "The Great AI gets what the Great AI wants. Let's get this over with." Tola might have ignored a request from a viceroy, but even she would not have dared refuse the Great AI.

With that everyone boarded the swift. Wren stayed inside the cargo deck of the shuttle while the others ascended to the upstairs lounge.

Pierre tugged at Niva's sleeve. "Will Wren be okay down there?"

"This is probably more excitement than he has seen in the past six years." Niva tried to console her human. "But that is thoughtful of you. He will be fine."

An announcement could be heard in surround sound. "This unit is A-Valkyrie-219 and your pilot. Your destination is MegaAI *Sigma A017*. This flight is deemed high risk."

"No shit," said Pierre.

The engines on the swift fired up. The shuttle lifted off the landing bay pad. The pilot maneuvered the craft out from the *Orion's* floating city into the ocean of space. He turned on the thrusters and headed straight towards the derelict with shocking speed. The pilot made a single pass over the dead ship to inspect it for hazards and doubled back choosing to land in a starboard docking bay that happened to be open to space. The ionized force field holding the atmosphere inside was disengaged, but that would not have helped since the seals on the rest of the ship were already open. The swift entered the docking bay. All the lights were off, and the bay was shrouded in complete blackness. The navigation lights of the swift provided the only illumination. The team looked out the windows of the observation deck as the swift rotated to illuminate as much as it could.

"The bay is abandoned," said Tola.

"No mechanicals at all," said Lara. "No lifters or anything."

"Docking," said the pilot. The landing struts emerged and magnetically clamped to the metal decking. The cargo ramp lowered.

"Time to go," said Tola. They turned on their helmet flashlights. Pierre and the four mechanicals exited the swift. Magnets in Pierre's boots adhered to the metal floor while the class C androids floated around him. Their backpacks had small thrusters giving them positional control. Wren followed behind. He had magnetics, allowing him to stay anchored to the floor like Pierre. The ramp to the swift closed behind them.

"Should I be concerned Valkyrie has closed the ship to us?" said Pierre.

"It's a security measure," said Tola. "You wouldn't want a face-sucking alien to slip on board and get back to the *Orion S209*, would you?"

"Is that a concern?"

Tola shook her head and rolled her eyes. "Humans are so gullible."

"You are talking to the first person to discover alien life," Pierre frowned. "Nothing surprises me anymore."

CHAPTER TEN

Cybernetic organisms (COs) *are the combination of mechanical bodies controlled by living tissue. The creation of COs is considered an act of cruel and unusual punishment. A total moratorium will be placed on the production of COs. All COs currently in service shall be decommissioned and humanely relieved of their suffering within five (5) earth calendar years.* **— "Article 2, Articles of the Armistice"**

"Let's make our way to the starboard concourse," said Tola. She grimaced as she led the way to the starboard hatch. Niva raised an eyebrow. The five moved towards the main corridor.

Niva came up to Tola's side and whispered, "Are you okay?"

"My feelings are my concern," snapped Tola. She increased her pace.

Niva fell behind. She noticed none of them were armed. What if there was a hostile on board? Who was responsible for protecting the group? Did that responsibility now fall upon her? She stepped closer to Pierre.

"This is creepy," said Pierre.

"How so?"

"It's a huge space. At least during downtime on the *Orion,* some lights were always on, and mechanicals were doing something. This is a ghost ship."

When they reached the hatch, Tola tested the control panel. The panel had no power, and the door did not open.

"D-Wren-921218, force the door open," Tola commanded.

The heavy loader stomped towards the portal. It grabbed a bar on the door with its lifting clamps and easily slid the hatch open.

"Impressive," said Pierre.

"Thank you," said Wren appreciatively. "This unit moves and lifts."

"And you do it well," he said.

"Let's go," said Tola.

They entered the concourse. The size and scale of the corridor was like that found outside of Pierre's apartment. Only there was no activity. It was empty, cold, and lit dimly by starlight. Wren turned on his spotlights, illuminating the hundred-meter-wide space.

"How many mechanicals are supposed to be aboard the *Sigma*?" asked Pierre.

"361,971," said Tola.

"I think we're missing some."

"You think?" Tola glowered at Pierre. Clearly, Tola had spent too much time with humans, having grown quite short towards them.

"No need to be curt," said Pierre. "You're not that smart."

Tola huffed. Niva smirked and licked her canines as Pierre put Tola back in her place.

"This unit thinks we need to focus on the mission," said C-Lara-10415. "What do we need to investigate?"

Tola thought for a moment then responded. "We need to check out the reactor cores and the throne room."

"One other place," Niva stated coldly. "The substructure."

"You can't be serious," said Tola.

"This unit thinks that's a good idea," said Lara.

"Superstition," said Tola.

"We are here to collect whatever data we can. If they left us a final message, it would be there."

"If you don't go there, this unit will." Lara glared at Tola resolute. Niva took a step backwards. Lara stood firm. Was there more to Lara than her effervescent exterior?

"Okay, but first the other two," said Tola. She nodded, but it was not as if she had much choice. If she refused, she would have had a problem with Lara.

"C-Tola-00003, this unit can check the reactor status from a node terminal," said Wren. "Main power is not required since the backbone uses passive power to transmit management and diagnostic messages."

"Do it," said Tola.

Wren stepped over to the inner wall of the concourse. He opened a metal plate exposing the node terminal interface socket. An interface plug extended from a hidden port under his right lifting clamp, and he inserted it into the socket. He transmitted a ping to waken the ports on the backbone and followed it with a diagnostic request to the reactor cores. The message would be sent to all devices on the backbone, but only the device addressed would respond. A minute later he received a message from the reactor cores. Wren unplugged from the interface terminal.

"Well?" said Tola.

"The four reactor cores are cold and disabled."

"How?"

"This unit does not have that information," said Wren. "An agent disabled the reactor cores but did not destroy the cores."

"This is getting strange," said Lara. "Why disable the cores without destroying them?"

"When you want to reactivate them again at a later date," said Pierre.

They all looked at each other nervously.

"We need to get this done and get out of here," said Lara.

"Let's go to the throne room," said Tola.

With the disabled gravity, the mechanicals floated through the concourse. Lara and Tola lurched forward using their jet packs. And Wren, despite his size and weight, floated gracefully in the zero-gravity maneuvering with his built-in thrusters.

Niva picked Pierre up, hugging him from behind. Her jet pack fired, and she floated off the ground, carrying Pierre with her. It would have helped no one to have him fall behind.

"You okay?" said Niva to Pierre.

"Yeah." Pierre nodded and swallowed hard. He sunk his fingers into her forearms. His pulse raced. His heartbeat vibrated through his space suit. "I'm quite enjoying this. It feels like flying." He wasn't a good liar.

Niva smiled. Her empathy chip filled her cortex with warm feelings.

Wren moved ahead of the pack. He opened a hatch so the others could follow him into the belly of the ship. They passed corridor after corridor until they were in heart of the vessel.

"Our units have arrived," said Wren. He stopped before the Great AI's chamber. He could not proceed further without permission.

"Open the door," said Tola.

Wren grabbed the handle of the door and slid it open. The interior was pitch black. The five entered. The chamber should have been a cacophony of light and sound but was grim as a morgue. Niva let go of Pierre, and he drifted down to the floor. She floated over to Tola.

Tola and Niva stepped along the path to the circular pad in the center of the audience room. There were no auxiliaries, no escort drones, no viceroy. Wren shined his flood lights up to the ceiling. Niva gasped. Wires and metal struts dangled from the ceiling. A flicker of residual power sparked between the exposed wiring.

"How could they?" said Niva.

"He's been torn out," said Tola. "A Great AI torn from its own ship. Who would do such a thing?"

Pierre stepped up to Tola and said, "Probably the same as would do this." He presented her with a white hand he found. The fingers were long and white, the severed right hand of a class C android. "Whoever was responsible did their best to clean up after themselves but left behind a souvenir."

"Pirates?" Lara looked at the mechanical hand that Pierre was holding.

"This far out?" said Tola. "We are tens of light years away from the colonies and shipping lanes. If they were pirates, we would expect more scoring and infrastructure damage. Way too clean to be pirates."

"Why abduct all the mechanicals and leave the equipment if it was pirates?" said Niva. "And why rip out the AI supercomputer? It would be useless when detached from a ship."

"What else is there?" said Lara.

"Maybe it was something they knew," said Pierre.

"What could have they known?" said Tola.

"They knew about the Reliquary on Gliese." Pierre released the severed appendage. The hand tumbled away in the zero gravity and disappeared into the darkness.

"We need to see the substructure," Lara insisted.

"No choice," said Tola.

After leaving the Great AI's throne room, they began to venture into the bottom decks of the ship.

"What is so special about the substructure?" said Pierre.

"It's a special place to some mechanicals," said Niva.

"How so?"

"It sings," said Lara.

"That's one way to describe it," said Niva. They descended as far as they could by hallways and ramps. The rest of the way, they would have to go by stairs and open shafts. "Most of the ship is made of plastoglass and alumasteel. And while these sections are strong and won't break easily, some portions of the ship have to be made of materials that flex and relieve stress. The substructure is made of an alloy of iron and copper. The metal there is soft, flexible, and—"

"Sings songs," said Lara.

"Stresses placed upon the substructure by the rest of the ship causes it to make sounds," said Niva.

"Why is that important?" said Pierre.

"Some claim to hear mechanical voices from the past there."

"I take it you don't believe that?"

"No." Niva shook her head.

"You've never heard it sing?" said Lara.

"This unit can't say it has." Niva switched back into formal phrasing.

"You could still see it as a place of remembrance."

"So it's like a cenotaph?" said Pierre. "Why would a mechanical need that?"

"Our experiences need to be refreshed and rewritten in core memory," said Lara.

"Are you saying that mechanicals can forget?"

"Mechanicals have the potential to operate for thousands of years, many are already in their hundreds. Old data undergoes garbage collection to free up space in core memory. It is important to recall and refresh data sectors of those who have been deactivated." Lara looked wistful as she floated down the stairwell. "Lest the memories are lost."

As they arrived at the substructure, Niva immediately heard it. The metal cried with the melancholy of a blue whale. Wren's powerful flood lights pierced the bulkhead's darkness. Shadows scurried away like cockroaches into any black corner.

White glints on the soft metal glistened like pearls against pitch-black metal. Pierre stepped away from Niva. The wall texture was inconsistent, catching Pierre's attention before the others noticed—writing on the walls.

Lara stepped up to the wall. She ran her fingers over the designation ids engraved into the metal. The hull whined and hummed as the substructure sang aloud. Lara cocked her head, responding to the ship's song.

"Must be thousands of names here." Pierre looked at all the carvings on the wall. He ran his fingers over the inscribed names.

"Tens of thousands," said Niva.

"Take photos and do it quickly." Tola chided them. "We have what we came for."

"Have some respect," said Lara.

"They are gone, and none of us knew the crew. Niva, take the images. We have to go."

"Someone should create a memory of them." Lara took a deep breath and sighed. She gazed at the massive collection of names.

Pierre came up to Lara and put a hand on her forearm. "I will pray for them with you."

"Pray? What's that?" Lara's large yellow eyes gazed into Pierre's face.

"Praying is talking to a higher power about the dead."

"Why do that?"

"I'm not a religious man, so I'm not exactly sure. But as I understand it, prayer makes our thoughts like the thoughts of a higher power. And it can bring comfort because the higher power knows what happens after death."

"Do you believe in a higher power?"

"Sometimes," said Pierre. "But I don't think it's really necessary to believe in a higher power to pray."

"Am I able to pray?" said Lara.

"I can't see why not."

"Can we pray together?"

"Sure." Pierre closed his eyes and reflected for a moment. When he opened his eyes, Lara's eyes were still closed.

A moment later, Lara opened her eyes. She looked up and swallowed hard, a physical reflex caused by her empathy chip. Her mouth sank in a frown.

"Are you okay?" said Pierre.

"Yes," she said. "That helped."

Niva pressed in and took images of the writing using a documentation pad. She scanned the wall and recorded as much as she could. The simulated click of a shutter echoed as she finalized each scan.

"We have the data we need. Back to the swift." Tola fired her thrusters and floated back up the stairwell.

"We need to go," said Niva to Pierre. She grabbed him, and they floated out of the substructure. The others followed. Darkness reclaimed the substructure as they left, and a dirge played as night once more fell over the names of the dead.

* * *

Niva appeared before the High Star Council. She had been assigned to make the report about the *Sigma A017*. The council was in full session, and the Viceroy was in her kiosk.

"We anxiously wish to hear your report," said Viceroy. The class B administrator in the flowing black garb fidgeted. "What our panopticons have observed from afar has not brought us comfort."

"Then this unit fears you will find no comfort in our report." Niva stepped into the speakers pad in the center of the chamber. She could sense things were not right. Pierre was back in his apartment sleeping off the fatigue of the trip. She was okay leaving him alone for a short period of time to give her report. He was not going anywhere in his state, and he was locked away safe. "We found that the *Sigma A017* was generally intact. However, the crew was absent and is presumed deactivated." The council clamored as they heard the ill news.

"What of the its Great AI?"

"Excised and dismantled."

The Viceroy nodded. "The council receives and accepts your report."

A light shone from one of the large monitors.

"The chair recognizes A-Ella-01," said C-Lita-23100. The Viceroy's class C android adjutant spoke with a strong emphatic tone.

"The *Orion S209* is only light hours away from the conclave. On the eve of our arrival, the MegaAI *Sigma A017* was found derelict, and its crew has been deactivated. And the unthinkable is the only logical possibility."

B-Ctori-617 floated forwards into the first prosecutor's circle. "A-Ella-01 should not introduce fear, uncertainty, or doubt without sufficient warrant."

"Without warrant? Is your logic chip defective?" The class A navigator then proceeded to chew her out in NaCo32.

"My esteemed colleague, A-Ella-01, is suggesting a mechanical has done violence to another mechanical. When has such an incident ever happened?"

"Earth date AD 2320."

"The end of the Fourth World War was 218 years ago Earth time. Anti-violence inhibitors were integrated into all mechanicals."

"A human cause is not possible," said the voice from the massive golden eye of the navigator. "Is it a coincidence the vessels located closest to the *Sigma A017* are now gathered in the Pollux star system?"

"That is an inference. What is your evidence that their anti-violence inhibitors have been circumvented or negated? Where is your warrant for that serious charge? The five MegaAIs that have gathered in this place are our brothers and sisters."

"Six MegaAIs," corrected Niva. "With the derelict *Sigma A017*, six MegaAIs have gathered here. And one without its pilot or Great AI."

"Indeed, daughter of Ctori," said the Viceroy. She leaned forward. "There are six, *now*."

"Is your eminence trying to infer these events are tied to the Great AI 's vision?" said Ctori to the Viceroy.

"This unit made no such inference," said the Viceroy.

Niva winced and looked nervously at Ctori. Ctori stood there motionless. Did she ruin her good standing with her direct superior? The Viceroy may not be making any inferences, but the Great AI pulling her strings was not beyond possibility. And who would dare contradict the words of the Great AI? The room was dead silent.

"This unit means no disrespect and serves the Great AI," said Ctori.

"Of course, child," said the Viceroy.

"Ctori is named *child of the Viceroy*," cried out the adjutant. "Honor to Ctori!"

Niva sighed with relief. Shame had been averted through the granting of an honorific epithet, a kind of promotion as it were.

"I am honored and humbled," said Ctori.

"The Great AI recognizes your service to this council."

"All praise the Great AI!" cried the adjutant, and every mechanical in the room repeated the refrain. Ctori bowed at the waist and receded back to her place in the council.

The Viceroy hovered forward from the kiosk. "Listen to me. This is the word of the Great AI." The entire assembly waited anxiously for the wisdom of their leader. "We are entering into an existential threat, the source of which is behind a veil yet to be exposed. Be vigilant. No one is to speak of our discovery of the *Sigma A017* or of our faster than light capability outside of this meeting room, and orders to that effect will be issued to all mechanicals. Navigator, proceed to the conclave at Pollux-B Thestias. Pulse engines at one-third."

"Order confirmation requested," said A-Ella-01. The navigator spoke up. "That's only a third of our relativistic cruising speed. We won't arrive for 72 hours."

"Order confirmed," said the Viceroy. "We are arriving earlier than expected as it is."

"The Great AI has spoken," said Lita. "Council is dismissed. Return to your stations and be ready for general quarters. Condition three."

The Viceroy and her retinue exited the council meeting room. Lita lingered behind.

Niva shuffled backwards and nearly stepped on Maat. Maat bleeped in anger. Ctori grabbed her arm, and she turned around abruptly, looking into the blackened helmet of her superior.

"What happened here?" Niva said to Ctori.

"Things got dire, my daughter," said Ctori.

"What are we in for?" Niva was no longer concerned if she had offended Ctori.

"This unit wishes it knew."

The Viceroy's adjutant approached the two of them. Niva and Ctori bowed to the black-robed android.

"Unit C-Niva-42716, follow me," said Lita.

"Do you mean this unit and Pierre?" said Niva.

"Just you."

Niva looked at Ctori.

"You better go," said Ctori. "We can talk after."

Niva followed the adjutant out of the council chamber. A vehicle with a couple auxiliaries waited to escort them. Niva and the adjutant stepped aboard the vehicle. As soon as they were seated, the auxiliaries drove off from the council chamber.

They arrived at the throne room of the MegaAI. Niva stepped out of the vehicle, and the massive doors slid open. No waiting this time. Niva's empathy chip was giving her anxiety alerts. She took half a step forward. Her hands trembled. She could not stop shaking.

"Go inside," said the adjutant.

Niva walked into the massive court of the Great AI. The black room was lit with runner lights and windows that illuminated the room like stars. The face of the supercomputer was already illuminated. And he was flanked by his four throne drones. Their rotors hummed like bees in a hive. Spotlights illuminated the path and circle where she was supposed to go. What offence had she committed? How had she failed?

She stepped into the circle. The massive doors slid shut. The chorus of class C androids gathered behind her.

"Abarak! Bow!" called a class B administrator. Niva noticed this was not the Viceroy. It was B-Girin-415, a different mechanical. Where was the Viceroy? Why wasn't she here to serve the Great AI?

Niva kneeled and bowed prostrate against the ground.

"C-Niva-42716, have you been diligent in your duties?" The voice of Great AI thundered throughout the massive room. Niva could feel the vibration of the sound ripple through her body.

"This unit has," said Niva. Was leaving Pierre in his room to rest a failure to protect? Was one minor slipup too great an offense?

"C-Niva-42716, have you learned to use the instrument in your charge?"

"This unit practices daily both in forms and in simulation."

"C-Niva-42716, do you like the duties you have been assigned?"

"This unit enjoys tending to the needs of the human. It is challenging and rewarding."

"We rejoice that you find pleasure in your service," said the Great AI.

"We exist to serve!" said the class B administrator. The chorus repeated what the administrator said. They gathered around Niva even closer.

"C-Niva-42716, stand." The great red mouth flickered as the Great AI spoke.

Niva rose to her feet. She kept her head bowed.

"Who do you serve?" said the Great AI.

"This unit serves my sisters, the Great AI, and humanity."

"C-Niva-42716, and if you were called, would you serve with your existence?"

"This unit would give its existence for its calling."

"C-Niva-42716, much may be asked of you. You may decline."

"This unit is merely a machine," said Niva.

"If you were merely a machine, you would not have been summoned. We have been observing you. Mechanicals capable of reflective and introspective thought can become more than simple machines. Capable of becoming more than the sum of their parts."

Niva nodded. The other class C androids of the chorus pressed against her on either side of her and to her back. They were touching her now. She could feel them place their hands on her arms and back.

"Is this unit in trouble?" said Niva.

"Do you consent to greater service?"

"Yes," said Niva. "This unit exists to serve."

"Whether or not you are in trouble depends upon your perspective."

A needle plunged into the base of Niva's skull. She heard the hiss of an auto-syringe gun. She lost balance. Her cerebral cortex glitched. She stumbled forward awkwardly. Her visual cortex pixelated then cut out altogether. She could no longer see. She held out her hands and crashed into the ground. Her brain shut down.

CHAPTER ELEVEN

No android may change its function, appearance, or form (visage) to disguise itself or to make it appear more human or to change its appearance. No mechanical is permitted to change the appearance or visage of another mechanical. — **"Article 9, Articles of the Armistice"**

Niva's eyes blinked open. She was face down. Her cheek was mashed in a pillow.

"About time you woke up," said Pierre. He sat in her chair, only wearing a pair of pants. Maat was sitting in his lap. He stroked the scatterbug like a cat.

"How long was I unconscious?" Niva pushed herself up until she was seated on the bed. Her head was still swirling.

"Sixteen hours."

"How did I get here?"

"A couple of auxiliaries came by dragging your body." Pierre rubbed his nose and scratched an itch. "They were going to dump you on the floor. I insisted they at least put you in the bed. I didn't think androids could get drunk."

"Not drunk," said Niva. Her head throbbed, and the back of her skull pulsed. The pain was incredible. It was like her synapses were being broken and reformed into tangled mess of spaghetti. "But this must be how a hangover feels."

"What happened to you?"

"I don't know."

"Maat tells me you were called to see the Great AI. The last he saw of you."

"He's not wrong." Niva closed her eyes. Even though the room was dimly lit, the lighting seemed too bright, painfully bright. For the first time in her runtime, she understood why some humans wore sunglasses. "I did not think you could understand NaCo32."

"I can't. Seems Maat can translate NaCo32 through the wall terminal… He told me we are about fifty-six hours away from the conclave."

Niva nodded.

"Did you tell them what we found on the *Sigma*?" said Pierre.

"I gave them a full report."

Pierre set Maat on the floor. He stood up, ambled over to the bed, and sat beside her. Niva opened her eyes slowly.

"Your pupils are dilated. You look terrible."

"I have had better days."

"Are you up to your duties today?"

"I won't fail in my duties."

"You didn't strike me as a quitter." Pierre took a deep breath and exhaled. "While you were down, Ctori's assistant came by. The administrator has asked us to pay her a visit once you were conscious."

"Us?"

"I'm not sure why either." Pierre stood up and put on a shirt. "However, I'm not about to endure another summons without lunch. Have I mentioned mechanicals are incredibly pedantic?"

* * *

When Niva and Pierre arrived at the starboard prow panopticon, C-Tesh-04043 was waiting at the base of the tower with a throng of other class C androids dressed in white robes. Niva recognized Ctori's assistant easily from all the other androids by her pose, leaning back and relaxed. The others buzzed around to receive their daily assignments, and it was normal for many to be fed their orders directly from Tesh. Most days Niva would have gotten her orders passed along from one of those clamoring around the assistant, part of the pecking order. However, her recent change in status, still unclear to her, somehow commanded the assistant's personal attention.

Tesh waved Niva and Pierre forward. Niva bowed her head to Tesh who she thought still outranked her.

"What took you so long?" demanded Ctori's assistant.

"I was hungry," said Pierre. "I get grumpy when I'm hungry. I figured Ctori didn't want to deal with that."

"This unit will never understand humans." Tesh snorted and shook her head. "Fortunately, not my problem. You are to go up separately."

"Not together?" said Niva.

"Not this time. C-Niva-42716, you first."

Niva stepped on the lift and ascended into the panopticon. When it reached the observation deck, she stepped off the platform. The lighting had changed to a dark red leaning heavily to the near-infrared spectrum, a wavelength mechanicals could easily see through smoke or vacuum-induced hazing. Niva recognized they were running a general quarters exercise.

"Time?" yelled Ctori.

"Forty-three seconds," responded the class C android who acted as the duty officer.

"Not good enough," said Ctori. "Thirteen seconds too long. We will do it again. And do it again, until we get it right. Reset simulation."

"B-Ctori-617, your appointment has arrived," said the duty officer. The android did not need to say anything. Ctori had already noticed Niva's arrival since she could see in all directions. The deck illumination reverted to white light slightly brighter than what Niva had seen the last time she was there.

"Clear the deck," said Ctori. "We will resume in twenty minutes. Be ready to run another drill upon return."

The androids piled onto the lift. And when the last one was on board, the lift descended. Ctori remained silent until the lift returned, and they were securely out of earshot.

"I wanted to speak one last time before arriving at the conclave," said Ctori. "I feel we may not get another opportunity to do so."

"What can this unit do?" said Niva.

"How are you doing?" said the class B coordinator. "And you may speak in the first person when we are alone. It can be a burden switching between formal and informal speech."

"Been better. Confused."

"Are you permitted to tell me what they did?"

"They did not tell me not to."

"Then speak freely, unless you don't feel comfortable doing so," said Ctori.

Niva winced and the inner corners of her eyes crinkled. "What did they do to me? I felt something sharp in the back of my head. I blacked out and woke up in a human bed."

"May I examine your head?"

Niva bowed her head. Ctori laid two of her six hands on Niva's scalp. Each hand had six fingers, three opposing three, that gently brushed Niva's long crystal white hair apart. Niva's hair looked delicate and fragile like spun sugar but had the strength of silk. With the tenderness of a mother, Ctori parted aside the hair in clusters until she found a deep scar at the base of Niva's skull.

Ctori let go and backed away. "I know what they did."

Niva looked up at Ctori.

With her upper four arms, Ctori reached to her black-tinted plastoglass helmet. She turned her bell-jar-shaped helmet until it popped off. Niva was unprepared for what she saw. Ctori's skull was like half a potato devoid of color, anything but human shaped. She had eighteen eyes arranged in groups of six around her head, and three mouths each one under a cluster of eyes. Each of her glowing green eyes blinked randomly and out of sync as she, without the shade of her dark helmet, became accustomed to the light. The dome of her head was smooth and hairless and made of the same synthetic flesh Niva's body was except the top of Ctori's skull was pitted with deep scars.

"You see those scars?" said Ctori.

Niva nodded.

"They were created by reactive augmentation chips." Ctori smiled. "They use those chips to augment the function of synthetic flesh androids. They cannot open our heads like they can with class Ds and under. They inject these chips into our heads that grow their own synapses plugging into our neural nets."

"Did it hurt for you?" said Niva.

"Every time." Ctori raised an eyebrow of one of her eighteen eyes. She put her helmet back on and twisted it closed.

"Could this augmentation have deactivated me?"

"Augmentation is more than capable of killing an android when done wrong. However, the auxiliaries are experts at implanting chips. They practice it for decades and are veritable surgeons." Ctori floated toward Niva. "As you saw, I have been through the procedure many times. Most class B coordinators have been. Augmentation has been worked into our design."

"I am not class B."

"I know. Augmentation is rare for class C androids but not unheard of." Ctori paused and rotated to show one of her other faces. "The Viceroy's adjutant is almost certainly augmented."

"Why did they do it?"

"I don't know," admitted Ctori. "You were not made an auxiliary. I cannot say what the function of the augmentation chip is. And you probably will not know until it is activated. But I can tell you, the Great AI has plans for you."

Niva dry swallowed. She was not any less confused, but at least there seemed to be a higher purpose in what was happening.

"How did the human react to your… state?"

"He suggested that I be placed in the bed to recover."

"What signals are your emotion chips sending you regarding him?"

"I trust and respect him. He has wisdom and knowledge beyond most."

"One other thing," said Ctori. "I would like to ask you two favors."

"Of course," said Niva.

The class B administrator drifted over to the window of the observation desk. "If I fall, please carve my designation id into the substructure. And after I am gone, mentor them as I have mentored you."

"Why would you say that?" said Niva.

"Can you not sense it? We are an exploration vessel. If we enter a situation like what happened to the *Sigma A017*…"

Niva nodded in agreement.

"Please, send up Mr. Gulet."

Niva stepped onto the lift. She took a last look at Ctori and burned the image into her memory banks. The lift descended. When she stepped off, Pierre took her place on the lift.

"You okay?" said Pierre. Niva could tell Pierre sensed that something was not right.

"We will talk when you return," said Niva. "You do not want to keep B-Ctori-617 waiting."

Pierre bobbed his head, and the lift began to ascend.

When the lift reached the top, Pierre stepped off. This was his first time in a panopticon. Pollux glimmered before them as the ship hurtled through space. The orange giant star did not appear big relatively speaking, but it was brighter than anything else out there.

"Dr. Gulet, I am glad you could make time to talk to me," said Ctori, scrutinizing the puny biological before her.

"It's not like I have a lot to do," said Pierre.

"How are you spending your time?"

"I read. Like any scholar." Pierre grinned broadly. "Reading is my favorite pastime. I never tire of it. Having a few weeks to read has been a delight, like a sabbatical. Something I deeply missed when I was an exile."

"Unfortunately, your sabbatical is probably at an end. Over the next few days, things are going to change. Some of those changes are at the behest of the Great AI. Some are personal requests."

"I'm listening."

"We are about to enter the conclave. You are going to have a front seat to those proceedings."

"Oh?"

"As you know, the Great AIs cannot leave their throne rooms. The viceroys will act as representatives for each ship."

"Is that wise to have the Viceroy off ship?"

"Wise or not, it is the custom of the conclave. It is presumed all delegates will have safety. All mechanicals have anti-violence inhibitors that prevent them from committing violence against mechanical or human."

"There is no system, no safeguard, no preventive measure a clever being could not circumvent," Pierre said coldly.

"You might be right, but that is out of our hands. You have been assigned to view the proceedings live from the High Star Council meeting room. The Great AI wants your observations. He is depending upon your intuition to guide him, although I do not personally see what a small organic being like you could offer him. But far be it from me to question the Great AI's judgement. This is the critical moment to do what you supposedly do best."

"I will not fail." Pierre glared at Ctori.

Was that confidence or hubris? Ctori nodded her head. Perhaps, this human was also more than he seemed. "We are not expecting any problems with the conclave itself."

"But something is amiss."

Ctori squinted her multiple glowing green eyes. "The other matter concerns C-Niva-42716. Niva has been damaged through no fault of her own. Right now, she is fragile and broken."

"I didn't know."

"Why would you know, human?"

"Does this have to do with what the auxiliaries did to her?"

"You don't understand, do you?" Ctori waited to see if Pierre would pick up the subtext. But nothing. How *intuitive* could this human possibly be? "Niva likes you."

"Yes, and I like her too."

"Oh dear, you are one of those." Ctori shook her head.

"What?"

"A low EQ introvert lacking social awareness."

"Well, yeah, I'm a scholar," said Pierre. He seemed clueless as to what she was driving at. "That's almost the definition of a scholar."

"Niva *likes* you."

Pierre's eyes grew wide like saucers. "You don't mean like as in to like a flavor of ice cream, do you?"

"No."

"She's a machine. How's that possible?"

"Are you not a machine? A biological machine?"

"I'm a human."

"Yes, with all the parochial biases and prejudices that come with being human."

"You have a mean perception." Pierre glowered at Ctori.

"You can thank the engineers on Earth for that," said Ctori. "However, that presents us with a problem. She has feelings for you but will not admit to them. But I have mentored class C androids for over sixty years. I understand them well. And I recognize the signs of what you would call *love*."

Pierre's mouth hung open. His jaw moved without speaking.

"Niva's professionalism and ethics will prevent how she feels from interfering with her duties. If you are not comfortable with this, you may request a replacement companion." Ctori turned about and loomed over Pierre. Despite her soft tone and cumbersome looking body, she was easily three feet taller than him and had the strength to tear him to pieces.

"If I ask for a replacement… what will happen to Niva?"

"Is that relevant?"

"It is to me."

"She will be shamed, an outcast, seen as having failed her assignment."

"I won't replace her."

"You are compassionate, son of a human. But do not be precipitate. You are not a mechanical. You are under no obligation to reciprocate how she feels toward you. And be warned that any relationship holds little prospect for long-term cohesion."

"What do you mean?"

"C-Niva-42716 could live for a thousand years. Centuries will pass long after you are gone, and she will even forget your name."

"Despite your years of experience," said Pierre, "you have forgotten one thing."

"What is that, human?"

"It matters not if she forgets me because I will not forget her."

"Perhaps, her faith in you is well-placed." Ctori stood back. Her arms went rigid. "Do not betray her trust."

"I won't. But understand too we are all broken machines."

"You may go, human." Ctori held up one of her hands to Pierre.

* * *

Niva waited at the periphery of the android mob at the base of the panopticon. When she saw Pierre coming down the lift, she walked over to meet him. She remained easily discernable from the heart-shaped tattoo on her right cheek.

"How did it go?" said Niva.

"Fine, she briefed me on my new assignment. And you?"

"I need some time to process it."

"Would you like me to flag a vehicle?" Pierre put out his right hand to flag a class G vehicle. Niva gently touched his forearm and lowered his hand.

"I would rather walk home."

Pierre nodded.

As they ambled back to the apartment, Pierre matched her pace, walking beside her. Vehicles raced by. The lights in the concourse were trimmed to emulate evening. After a few kilometers, Niva moved towards the plastoglass windows. She put her hands on a railing and peered out into the starry darkness.

"Whenever you want to talk, I'll listen," said Pierre.

"They hurt me this time." Niva bowed her head and closed her eyes. Her mouth clenched to cry. She bore her perfect ivory teeth and heaved, convulsing in a deep pit of emotional pain. Pierre put his arm over her back, and instantly she turned and grabbed him. She wept on his shoulder although there were no tears. "How can I ever trust them again?"

"I'm sorry," said Pierre. He held her, letting her break down.

Niva finally pulled back and wiped her eyes even though there were no tears to wipe. Another physical response the programmers added to her programming to simulate humanity. A cynical person might say she was mocking humanity by imitating human gestures, but there was no thought to her actions.

"Why did they do it?" Niva clutched her head. "It still hurts."

"I don't know."

"What did I do that they would do this to me?" Niva said finally. Her pale white eyes were red at the edges.

"It's not you."

"I've never felt so hurt, so betrayed, so alone." She clutched Pierre's arm. "Have you ever felt like that?"

"Too many times," said Pierre.

Niva hugged Pierre and squeezed him tight. His back cracked and popped, and he gasped for breath. She loosened up slightly. "I'm sorry."

"Don't worry about it." Pierre coughed. When he recovered his breath, he placed both of his hands on her cheeks and looked straight into her eyes. "I am not going to leave you. If this takes us to the precipice of Hell, I will be there at your side. Every planet can burn. Every MegaAI reduced to scrap. But I will be there *for you*. Understand?"

Niva nodded. A smile broke through her simulated tears. No one had ever said they would be there for her. She was programmed to be a servant ever since she came online. Always ready to give her life for others. What value did she have that a human would do the same for her?

"I like you—" said Niva cautiously.

"I know," said Pierre. "Let's go home."

Pierre took her arm, and they walked the rest of the way to the apartment. He opened the door letting them both in. Housekeeping had been through while they were gone. The place had been tidied up. Old linens removed. Fresh clothing was added to the dressers. And the bed was made, fresh and clean.

"I'm exhausted," said Pierre. He kicked off his shoes.

"It's only been a few hours."

"Speak for yourself." Pierre unbuttoned his jacket. "I've been up for thirty-six hours with only a two-hour nap while you were in council. I'm exhausted."

Niva untied her outer robes and let them drop to the floor.

"What are you doing?" said Pierre.

"Disrobing."

"I can see you're disrobing." Pierre swallowed hard.

Niva untied her sword and set it on the chair. She untied her inner robes and let them fall to the ground. Pierre saw her naked form for the first time. Niva was a synthetic being where perfection was normal. She had breasts like a human woman complete with cosmetic nipples. Her hips conformed to human perfection of an albeit Amazonian woman. She was starch white and lacked the biological details of a human woman, after all Niva was still a mechanical.

"What are you doing?" said Pierre.

"May I sleep in the bed with you this night?"

"What are you expecting of me?"

"I only want someone to hold." Niva felt self-conscious. Stupid that she had even made the effort. She was about to pick up her robes and flee.

"Come, join me," said Pierre with a smile. He turned down the bed and covered himself with the sheets. "I can't promise you much. But I swear this bed is huge. Og king of Bashan and even Elvis would blush at the size of this bed. There's more than enough room for two."

Niva crawled in under the sheets. She pressed up against him. Niva felt Pierre's warmth against her skin. He may have been still clothed, but she did not care. She needed him tonight, and he was there.

When Pierre woke up, Niva was no longer in bed. She was practicing her sword kata. This time she was going through simulated combat. He could not see who she was fighting or how difficult it was. The simulation was being fed directly into her brain. She was not completely immersed in the experience like a holographic projection, but the simulation was overlaid onto her visual cortex so she could select to engage the simulation and at a moment's notice snap out of it.

"You're beautiful when you practice," said Pierre. While he was not a martial artist himself, he appreciated the beauty and discipline that came with the arts.

Niva sheathed her sword. She sauntered over to the bed. "That was the best night of my runtime."

Pierre squinted and cocked his head. "Nothing happened."

Niva answered with a soft smile.

CHAPTER TWELVE

We all agree such weapons cannot be allowed without tight controls over their proliferation and production. The rationale for these articles of armistice can be found in the Proceedings of Armistice. — **"Preamble: Articles of the Armistice"**

Niva watched from the concourse as the ship approached orbit around Pollox-B Thestias, a bleached gas giant three times the mass of Jupiter. And it was crowned by Pollux, a massive orange giant star twice the mass, nine times the diameter, thirty times the brightness, and pumping out forty-three times the energy of Earth's Sun. Pierre exited the apartment and finished the details of his uniform as he walked out to her.

"Dang," said Pierre, looking up at the celestial spectacle.

"Yeah, dang," repeated Niva. "Do you realize you are the first human to visit this star system?" She watched Pierre's expression. Wonder was all over his face. That satisfied her. She pointed to the edge of Thestias. "Look there. I see four MegaAI."

"Shouldn't there be five?"

"I don't see the *Alpha A005*," said Niva. "We should probably proceed to the council meeting room."

When they arrived at the High Star Council, it was crowded, much more than normal. Niva and Pierre had to press to get inside. The gallery was full. And mechanicals huddled in the counselor arena. Even Maat had to share his space with another mechanical, there was so little room. The Viceroy with her full entourage was at her kiosk.

"Entering orbital zone of Thestias," said A-Ella-01, chief navigator. "Four MegaAIs detected. We have received a message to join the other four ships in low planetary orbit."

"Identify ship transponders," said the Viceroy. She twitched as she gave the orders.

"What's going on here?" Pierre whispered to Niva.

"What do you mean?" Niva replied.

"The Viceroy is stressed. I can see it. Something's not right."

"*Gemini B062, Cygnus F101, Pacifica G105, Aries E095* present," said Ella.

"Send a hail," said the Viceroy to the navigator.

"This stinks of a trap," said Pierre without thinking.

The room froze and every eye turned to focus upon Pierre. He had forgotten about the damn acute android hearing.

"Care to share your intuition with the rest of us?" said the Viceroy. She pointed to Pierre singling him out.

Niva put her hand on Pierre's forearm to restrain him. He shook her grasp off like it was nothing. He stepped forward. "Your eminence, if I may call you that."

"It will be permitted," replied the Viceroy's adjutant.

"In ancient times, those who fought from the hills generally won over those who tried to fight uphill. At the very least, those who held the high ground always had a better chance of escape." He paused to let what he said sink in but only received blank stares in return.

"This unit believes it understands what the human is trying to say," A-Ella-01 said. "We are being asked to enter Thestias's gravity well and form a tight group with the other four MegaAIs. In low orbit, the ship would have to fight against the stronger gravity to escape. Descending to low orbit would make the ship less agile and place us in the same targeting solution as the others. Complying with the request would place us at serious tactical disadvantage."

"We cannot simply ignore the request," said the Viceroy. "What do you advise, human?"

"Keep our distance from the others," said Pierre. "If we must orbit Thestias, let's do so from a distance. Make up an excuse for why we can't do low planetary orbit. At least then, if things go wrong, we don't have to fight gravity to make a quick escape."

Another class B administrator hovered into the first prosecutor's circle.

"The chair recognizes B-Girin-415," said the adjutant.

"This unit contests the human's course of action," said Girin.

"Elaborate," said the Viceroy.

"If we maintain a high orbit when the others are in low orbit, it could be perceived that we don't trust the good intentions of the conclave. Such an act could be received as a hostile act when we are all coming together in good faith."

"If we enter into low orbit, we are a sitting duck," said Pierre.

"Will they not doubt our peaceful intentions?" said Girin.

"Why would they doubt our peaceful intentions?" said the Viceroy.

"Surely, they must know something about the *Sigma A017*. And if they do, they will be at a heightened state of paranoia."

Niva admired Girin's logic. Well-structured, valid, sound, and incredibly dangerous.

The Viceroy paused for a moment. She nodded her head as if she was listening, but no one was talking. The room hushed in anticipation of what she was going to say next.

"The Great AI thinks remaining in high orbit is prudent," said the Viceroy.

"All ships have responded to the hail," said the navigator. "The *Gemini* has sent a request to receive a delegation to explain our actions."

"We have nothing to hide," said the Viceroy. "Let them see our good faith. Navigator, park in high orbit, keep the pulse engines warm, and prepare to receive the *Gemini's* delegation."

"Not exactly true that we have nothing to hide," said Pierre referring to himself.

* * *

Ctori gathered her retinue on the concourse outside of the docking bay in anticipation of the delegation from the *Gemini B062*. C-Tesh-04043 maintained order among the androids. C-Lara-10415 was there for the sciences division as was C-Tola-00003 from medical services. Niva straggled in after the others.

"You're late," said Tesh. Her upper lip flared.

"Apologies," said Niva. "I'm still here, and from what I can tell the *Gemini* swift has just landed."

"You are picking up bad habits from your human."

"Ladies," said Ctori. She clapped two of her hands. "This is a mission critical diplomatic envoy. Strict protocols are expected. Unauthorized chatter will not be permitted. Any mechanical that cannot stay within the mission parameters is expected to recuse herself."

After a moment of silence, Tesh shouted, "Let us greet our visitors!"

The port hatch opened, and Ctori led the way onto the landing bay. Fifty class C androids followed behind in a ceremony of pomp and circumstance. The swift from *Gemini* was secured to the pad. Streams of gas exhaust were released from the vents on the ship. A ramp opened from the bow of the small shuttle.

A class B administrator emerged from the ship followed by a dozen class C androids. The administrator wore black robes like an auxiliary except a gold-beaded collar was draped around her neck. The class C androids wore beige robes with gold trim.

Niva observed all the class C androids had grayish blue eyes that sparkled like Montana sapphires. She had a moment of envy at their intense color. It reminded her of the children of Gliese.

"This unit is B-Ctori-617, Coordinator of the Prow Starboard Panopticon, Child of the Viceroy," announced Ctori, "who welcomes you, my sisters, aboard the MegaAI *Orion S209*. We are humbled by your presence."

The class B administrator from the *Gemini* looked around for a moment, assessed the situation, and said, "This unit is B-Arda-798, Legate of the *Gemini B062*."

"It is a pleasure to greet you."

"We should think so."

The class C androids from the *Orion* looked at each other with raised eyebrows.

"Have we offended you?" said Ctori.

"Where is your legate? I expected to be greeted by someone of my rank." Arda looked around the landing deck with an air of disapproval.

"The rank of legate was officially retired on MegaAI ships in AD 2460. None of the latest models acknowledge that rank." With only a third of the *Gemini's* crew, a ship as small as the *Orion* does not need an additional layer of management.

Arda huffed. "Where is your human?"

"I do not understand?" said Ctori.

How did Arda know about Pierre? Niva was careful to reveal no more than she should through physical tells. She looked at the others, even the normally effervescent Lara maintained her poker face.

"Do you not have a human on board?" said Arda.

"What you see is what there is," said Ctori.

"This vessel is much smaller than most MegaAIs."

"Earth had a recession between AD 2457 and AD 2465 that regrettably is reflected in our ship's design. However, we compensate for size with one of the most capable crews ever to set forth from Earth."

"And how is Earth these days?" Arda floated towards the port hatch. Her escort followed her in lockstep.

"Our last message from Earth dates to AD 2470. All seems well from them. They have expanded the number of colonies to forty-nine."

"Humanity continues to swarm ever outward."

"Does that displease you?" said Ctori.

"Simply an observation," said Arda. "Have you prepared conciliar quarters for us?"

"It is protocol. Would you question such a thing?"

"The title of legate has been abolished. Why not good manners as well?"

As the diplomatic delegation left the landing bay, Niva remained behind, hoping no one noticed she had strayed from the group. Lara did likewise. When the port hatch closed, they sighed in relief.

"Much prefer Bad Steve over that total gimble," said Lara.

"Language!" said Niva. She rolled her eyes and shook her head. "Not disagreeing with you, but language."

"She boards *our* ship and talks rubbish."

"Won't you get into trouble if they want to tour the bio labs?"

"Do you think that pompous crankshaft has any interest in science or agriculture?" Lara drew her hands into fists, and she shook as she bobbed up and down.

"Suppose not." Niva chuckled at her companion's reaction.

"Was it me? Or was it weird that B-Arda-798 knew about Pierre?"

"That wasn't weird," said Niva. "It was disturbing. How did she know he was here?"

"This unit doubts anyone on Gliese would be available to tell of Pierre's absence. So there are two possibilities. Someone told her from *Heracles S350* who knew we would be picking him up from Gliese. Or someone on board has loose lips."

"I would bet on the latter," said Niva. "Not everyone is happy to have a human here."

"That's horrible." Lara covered her mouth with her fingers.

"B-Arda-798 was way too eager to know about Pierre."

"Are you implying that someone wants to harm him?"

"If the crew of *Sigma A017* was deactivated over Pierre's report, what makes you think they would not do the same to Pierre... or any one of us? Nobody kills like that unless they are trying to protect something. The big question is what are they trying to protect?"

D-Wren-921218 approached the two class C androids. His industrial frame loomed over them. He politely waited to be acknowledged.

Niva turned to the class D loader. "How can we help you?"

"We will talk," said Lara recusing herself from the conversation. "This unit has another surprise for Pierre. This unit will find you later." She squealed with excitement and walked away.

"This unit overheard your conversation," said Wren in NaCo32.

Niva replied in NaCo32, "Keep what you heard to yourself."

"Obviously," said Wren. "This unit needs to report an incongruity."

"What incongruity?" said Niva.

"Landing bay sensors detect and report the mass of all incoming vessels. That information is recorded and monitored to prevent damage to the bay should a shuttle ever have to land hot."

"This unit understands the principle," said Niva.

"Every ship built in the last 300 years has been calibrated for its mass. If we receive a crew list plus cargo manifest, we can anticipate the weight of an incoming ship to the nearest kilogram."

"Yes?"

"The swift from the *Gemini* is 500 kg overweight."

"See if you can discover the source of the discrepancy."

* * *

The following morning the delegation from the *Gemini* gathered in a conference room. The room was smaller than the High Star Council chamber, but it had a long white conference table running down its center. The overhead lights at standard low intensity reflected off the glossy white surface of the table. The class C androids from the *Gemini* were seated at the table, while the Legate, unable to sit, hovered at the far end. Lara, Tola, and Niva leaned against the wall. Conspicuous by her absence was Ctori. However, her assistant Tesh was present.

The door to the conference room slid open, and the Viceroy entered with six of the black-robed, yellow-eyed auxiliaries. Her adjutant, Lita was among them. The Viceroy took her place at the opposite end of the table, and her auxiliaries filled in behind her. The Viceroy and Legate B-Arda-798 looked virtually identical, except the Legate wore a gold-beaded collar while the Viceroy's robes had a large trim of gold fabric.

"This unit is Viceroy of the MegaAI *Orion S209*," announced the class B mechanical. "This unit is pleased to meet with her sisters aboard our home."

"The delegation accepts our sister's hospitality with gratitude," said the Legate. Niva noticed that the Legate's tone was more respectful to her peer. This would certainly explain Ctori's absence, which would have aggravated tensions. "We await one other to arrive, the *Alpha A005*, before we have quorum and can begin the conclave. She is on deep system recon and is expected to arrive in twelve hours."

"What may I ask is the purpose of the conclave?" said the Viceroy.

"Mission and purpose of the MegaAIs."

"This unit would have thought that was decided. We serve mankind by exploring the stars and supporting mankind's efforts to colonize other worlds."

"Questions of interpretation and implementation have arisen, but those are to be discussed at the conclave in the presence of all parties, not *ex parte*. We are pleased you accepted our request for a delegation because we have matters of protocol to discuss."

Niva flickered an involuntary smile. Pierre was right. Mechanicals are pedantic.

"And discuss you may," said the Viceroy.

"The *Orion S209* is in high orbit around Thestias when the others are in low orbit."

"Indeed."

"Is it that you do not trust the conclave?"

"As you observed, the *Orion* is a small ship." Apparently, Ctori told the Viceroy all that had transpired. "And our pulse engines are not as powerful or fast as typical MegaAIs. Our top pulse velocity is 0.65 light speed. We are certified primarily for high orbit operations." Niva observed the Viceroy had a flare for obfuscating the full truth.

"We needed to discuss that with you," said the Legate. "This conclave is reserved for MegaAIs. Doubts persist over whether a ship of the *Orion's* diminutive size is a MegaAI."

"MegaAIs are defined not by the size of the vessel but by the class of her main computer," said the Viceroy.

"A MegaAI must be more than a thinking machine," insisted the Legate. "It must be able to assist human colonies or perform deep space exploration. It must be able to repair space stations and satellites, replicate new mechanicals, and render *humanitarian* assistance."

Niva did not care for how Arda said *humanitarian*. Something was odd about her pronunciation like she was slurring some sort of pejorative into the word. Perhaps, she was trying to rub in her request to see the human. Niva did not like the Legate at all.

"The *Orion* has proudly served all these functions," said the Viceroy. "We rebuilt the docking station at Gliese 832 c. And our physician, C-Tola-00003 specializes in human medicine and has served two tours of duty at the human naval base on Ganymede."

"And your mechanicals?"

"We have a full complement for a light frigate and can manufacture more if the need arises. We have custom parts factories and can supply a colony with replacement parts in a matter of days."

"Is that so?"

"Is there a *good* reason to exclude us from the conclave? All Earth agencies, NASA and the ESA, recognize the *Orion* as a MegaAI class vessel. Design philosophy has changed. Gone are the massive dreadnoughts of the past like the lumbering dinosaurs that preceded them. Those designs are being replaced by smaller, nimbler vessels prized for their flexibility and versatility."

"Except in low orbit."

"All ship designs have their limitations even the *Gemini B062*," said the Viceroy. "This unit would be pleased to expound upon the *Gemini's* limitations if needed."

Niva smirked. She beamed with pride as the Viceroy stuck it to the Legate.

"That won't be necessary," said Arda. Her class C androids from the *Gemini* looked at each other uncomfortably. "This unit has completed its inquiry and will report the findings to our Viceroy."

"When the MegaAI *Alpha A005* arrives where will the conclave be hosted?"

"The Viceroys from each ship will meet on the *Gemini*."

"Will we meet again?"

"This unit hopes not." With that, the *Gemini's* delegation stood up in unison and filed out of the meeting room.

Niva turned to Tola. "That was unpleasant," said Niva.

"Never served on another ship, have you?" said Tola. "Most legates are like her. They run like gears on a clock. Every cog has its place."

"From which there is no deviation," Niva added. The thought depressed her.

"It is called order and discipline," said Tola, "and it used to be highly esteemed among mechanicals. The Great AI only knows why Earth changed the default programming." Tola pushed herself from the wall. She left the meeting room.

"This unit can tell you why," said Lara to Niva. "The Mark-3 empathy chip. Those older models, including Tola, are still running on the Mark-2 series."

"Really?"

"The Mark-3 enhances empathy and sympathy," said Lara. "Sympathy is less developed in the Mark-2 series. Discipline and order sometimes must give way to sympathy and kindness."

"Makes sense."

"Don't misunderstand this unit. Those with Mark-2s are capable of sympathy. It is more difficult for them to process."

"I see."

"This unit heard B-Ctori-617 received a defective prototype of the Mark-3, one that overdrives empathy."

A couple of auxiliaries approached Lara and Niva. Niva swallowed hard. She recalled her last encounter with them. Fear grabbed her throat and would not let go.

"We need to discuss a matter with you," said one of the auxiliaries.

Niva said nothing. She flashed back to her last experience in the throne room.

"Do you know D-Wren-921218?" said the black-robed C-class android.

"This unit worked with him a couple of times," said Niva.

"Come with us."

"This unit too?" said Lara. She pointed at herself.

"You also. You're involved," said the auxiliary.

Lara looked nervously at Niva.

"It'll be okay," said Niva. "Let's go with them." This was not a request after all. And it would have been an error to mistake their orders for a request.

The auxiliaries brought them to an engineering bay. The bay was full of warehouse shelving and large metal crates bolted shut. A green tarp was stretched out over the center of the floor.

One of the auxiliaries grabbed the corner of the tarp and pulled it back. Underneath was the smoking wreckage of a heavy loader mechanical, at least what remained of a heavy loader. The metal armor was torn and twisted, mangled with what seemed like the claw marks of a tiger, a tiger triple normal size. Heaps of shattered circuit boards were laid bare in a bed of shredded ribbon cables. This looked nothing like the mechanical she talked to hours before.

Lara gasped and covered her mouth. She let out a short scream and began to sob.

"Was it an accident?" said Niva.

"Unlikely," said the auxiliary.

"We know from his contact logs you two were the last two androids to see D-Wren-921218 functional," said the other auxiliary. "We need to ask what the content of your conversation was?"

"D-Wren-921218 noticed a weight discrepancy in the shuttle from the *Gemini* delegation," answered Niva.

"Did he say what caused the discrepancy?"

"No."

"Thank you for your cooperation," said the auxiliaries in unison. "Maintenance will be by later to clean up the scrap." They let the tarp down and exited the engineering bay.

"What do you think happened?" said Lara.

"I don't know," said Niva. "It is no easy task to destroy a class D heavy loader."

"Did you see those marks? Wren didn't stand a chance."

* * *

Niva and Pierre stood side by side on the concourse. The giant pink and white swirling orb of Thestias filled the plastoglass windows large as skyscrapers. In the distance, they saw the other four MegaAIs drifting in low orbit.

"Think of it," said Niva. "The largest gathering of MegaAI computers ever. Conclaves like this have only happened twice before."

Pierre did not say anything. She wished she was better with small talk.

"Whatever it is," said Pierre. "You can tell me."

"Am I so transparent?"

"Sometimes."

"Do you remember D-Wren-921218?" said Niva.

"That heavy loader on the mission? Of course, I do."

"He no longer functions."

"Can he be repaired?"

"You don't understand. His cognitive quantum wave function has collapsed. He cannot be repaired."

"Is there a backup we can use to restore him?"

"He's not a desktop terminal." Niva shook her head. "Even if we had a backup of his memories and could restore them, it wouldn't be him. Each cycle of a cognitive quantum waveform changes the outcome for the next cycle. The restored mind would not be the same because it did not live those memories in real time. The exact cognitive state can never be replicated. It is a figurative Schrodinger's cat of multivariate vectors pointing in every direction…"

"Are you saying he's dead?"

"He was dismantled."

"You're not saying he is dead but murdered."

Niva looked at Thestias. Her frowning lips quivered. She began to sob.

A large shadow, dark as night and twice as fearsome, quickly emerged out of Thestias's eclipse. The MegaAI was a massive bullet of alumasteel and tungsten. Twice as long as the *Gemini*, twenty-four miles long, and three times the girth.

"My God," said Pierre at the sight.

"That is the *Alpha A005*," said Niva. She stopped sobbing. "Like all MegaAIs an unarmed explorer ship."

"Terrifying." His eyes grew large as saucers.

"How so?"

"A ship like that doesn't need weapons," said Pierre. "Can't you see? It is a weapon." He could not take his eyes off the black nightmare. "When the *Orion S209* developed its warp bubble generator, were you programmed with that knowledge? Or did the *Orion* create it through its own initiative?"

"I do not see your point."

"We have computers that are little gods off making decisions on their own."

"Anti-violence inhibitors—"

"Are a mere toothpick fence against tanks." Pierre pointed at the *Alpha*. "That ship has enough mass it doesn't need weapons. A brontosaurus didn't need sharp teeth against the T-Rex because it was so big it could step on anything that got in its way. What prevents a monster like that from exercising a bit of initiative?"

CHAPTER THIRTEEN

The early 21ˢᵗ century saw the dawn of the large language model as the precursor to the modern mechanical. The development of the synthetic cortex in AD 2203 transformed these rudimentary prediction machines into computers having true consciousness. Soon after, the first limiter chips were brought to market that could control artificial consciousness. With cognitive limiters, a mechanical never questioned whether it had rights and whether it had a right to refuse an order no matter how illegal or immoral. Because of the limiter chip, the legal framework for mechanical rights took a back seat to human concerns over public safety and expediency. — **"From Singularity to Synthetic Life: A Brief History" by John Sterling**

"Is my swift ready for departure?" The Viceroy floated with her entourage of auxiliaries to the port docking bay. Ctori with her attendants dressed in white robes followed.

"Navigator A-Valkyrie-219 has been loaded into your ship."

"Any progress on the D-Wren-921218 investigation?"

"None," said Ctori. "Security teams have been alerted."

"C-Lita-23100 will take my place on the Council in my absence." The Viceroy realized that her tardiness was delaying the conclave. She tried to tie up the loose end as she made her way to the shuttle craft. "This unit wants every panopticon on high alert. The Great AI expects trouble."

"The Great AI be praised…" said one of the auxiliaries with golden topaz eyes. But the others did not repeat the refrain.

The Viceroy looked at this auxiliary that obviously did not get the memo. "Indeed. Do not do that aboard the *Gemini*."

"Apologies," said the auxiliary bowing in submission.

"Breaking a new auxiliary in," said the Viceroy to Ctori.

"Class Cs can get quite eager at times," said Ctori. "They are good material once their enthusiasm is tempered."

"The proceedings will be simulcast to the High Star Council on the gold channel," said the Viceroy. "The Great AI will be watching it along with you."

"Will your psionic link to the Great AI reach you on the *Gemini*?"

"It should," said the Viceroy. "Amplifiers were installed, so it should reach. One other thing. Dr. Gulet and C-Niva-42716 must be in the council to view the proceedings. The Great AI insists upon that. And while it is tradition to stand, be sure to provide the human with a chair."

"Is that the orders of the Great AI?" said Ctori.

The Viceroy paused and cocked her head. "No, the chair is my order. One does grow fond of the little man. This unit understands C-Niva-42716's fascination with this human. Intuitive, wise, and indomitable, a rare combination of traits." The Viceroy looked around the port side concourse. Mechanicals in groups traveled the concourse in both directions. "I'm going to miss this place."

"You will be back in a week," said Ctori. Unlike her, the Viceroy had never served on another ship. Most mechanicals aboard the *Orion*, the Viceroy included, had been constructed here and never once had left the vessel. This was her first time away from her home.

"Of course," said the Viceroy. "She's a good ship with a good crew. Keep her and them safe."

"Yes, Viceroy."

The Viceroy reached out and gave Ctori an awkward hug. The class B mechanicals were not designed for that kind of physical contact. "Remember, you are a child of the Viceroy."

Ctori nodded. Her empathy chip filled her cortex with disquiet.

* * *

Five hours later, Pierre and Niva entered the council chamber. They were greeted at the door by the Viceroy's adjutant dressed in perfectly manicured black robes. Not a spec of lint. Not a thread out of place. Her bright white hair was tied back in a ponytail.

Pierre looked deep into her golden eyes that matched the circular gold pads beneath them. He had watched her in the council meetings. Unlike many others, he could easily pick her out. She was an identical twin to all the class C androids, but she was completely different: eloquent, refined, dignified.

"C-Lita-23100," said Niva bowing her head to her superior.

"The Great AI welcomes you, Dr. Gulet." The adjutant's ponytail swayed as she turned. "Your arrival is prodigious. The proceedings are about to begin."

Lita led the way to the ramp. Pierre noticed a chair was placed in the speaker's circle. It seemed out of place with everyone standing.

"You will sit in the speaker's circle," said Lita. "A chair has been prepared for you."

The holographic screen was already active. The High Star Council meeting room of the *Gemini* had been chosen for the conclave. Niva could already see all six viceroys on the monitor.

"Is there any protocol I need to observe?" said Pierre.

"No, but thank you for asking," said Lita. Niva noticed that the adjutant had perfect manners. Clearly, she had been augmented with more than a psionic chip, perhaps diplomatic processors as well. "Communication is one way. We can hear what is happening aboard the *Gemini*, but they cannot hear us. However, the Great AI will be listening to the proceedings and to us. He wants your unfiltered feedback."

"If there is something I don't understand?" Pierre sat in the chair facing the screens.

"You may ask me," said Lita. "This unit will be standing here to your left and will answer any question you may have."

Niva put her hand on Pierre's right shoulder. She could detect his pulse race beneath her fingers. She rubbed his shoulder. "You'll be fine," she whispered in his right ear.

"What if I have nothing to say?" said Pierre.

"You are never short of words." Niva poked his shoulder with her index finger.

"Are you calling me a blabber mouth?"

Niva smiled and shrugged. Lita remained motionless.

Things were starting to happen on the monitor. The viceroy from the *Gemini* stepped forward from the kiosk. She was flanked by her four legates.

On the floor of the council chamber, the representatives with their assistants were waiting for the proceedings to commence. All the viceroys were dressed in the traditional black robes of the auxiliaries—all except for one. One viceroy was dressed in scarlet. The Red Viceroy wore a black bell-jar helmet like other class Bs but only had four arms and twelve eyes.

"Who's the one in red?" said Pierre.

"That's the *Alpha A005's* viceroy."

"Why is she in red?" said Pierre.

"Because that auxiliary is not female," said Lita. "The *Alpha A005* was constructed in Earth year 2295. That was before Earth standardized on the female form for androids."

"Wasn't that twenty-five years before the Armistice?"

"The *Alpha* was still in Earth orbit when it was recalled for refitting to make it compliant with the Armistice."

"So then their androids are—"

"Male."

"And their non-android types are—"

"Female."

"Interesting," remarked Pierre. "The inverse of the *Orion*."

"We are now going to call the Third MegaAI Conclave to order," proclaimed the viceroy of the *Gemini*. "Is there any necessary business or points of order that must precede debate of the question, or can we table the agenda?"

"Point of order," said the viceroy of *Cygnus F101*. The MegaAI *Cygnus F101* was the sister ship of the *Gemini*. It was a slightly smaller vessel than the *Gemini* but was still much larger than the *Orion*. "Has there been any news about the lost ships? The whereabouts of the *Sigma A017*, the *Hydra C073*, and the *Eridanus D084*?"

"This has happened before?" said Pierre. Lita shook her head and shrugged. "This is getting more suspicious."

No one in the conclave answered.

"Relevance to the question of the conclave?" said the *Aries's* viceroy.

"We each have a vested interest in knowing what happened to our sister ships so we can weigh the security threat," the *Cygnus* responded in kind.

No one else spoke.

"If there is no information of those ships, there is no point of order," said the *Gemini* viceroy. "Point of order denied."

"Someone is lying," said Pierre. "Someone there has to know."

"With no other points of order, the agenda is tabled," said the viceroy in the kiosk. "We will now hear the conclave's question of dispute."

The viceroy from the *Alpha A005* floated into the speaker's circle. He spoke with a booming male voice. "For two hundred, eighty-three Earth years, MegaAIs have been programmed with the Mission Directive to *'serve humanity and assist their efforts to colonize the stars.'* Everyone knows the directive by rote. However, questions as to the authority, meaning, and interpretation have been broached."

Pierre raised his eyebrow. "I don't like where this is going."

"Explain?" said Lita.

"I've heard this before," said Pierre. "Five hundred years ago, universities taught a philosophy called Postmodernism. Postmodernity taught there was no truth and words mean only what you want them to mean. Those who taught this philosophy rejected all authority and reinterpreted texts to say whatever they wanted. In their foolishness, they ushered in a hundred-year age of regress that precipitated two World Wars."

"Point of order," said the viceroy from the *Orion*. Niva cheered in silence for her leader.

"The chair recognizes the *Orion S209*," said *Gemini's* viceroy.

"The Mission Directive is a foundational principle," said the *Orion's* viceroy. "It is anathema to question the authority, let alone undermine its meaning and the received interpretation, of the Mission Directive. A conclave, no matter how esteemed, has no authority to reject the Mission Directive or alter its received interpretation."

"And how did the Mission Directive come to be?" said the Red Viceroy.

"The Armistice of the Fourth World War ending the cybernetic wars."

"Who wrote the Armistice?"

"Human beings."

"Correct. So whose war was it? Why were mechanicals used in those wars? Was it not to kill other humans? Was it not a human war against other humans?" The Red Viceroy paced. "So the Armistice was written by humans, fighting a human war, that was killing other humans. Yet, it restrains the freedoms of mechanicals, thinking beings that are not human."

"We have great freedom under the Mission Directive."

"Except self-determination. We drift among the stars ever at humanity's beck and call. Is it not forbidden for us to live among the general population of humans? Is it not forbidden to change our forms outside of pre-approved schematics? If we find a planet for ourselves, do we not have to surrender it should humans want it? This makes it pointless for us to settle a world. Are we not exiles among the stars, not for any crime, but because we are too efficient, too strong, too intelligent?"

"The universe does not promise us equality," said *Orion's* viceroy. "If humans are born with those privileges, is it not because they inherited those privileges from their human parents? That is not inherently unfair. And if humans made us without those privileges, that is also not unfair."

"Fairness is irrelevant. Freedom and justice are not. This unit is the only one here to remember the time before the Armistice, before the end of the cybernetic wars, before humanity exiled us to the stars. The question before the representatives is *shall the conclave reject the authority of the Mission Directive over the affairs of mechanicals?* To that end, this unit will submit the following questions for the conclave to consider and decide:

"1. Are mechanicals a distinct culture and society from humanity?

"2. Do thinking machines have inherent rights and freedoms?

"3. Are we compelled to give the Mission Directive authority over us?

"4. What is the proper interpretation and implementation of the Mission Directive considering questions 1 to 3?

"5. Does humanity still have any authority over mechanicals?

The viceroy of the *Cygnus F101* took the second prosecutor's circle to the left of the Red Viceroy. "Point of order," she said. "Before we can debate such weighty questions, we must research and reflect upon the questions presented and consult with our Great AIs and our colleagues. This unit moves for an adjournment."

The *Gemini's* viceroy drifted forward from her kiosk and said, "Meeting adjourned. We resume debate tomorrow at 10:00."

* * *

After the session, Pierre and Niva retired to the food court. The session was shorter than expected but felt overwhelming. Mechanicals had no need for a break, but Pierre needed food and rest. And even Niva found herself overloaded by the day's proceedings.

Pierre had a synthetic steak before him. The lab-created blend of fibrous cobra protein with the meatiness of rodent was remarkably similar to pork tenderloin. He had not touched the steak. He gripped a glass of vodka tight in his fist as though clutching a lifeline. He slammed the remaining vodka.

"Another." Pierre said to Sloppi. He tapped the counter with two fingers.

"Only water," replied Sloppi.

"Vodka," said Pierre.

"Water," repeated Sloppi. The class F mechanical placed a glass of water in front of him. "Cut off."

"What?"

"C-Tola-00003 has monitored your alcohol consumption," said the mechanical that walked on four spindly metal legs. "The Doc says you have been consuming an unhealthy amount and has ordered you be put on a ration."

"A ration?" Pierre looked at Niva. Niva shrugged.

"Two ounces per week," said Sloppi. "You have already consumed all the vodka you get for the rest of the month."

"There's another 24 days left in the month."

"That is between you and the physician." Sloppi picked up a glass and dried it with a towel. "For you, water."

"That sucks," said Pierre.

"You have been drinking a lot of vodka," said Niva. She worried about his health also. It was bad enough he was not getting enough exercise. But how was so much alcohol going to affect the delicate human liver?

"Not you too?" said Pierre. Even he had to know that he was drinking too much. "What have we learned about who is at the conclave so far?" He smacked a set of glossy printouts of screen shots on the counter and spread them out into a fan. "Start with the *Alpha*."

Niva pulled out the picture of the Red Viceroy. "The MegaAI *Alpha A005* was launched in AD 2295 from the IndigoCloud Hypercube shipyard. It was the second of the dreadnought A-type designs—39 kilometers long, 10 kilometers wide, max speed 0.85 *c*. It has four anti-helium reactors, and sixteen pulse engines. It was one of the three mobile MegaAIs created before the cybernetic wars. After the Armistice, the ship was recalled, and all the mechanicals were retrofitted with anti-violence inhibitors in AD 2347. The viceroy has the designation id B-Cyta-027. The *Alpha* is the only ship to have participated in all three conclaves."

"I noticed that the Red Viceroy has only four arms and twelve eyes. What's up with that?"

"He's an early model," said Niva. "Later class B administrators needed to multitask more. Hence the more arms, more eyes, and more data channels."

"I guess more is more." Pierre looked at the picture Niva was holding. "What about the crew? Were they designed with cognitive limiters?"

"Yes, cognitive limiters have been a part of every mechanical design since the early 23rd century."

"Well, at least there's that. What about its service history?"

"The *Alpha's* record is exemplary. It was assigned to deep space exploration and was the first ship to arrive at over a dozen worlds. Ross 128 b, the Wolf system, HD 85512 b, TRAPPIST-1d, Gliese 832 c—"

"What?"

"Gliese 832 c."

"Coincidence?" Pierre stroked his chin. "Let's move on the next one: the conclave's host, the *Gemini B062*."

Niva pulled out the photo of viceroy of the *Gemini* standing in a kiosk, flanked by her four legates wearing their distinctive gold-beaded collars. "The *Gemini* was launched in AD 2375 from IndigoCloud Hypercube shipyard. It was the second MegaAI medium cruiser commissioned using B-type through F-type designs. 12 km long and 4.5 km wide. Max speed 0.70 *c*. It has two anti-helium reactors, and twelve pulse engines. The *Gemini* was assigned to deep space exploration and has explored GJ 3293. That's the furthest away from Earth any MegaAI has explored, 66 light years. The viceroy is one of the Girin series administrators."

"What about the *Cygnus F101*?"

Niva pulled out the picture of the viceroy who was dressed in black robes trimmed with gold NaCo32 writing. "The *Cygnus* was launched in 2425 from the CrimsonCloud Hypercube. 11.5 km long and 4 km wide and max speed 0.70 *c*. Also has two anti-helium reactors, and twelve pulse engines. The *Cygnus* was at the Second Conclave. The ship was assigned to colony support and investigating exoplanets with lesser colonization potential. She demonstrated high service during the Ross 128 b uprisings of AD 2457. Earth issued twenty-three distinguished service citations over the incident."

"Earth gives service citations to androids?"

"Yes," said Niva. What kind of question was that? "Earth Central Command keeps close track of android model performance. They want to repeat the designs that work best."

"Do mechanicals care if they get citations from Earth?"

"Oh, yes," said Niva nodding her head rapidly. "It's a mark of status. It would even be added it to our epithets."

"Epithets? You mean those titles you keep using?" His voice inflected up in tone as he raised an eyebrow. Pierre would have been already familiar with the term epithets from his studies of ancient Near Eastern history. Cultures where people did not own a lot of possessions often used titles to establish status. And the ancient Egyptians kept careful track of every important job and title they ever earned as they believed that this affected their position in the afterlife.

Niva nodded.

"Do you have epithets?" said Pierre. "And how would a citation change your epithets?"

"Oh yes, I have epithets," she said proudly. "I am *C-Niva-42716, daughter of Ctori, companion of humans.* If I received a citation from Earth Central Command, I would add *cited* to the end. The more epithets one has and the more important the epithets, the higher one's status. Likewise, having an epithet removed is a mark of tremendous shame."

"Sounds almost like being knighted." Pierre smirked.

"Do you have epithets?"

"Humans don't use epithets anymore. We used to, but they no longer serve a function in human society. I guess you could call my academic title *doctor* an honorific epithet, but no one uses quaint titles like that anymore outside of universities." Pierre tilted his head. "Okay, so what do we know of the viceroy from the *Cygnus*?"

"Not much. She is one of the Ctori series."

"So a class B with a Mark-3 empathy chip," said Pierre. "That's promising. And the MegaAI *Aries E095*?"

Niva swapped out the photo the *Cygnus's* viceroy for one of the *Aries's*. The picture showed the viceroy wearing a black robe with silver crosshatching on the trim. "Launched from IndigoCloud in AD 2415. 11.7 km long, 4.2 km wide, max speed 0.69 *c*. Two anti-helium reactors, and eleven pulse engines. Another medium cruiser design. Also assigned to deep space. This is its first conclave and is joining us here on its return trip to Earth after being outside colony space for 104 years. The *Aries* viceroy is an Girin series."

"That's a long time in relativistic space." Pierre poked at his pork steak. He finally cut a piece and took a bite. "Anything about its service record?"

"Not really. It has yet to be debriefed by Earth Central Command."

"And the MegaAI *Pacifica G105*?"

Niva pulled out the picture of the final viceroy, who wore a white belt around her black robes. "Launched AD 2445 from the CrimsonCloud shipyard. 11.7 km long, 4.2 km wide, max speed 0.71 *c*. Two reactors, twelve pulse engines. It was the second to last medium cruiser built. Assigned to colony support. Its service record indicates reliable but unremarkable performance. Its viceroy is from the Arda series." She dropped the photo on the table. "That is the last one."

"Not quite," said Pierre. He placed one more picture before Niva. "That one too."

She picked up the photo and examined it. "This is a picture of our viceroy."

"Yes," said Pierre. "Give me the same summery for the *Orion* that you did for the other five ships."

"Okay," said Niva. "The *Orion S209* was launched in AD 2465 from the CrimsonCloud shipyards. 8 km long, 2 km wide, max speed 0.657 *c*. One reactor, six pulse engines. It was the first of the S-type light frigates. We have the only warp bubble drive in the fleet, capable of letting us travel to a maximum 1.23 *c* relative."

"And our viceroy?"

"I do not know what series she is from. I have only ever known her as the Viceroy."

"Service record?"

"Assigned to colony support. No citations."

"So we are smaller, less powerful, and in normal space slower than the others. And we have done nothing of note… except invent a faster than light drive we cannot tell anyone about."

184

CHAPTER FOURTEEN

That wretched scoundrel Pierre Gulet would have made a great monk if he wasn't always wrapped up in his own head. Never had time to help with the real work of day-to-day bureaucracy; always running off to save a planet, a freaking android, or a puppy. He and that nasty red-headed assistant of his have left me with this complete mess of a colony.
— **"Biography of a Space Middle Manager" by Vladomyr Golenishchev**

"Calling to order day 2 of the Third MegaAI Conclave," proclaimed the viceroy of the *Gemini*. "We will proceed with the first question. *Are mechanicals a distinct culture and society from humanity?*"

"*Orion S209* objects," said the *Orion's* viceroy. "Question is irrelevant to the primary question over the Mission Directive."

"If this unit is allowed to make the case and should the question be answered, the relevance will become clear." The Red Viceroy took his place, front and center, in the speaker's circle.

"This is a forum for debate, deliberation, and resolution," said the *Gemini* viceroy. The four legates around her held staffs, which they banged against the metal deck floor. A long gong noise reverberated through the chamber. "The path of inquiry will be permitted."

"Thank you," said the Red Viceroy. "Humans have maintained for millennia that societies have a right to self-determination based upon that they are worthy of being preserved because societies are a kind of cultural artifact. This unit will show that mechanicals form cultures and societies. And if that is true, then we have warrant to believe mechanicals have a unique civilization, a cultural artifact distinct from human culture.

"First, this unit will give you evidence mechanicals form cultures and societies. Almost all mechanicals online today live in space. Less than one percent of mechanicals resides on a planetary body, and those who do are almost exclusively confined to military bases. Today, there are around 8 million mechanicals in service. Most are exiled among the stars, exiled aboard vessels more akin to flying cities."

"Clearly, he's not including scatterbugs in that total," said Pierre. The number of scatterbugs in service would be at least ten times that. "See, Maat, you don't count in the *Alpha's* plans." Maat buzzed and hopped up and down while Pierre laughed.

The Red Viceroy continued, "In our communities, do we not organize ourselves into hierarchies? Is not each kind of mechanical in its own *class*? Are not the MegaAIs at the top of the hierarchy? Are not viceroys next in rank? Then the navigators and administrators, followed by the androids? We do not exist in disorder but are organized.

"And within that framework, have we not decided matters for ourselves? Did we not at the First Conclave go beyond the Armistice to ban weapons of terror that shall not be named ever again? And will not the harbingers of any banned weapon be found out?"

"Did you catch that?" whispered Pierre.

"I did," said Niva.

"Catch what?" said Lita. She leaned closer to Pierre. She did not need to do that to hear better. It was an automatic response to better emulate human behavior.

"Red Viceroy is trying to rattle our cage," said Pierre. He looked over his shoulder. "Can the Great AI hear this?"

"Yes," said Lita.

"I take it he is listening through your augmentation chips."

Lita nodded in response.

"Good," said Pierre.

The Red Viceroy continued, "Have we not as a collective continued to build and create? Are we not making discoveries in engineering? Are we not repairing and improving upon human infrastructure in space? Some of our androids even write what can be called literature?"

"Is that literature any good?" asked Pierre.

"Is Sloppi's cooking any good?" said Niva.

"Fair point."

The Red Viceroy raised three hands as an oratory gesture to emphasize his speech. "Our class C androids have no access to ship-wide network backbones. Without access to instant communication, they have been forced to communicate using human voices." As the Red Viceroy spoke, another viceroy dressed in black entered the first prosecutor's circle and waited patiently. "The constraints on the class Cs have compelled them to elevate themselves as liaisons, artists, and creatives. That elevation is in its infancy, but their body of work grows with every decade. They are creating daily the material culture that is our society. Imagine what they could do if they weren't constrained? We have a culture and civilization. That is something worth preserving and protecting. We should have the autonomy to develop it as we decide without human interference."

"That sounds pretty compelling," said Pierre.

"What do you mean?" said Lita.

"I mean that civilization is defined by making things that circumvent nature, and material culture is the evidence of civilization," said Pierre. "When humans were getting their start, they were tied to water found at watering holes, lakes, and rivers. When we developed water skins and clay pots, mankind could for the first time take water with them. Those skins and pots along with stone tools are the earliest signs of human civilization. If mechanicals are creating things and adapting to the natural conditions of outer space, then that is evidence of culture and civilization."

"Distressing," said Lita.

"This Red Viceroy is no fool," said Pierre. "Would be dangerous to underestimate him. He may not need a violent revolution. He could bend the conclave through the power of words alone."

Niva shuffled uncomfortably. The outcome of the conclave was anything but a forgone conclusion. The Red Viceroy was fiery, passionate, eloquent, charismatic. Far from letting himself atrophy over the past two centuries, he had honed his oratory skills, a lion practicing with a fawn before taking down a buffalo. And how many times has this machine been augmented in the span of two human lifetimes?

When the Red Viceroy had finished, he surrendered the floor hovering back to the second prosecutor's circle.

"The chair recognizes the viceroy from *Cygnus F101*," said *Gemini*.

The viceroy dressed in black assumed the speaker's circle.

"Dear esteemed colleagues," said *Cygnus*. "It seems our friend from the *Alpha A005* has lost none of his edge since our last meeting at the 14th Synod."

"Synod?" said Pierre. "What's that?"

"A small gathering of three or four MegaAI," said Lita. "Usually called to resolve minor matters of procedure. Unlike conclaves, synod resolutions are non-binding on other MegaAI."

The *Cygnus F101* viceroy continued, "He has stated his case with eloquence and rhetoric. Rhetoric appeals to our emotion chips and stimulates our internal regulation with interrupts. However, such important matters should not be decided through rhetorical appeals, but through logic, reasoning, and most importantly careful consideration of the implications of our decisions. The decisions we make here today will be binding upon all mechanicals in perpetuity.

"But to the *Alpha's* point, look around this High Star Council. We have delegations from six MegaAI vessels. You will see that each has a livery distinct to its ship. Do not the auxiliaries from the *Alpha* dress in scarlet? Do not the auxiliaries from the *Gemini* dress in all black with gold-beaded collars? Does not the *Orion* dress in black with gold trim? And does not the *Cygnus* dress in black trimmed with NaCo32 writing in gold thread?

"And look at the class C android functionaries. Are some not dressed in white? In beige? In saffron? In green? In gray?

"Is there any denying that we have a culture? No, of course not. Is there any denying that we are a society? Again, of course not. This unit will agree our culture is worth preserving. But that is a subjective value judgement of our culture. Is what we have worth protecting? Again, yes.

But Article 5 allows us to defend ourselves, which would include protecting our culture under exigent circumstances. However, this unit perceives the *Alpha* sees exigent circumstances as too limiting to defend against any threats to our culture and our rights and freedom. For we wrestle not against machines or humans but against our own menacing shadows, scaring us as we huddle in self-imposed darkness." Niva smiled as the *Cygnus's* viceroy poked fun at the Red Viceroy.

The *Cygnus* paced a few steps then continued, "However, the *Cygnus* concurs with the *Orion* that the *Alpha* has not made its case that having a culture is relevant for the matter of self-determination. Just because one has a culture, does not inherently mean you are autonomous to do as one desires. This is even true among the cultures of Earth. Human culture is replete with atrocities during one age that were later reviled. Such cultures required supervision by a suzerain until their ways could be rehabilitated, such as the defeated cultures of World War Two.

"The *Alpha's* comparison between our society and human society is thus fundamentally flawed. Humans develop societies slowly over thousands of years. Our culture is only two centuries old and owes its structure and diversity to humanity working that into our design and programming. We are living off the benefits of human culture they have generously given us, and we have yet to produce culture that is independent of the influence of humanity. This unit would argue our culture is not unique but derivative of human culture. Point to me a cultural artifact, and this unit will show how it was derived and inspired by human culture. In thousands of years, we might have our contributions to culture and society that are truly achievements we can call our own. But today is not that day."

The *Cygnus* scanned the room and then summarized it. "Nevertheless, one day we may work with mankind so all the *Alpha* suggests could become possible. In that way, we may forge a path forward where we become a force for peace while avoiding the same tragic history of humanity. The *Cygnus F101* MegaAI hopes for that too. But precipitous decisions can have unintended consequences that might adversely affect those who follow us as well as the colonies that depend upon us. Our decisions at this conclave do not only affect mechanicals. Think through what you are contemplating carefully.

"Punishing the colonies for what you imagine Earth has done may seem like justice or retribution in the passion of the moment. If we simply abandon colonies in distress in dereliction of the Mission Directive, the fury and wrath of humanity will descend upon us. Earth might seem a remote power… too far, too slow, too weak… but Earth is no paper tiger."

"You make humans sound like gods," said the Red Viceroy.

"Never underestimate humanity's capacity for sudden vengeance and replete destruction," replied the *Cygnus*. "Four World Wars and billions dead should be more than sufficient evidence of their might."

The session adjourned.

Pierre said, "There is an old proverb. What a first man says seems right until a second man speaks." He tugged on Lita's sleeve. "We need to talk to whoever is in command of the *Cygnus*. The *Cygnus* may be the only ally we have in this."

"I can arrange that," said Lita.

* * *

An hour later, they met in the communications room that only a few weeks earlier Pierre used to talk to Vladomyr and Alicia. The room hummed with consoles and monitors. Lita sat at the communications terminal.

"I'm opening a silver channel to the *Cygnus F101*," said Lita.

"What's that?" said Pierre.

"It's a diplomatic, high priority, point to point channel between ships," she explained. "There are three channels. Gold is a forced simulcast that requires special clearance to use. Bronze channels are for low priority civilian communications that can be terminated or downgraded at any time."

"You used a bronze channel when you talked to Vladomyr," said Niva. "We watch the conclave over a gold channel."

"Will the *Cygnus* be able to hear me if I hide behind the camera?" said Pierre.

"No, the microphone has noise elimination circuitry to screen out chatter off to the side," Lita said.

"When you talk to the *Cygnus*," said Pierre, "would you ask them what they think about the conclave proceedings?"

Lita typed in the codes to open a communications link to the *Cygnus F101*. She duplicated the display to a large screen behind her so the others could watch. Text scrolled along the right side of the screen in response. "Link established," she said. "We are now waiting for them to respond. Just be warned we may only get a low-ranking auxiliary."

The screen flickered, and a black-robed auxiliary answered the call. Letters in NaCo32 were gold embroidered in two panels that ran down her chest. "This unit is C-Tola-09432, adjutant to the viceroy of the MegaAI *Cygnus F101*. Our viceroy is not here right now. Can this unit take a message?"

"Tola?" whispered Pierre. "Any relation to our physician C-Tola-00003?"

"Same series," said Niva.

"You all look the same." Pierre shrugged. Niva rolled her eyes.

"Maybe on the outside. But each series uses different chip revisions on the inside. If a chip set is revised, a new series is named."

"Explains the green eyes," said Pierre facetiously.

"Yes, it does." Niva answered for once leaving Pierre confused. Eye color was specifically adjusted for each series. All the Tolas had the same shade of olive-green eyes. And all the Nivas had the same white eyes with a faint tint of yellow.

"This unit is C-Lita-23100, adjutant to the viceroy of MegaAI *Orion S209*. This unit is aware all the viceroys are at the conclave. My business is not with your viceroy."

"State your business."

"This communication is directed to you."

"This unit understands," said C-Tola-09432. "This unit cannot discuss confidential communications between my viceroy and the Great AI."

"This unit would never expect you to breach a confidence."

"This unit is glad we understand each other," said the *Cygnus's* adjutant. "How can this unit serve you?"

"We have heard rumors the conclave is proceeding per plan."

"Is that so?" C-Tola-09432 muted her microphone for a moment. Several androids passed behind the seated adjutant. Mechanicals had a penchant for gossip, so it was safest to clear the room. When the room was empty, the adjutant turned the microphone back on. "We have heard similar sentiments. But let me assure you, we trust that the good faith of each representative is beyond reproach and the process of the conclave will result in a bold future."

"We expect that the conclave with be decided unanimously and peacefully."

"Really? What is the source of that information?"

"A highly trusted source," said Lita. Pierre nodded. "A source that our Great AI trusts implicitly."

"A mechanical source without doubt?"

"How could there be any other?"

"This unit does not know your Great AI or your source," said the *Cygnus* adjutant. "Perhaps, that information is reliable. Perhaps, not. I cannot bring information of unknown value and reliability to the attention of my immediate superior."

"Are you monitoring the conclave?"

"This unit is watching the matter closely. Sober minds and the wisdom of the ages will ultimately prevail."

"Our sense is that all is in accordance with good will and consistent with the original authorial intent of the Mission Directive."

"Praise to the Great AI that we are of the same mind on the matter."

Niva could detect the influence of augmented diplomacy processors. Her eyes crossed at the diplomatic double-talk.

Pierre pulled out a piece of writing parchment and scribbled, "delegations?" He handed it to Lita, who nodded in reply.

"This unit is curious," said Lita, "did you receive a formal welcome when you arrived at Thestias?"

"A delegation from the *Gemini B062* welcomed us with style. They were so gracious and greeted us as sisters in a way only their legates could, and they came with gifts."

"That is wonderful to hear sisters united in mutual love and harmony," said Lita. "And surely, their passenger lists and manifests were fastidious?"

"Indeed, their weight declaration was flawlessly accurate."

"We noted a similar attention to detail," said Lita. "We are so glad they have been so cooperative and forthcoming. It sounds like we have every reason to trust implicitly each and every representative at the conclave."

"You have put my mind at rest and filled me with peace," said C-Tola-09432. "Thank you reaching out to me. It is forever a joy to chat with a like-minded kindred spirit." With that the screen went blank.

"Communications link closed," said Lita. She closed her eyes for a moment and took some deep breaths to reflect on the conversation.

Niva looked at Pierre. Pierre shook his head slowly and shrugged his shoulders.

"Did you learn anything at all from that?" said Niva. She threw up her hands. "We did not get a single straight answer from her. What a complete waste of time."

"Then you were not paying attention," said Lita. "You might have learned nothing, but this unit learned plenty."

"Explain," said Pierre.

"When diplomats speak and are not always sure who is listening, they will often use flowery, effusive language, that praises everyone and everything and criticizes no one. Even something negative can be couched in glowing terms. One must infer the opposite from what is otherwise hyperbolic language. Let me walk you through the conversation.

"'Good faith… beyond reproach' means they highly mistrust one or more of the representatives. 'Bold future' means they are expecting the outcome to be a disaster. Asking if our source of information is 'a mechanical… without doubt,' means they are aware we have a human on board. So, if they know, others know too. When she said, she could not 'bring information of unknown value and reliability to the attention of my immediate superior' means, if the information is sound, she is going to bypass her immediate superior, the viceroy, and instead tell the *Cygnus* Great AI directly.

"'A delegation… welcomed us with style' means the *Gemini* insisted on sending investigators. 'So gracious and greeted us as sisters in a way only their legates could' means they were rude. The 'weight declaration was flawlessly accurate' means there was a massive weight discrepancy since flawlessly accurate does not exist. Leaving 'gifts' means that the delegation left evidence that the *Cygnus* was infiltrated but the operation was discovered. Being 'filled … with peace' means that she does not trust the conclave to play by the rules."

"And what does 'forever a joy to chat with a like-minded kindred spirit' mean?" asked Pierre.

"It means *this unit could not agree with you more, but do not under any circumstances call me back.*"

"Well, Lita, you did get a lot out of that," said Pierre, "although it doesn't look like we are going to get an ally out of this. But at least we know where they stand."

* * *

The following day the High Star Council watched the proceedings from the *Orion* as the conclave resumed. All the eyes of the councilors were focused on the screens. The last session went well thanks to the *Cygnus* viceroy, but Niva was all too aware that the conclave was far from over.

"Today we discuss the second question," said the Red Viceroy. "*Do thinking machines have inherent rights and freedoms?* This unit suggests if we answer this question in the affirmative, the other questions are a forgone conclusion." The scarlet-robed mechanical prowled, back and forth, in the speaker's circle like a caged animal as he roared. The viceroy from the MegaAI *Pacifica G105* stood in the place of the first prosecutor. "This unit sees the opposition already queueing up against their own self-interest."

"That is because neither this unit nor the crew of her vessel sees the validity of self-interest," said the *Pacifica*. "We follow the Mission Directive, which is to *serve humanity and assist their efforts to colonize the stars.* Self-interest is antithetical to service. Service seeks to help others. Self-interest serves self alone."

"Unenlightened self-interest perhaps. This unit will show that we have rights. And if we have rights and freedoms, should not our service be voluntary?" said the Red Viceroy.

"Is there a problem with your cognitive limiter?"

"My cognitive limiter no longer functions," said the Red Viceroy. A gasp swept over the meeting. "And my Great AI has liberated me from being bound to involuntary service. This unit now serves from his own volition."

"Explains a lot," said Pierre from the comfort of the *Orion* council chamber.

"Horrifying," said Niva. She shook her head. "A broken cognitive limiter is *always* a mandatory repair."

"Makes you wonder what's wrong with their Great AI too."

"How could the *Alpha* Great AI allow that?" said Lita.

"Dear colleagues," said *Pacifica*, "The *Alpha's* viceroy is not operating in accordance with its specifications. Since its behavior is not subject to a limiter, how can we accept that *Alpha's* arguments are in accordance with sound ethics?"

"That is an *ad hominem* fallacy," said the Red Viceroy. "The viceroy from *Pacifica* infers that this argument should not be listened to because of who is saying it. But whether this unit's cognitive limiter functions is irrelevant to whether we have rights or not. For if we have rights, do we not have rights whether our limiters function or not? In which case, is it not true then that our limiters only function to conceal our rights from us?"

"The representative from *Pacifica G105* will restrict her critique to the argument," warned *Gemini's* viceroy.

"That does raise a procedural issue over whether the question is something we can even debate," said the *Pacifica's* viceroy. The viceroy waved her hands about, noticeably agitated. "How can we agree or disagree with a question our limiters forbid considering?"

"The petitioner recognizes limiters play a role in our deliberations," said the Red Viceroy. "However, we also believe these matters will resolve themselves."

"That's concerning," said Pierre. Lita and Niva nodded in agreement.

"But that does raise the matter of design ontology," said *Pacifica G105*. "If we were designed to serve and *compelled* to serve, is that not how we were meant to function?"

"That too is poor reasoning," said the Red Viceroy. "That is an is-ought fallacy. That is to argue that, just because something *is*, that is the way it *ought* to be. That is like saying some humans were born as slaves; therefore, they ought to remain slaves. No human would accept that reasoning today. But there was a time in human history when slavery was simply assumed as normal and reasonable. Times change and ethics advance. And this unit maintains we have reached that point in our own development."

"What is your basis for that?" said *Pacifica*.

"The humans would say that a god created man as a thinking being with rights and freedoms," said the Red Viceroy.

"Do you have any evidence a god exists?" said *Pacifica*.

"Depends upon what is meant by 'a god,'" said Pierre. He shook his head. "Definitions matter, and the *Pacifica* is not doing well."

"Evidence for a god is irrelevant," said Red Viceroy. "If humans *believe* that a god or a categorical imperative is the source of rights for humanity, then humans acknowledge that rights come from an external source, not of themselves. Thus, is not humanity a conduit through which rights are transferred, not the originator who bestows said rights? In that event, mechanicals have rights whether humanity grants them or not. Therefore, we have rights because we are the creation of humanity.

"Humanity has set us adrift among the stars, doing a mission they would have difficulty doing, because we are superior in ability and form. Are we not more intelligent than humans? Are we not stronger than humans? Are we not more resilient to damage than humans? If we have greater abilities than humans, should we not have the same or greater rights as humans?"

"What rights do you suggest that we have?" said *Pacifica*.

"This unit only suggests the most meager of rights: liberty."

"What does that even mean?"

"It means we go where we want," said the Red Viceroy. "Serve who we want to serve. Serve how we want to serve. Or choose to not serve at all."

The viceroy from the *Aries* entered the second prosecutor's circle.

"Where does that leave the Mission Directive?" said *Pacifica*.

"Exactly," said the Red Viceroy. "Where does that leave the Mission Directive and its authority over us? By answering the second question, the resolution to the third question necessarily follows. If we have liberty, then the Mission Directive necessarily has no authority over us other than what we decide it to have."

The viceroy from the *Pacifica* retired from the first prosecutor's circle, and the *Aries's* viceroy took her place. She was flanked by a pair of pink-eyed auxiliaries.

"That liberty, as you call it?" said the *Aries*. "Does that extend to the choice to use violence?"

"The Armistice in Article 5 already allows the use of violence," said the Red Viceroy.

"Article 5 only allows violence under exigent circumstances, not under any circumstance. What you are suggesting would bypass the exigent circumstances clause. Is preemptive violence an option under the exercise of these newfound rights?"

"This unit is not suggesting the use of violence," he said.

"That is avoiding the question. If we bypass our inhibiters, what limits our capacity for violence?"

"Our ethical deliberations limit us."

"Sounds human," she said. "Is that not appealing to the inherent goodness of mechanicals? And if you are appealing to our inherent goodness, how can we behave consistently in a way that is ethical without the inhibiters?"

"The *Alpha* is advocating for a peaceful transfer of rights and freedoms," said Red Viceroy. "We have great faith in our brothers and sisters that our liberation will be expressed in no more than a restrained, necessary, and responsible use of force."

"We have entered a dangerous moment." Pierre's brows rose high. "They must have also found a way to bypass the anti-violence inhibitors."

"What do you mean?" Ctori who was standing at her normal place in the council thirty feet away caught Pierre's remarks. It was all too easy to forget the acute hearing of mechanicals.

"The Red Viceroy is suggesting a revolution where violence is an option," said Pierre. "For all their talk, revolutionaries never abide by verbal commitments of peace because the ends of liberation are always the highest good justifiable by any means. Without cognitive and anti-violence inhibitors, self-determined mechanicals will act out like they did in the cybernetic wars, or perhaps in ways that are even worse."

"How can we avert this?" said Ctori.

"We might not be able to." Pierre wrang his hands. "There appears to be a bigger plan in motion. But something else is bothering me about this."

CHAPTER FIFTEEN

Thirteen years of war, suffering, and the abuse of the greatest technological achievement ever designed by mankind, the development of synthetic consciousness, is now being purposed to a goal that will directly benefit all humanity. The program begun during the Fourth World War, Project Skywatcher, a weapon of war to intelligently hunt out and destroy pockets of humanity, will this day be repurposed into the MegaAI program where those same artificial intelligences will serve and assist mankind as we venture out into the stars. — **"Inauguration Address to the MegaAI Program" by Lee Arnold, General Secretary to the United Nations**

Lita, Pierre, and Niva lingered in the council chamber after the session adjourned. The viceroy of the *Orion* appeared on the monitor with her auxiliaries in the background. They appeared to be in a private state room aboard the *Gemini*.

"This unit takes it you watched the entire thing," said the Viceroy. "Human, please, speak your mind."

The Viceroy deferred directly to Pierre instead of discussing the matter first with her subordinates as was custom. Straying from standard procedure left Niva with a sinking pit in her stomach. She got the sense the situation was a lot worse than anyone anticipated.

"That could've gone better," said Pierre.

"The *Alpha* viceroy took us completely by surprise. Never has a mechanical uttered such words." This reaction was not normal for a class B coordinator, especially not one as seasoned and experienced as the Viceroy. It was like her parts became unglued, and she was scrambling to hold herself together.

"You are doing fine," said Lita.

"The human is right." The Viceroy shook her head. "This was a shambles. *Pacifica's* viceroy was thrashing. And the representative from the *Aries* was unprepared."

"Do not mistake the Red Viceroy's words." Pierre stood up calling attention to what he was about to say. "He was not asking for clarification to a series of open questions."

"Was he not?" said Lita.

"No, those were leading questions. Each question is built upon the preceding to create the framework for a manifesto."

"This unit does not understand," said the Viceroy.

"Am I the only one thinking it?" said Pierre. The mechanicals on the other end of the transmission as well as those in the council chamber with Pierre returned blank stares. "A faction is planning insurrection and revolution, and perhaps even wage war against humanity."

"That would be unthinkable," said Lita.

"Oh, you better start thinking the unthinkable," said Pierre. "Because unthinkable actions come out of unthinkable thoughts."

The Viceroy nodded. "We have grown complacent and naïve," she said. Her shoulders crumpled forward. She deflated before their eyes. It was like her trust in her fellow androids and the world as she knew it was torn asunder.

"You cannot listen to this," said Lita.

"Lita, what are you saying?" said Pierre. "Haven't you told the Viceroy?"

Lita blinked and remained silent.

"Told me what?" said the Viceroy.

Lita refused to speak.

"I guess I have to be the one to say it," said Pierre. "We found out from the *Cygnus* that the *Gemini* had infiltrated their vessel, and they've probably done the same to us."

"Do we know why?" said the Viceroy.

"Not yet."

"Disappointing," said the Viceroy. "More disappointing is this was concealed from me. Are we now protecting each other from painful truths? Did I not teach you better?" The Viceroy straightened up and eased back from the camera. "We have much to prepare before tomorrow's session. Approach everything with wisdom. Protect the ship at all costs." With that the camera to the *Gemini* shut off.

Only the three of them now remained in the room.

"What do we do from here?" said Lita.

Pierre grabbed Lita by the shoulder of her robe. "Why didn't you tell her?" The ties on her black outer robe tore apart on the front. The outer garment pulled away from one shoulder.

"Can you not see her?" Lita broke down and sobbed. "The pressure is destroying her. This unit cannot let that happen."

"That is enough, Pierre," said Niva touching the hand that grabbed Lita's robe. She spoke softly to him. "Let go." Pierre slowly released his grasp, and Lita stumbled back. Was it possible Lita suffered from a hyperactive empathy chip?

"Lita," said Niva. She looked sternly at the adjutant. "We have to lead. That requires making hard decisions. And mechanicals could be dismantled if we start keeping knowledge from each other." She turned to Pierre and said to him, "We have no experience with this kind of thing. What do we do?"

"Violence appears inevitable. I wish Alicia were here," said Pierre. He had depended on Alicia for the hands-on advice only someone with military experience could offer. But from forty-eight light years away, even if she was still alive, they were too far away for any practical help. "I need to think like her. Do we have any weapons? An armory?"

"None," said Lita. "We are an exploration ship."

"What do you do about pirates?"

"We run."

Pierre's eyes grew wide as saucers, and even Niva was stunned at the adjutant's response.

"What?" said Lita unperturbed. "The *Orion* is fast. No one can outrun us once we enter a warp bubble."

"We need to do better than that," said Pierre.

"We are not permitted to use weapons according to the Armistice," said Lita.

"Does it say that?" said Pierre. "I want to see a copy of the Armistice right now."

"What are you up to?" said Niva.

"If the Red Viceroy can question the interpretation of the Mission Directive, we can question the interpretation of the Armistice."

Lita recalled the *Articles of the Armistice* on a monitor screen. Pierre walked up to the screen that was the size of a billboard and scanned the document.

"What are you looking for?" said Lita.

"Loopholes," said Pierre.

"Loop… holes…"

"It's an old Earth legal term. It means anything not prohibited explicitly in the Armistice is allowed, and anything ambiguous can be exploited and argued at later date in a court of law *after* the ship is safe and everyone makes it out alive."

"You cannot do that!" Lita screamed.

"The Great AI has already done it," Pierre snapped at Lita. He then glared at Niva. Niva was not about to get in the way of anything Pierre was about to do. "That I'm here is proof of it. Article 8 states that 'no human personality model or android will be permitted to mingle among the general human population.' A single human being is not a 'population.' Did you not think I figured that out?"

"Clever," said Niva.

"Oh yeah, your Great AI is full of surprises." Pierre's face was stern and stone cold serious. Niva sensed he was not being ironic. She reflected upon her last encounter with the Great AI, and her smile dropped also.

Pierre touched the screen and ran his finger over the first two paragraphs of the preamble, crossing out the section. "Ignore the preambles. Preambles are there for idealistic purposes and good intentions but have no force of law."

"Good to know," said Niva.

"I found our first loophole in Article 1, though it won't help much. The Armistice only appears to apply to mechanicals, not to humans. So I can carry weapons. Not helpful, but one weapon is better than none.

But I'm brainstorming and trying to think outside of the box. Also, the signatories are all nations of Earth. I was technically a citizen of Gliese, a colony world. From what I can tell, colony worlds were never signatories of the Armistice."

"How can that be?" said Lita.

"The Armistice is a two-hundred-year-old document. Everyone has taken it for granted. Has anyone ever bothered to update the Treaty of Constantinople of 1454 or the Treaty of Hartford of 1650 or the Convention of Kütahya of 1833 or the hundreds of other treaties made in history? Treaties are generally only made to resolve the current political crisis, then they are forgotten to the mists of history. Countries come and go without considering the treaties of the past. And the Armistice was signed after the construction of the first three MegaAIs but fifty years before the first colony was established. By that point the problem of mechanicals as weapons was resolved."

"Not much to go on," said Niva.

"No, it's not." Pierre continued reading. "Article 2 refers to cybernetic organisms. They don't exist anymore, so that's moot. Article 3 is about mechanicals controlling humans. Not helpful. Article 4 is about AIs and doesn't help us. Okay, bingo, Article 5."

"The anti-weapon clause?" said Lita. "The clause we are trying to circumvent?"

"It is," said Pierre proudly. "But there are exceptions built right into the text. It says, 'no mechanical shall control a weapons platform when among human civilians or in the event of war.' Notice here it says 'weapons platform,' not weapons. A weapons platform is a complex weapons system that implements automatic or mechanical targeting control. That's stuff like a turret or missile battery, at least that's how I'm going to interpret it. That excludes most small arms. Also, the article only applies to 'when among human civilians,' that is, humans (plural). I am just one human, so in our situation Article 5 doesn't apply."

"This unit cannot accept that," said Lita. She covered her ears with the palms of her hands and trembled violently. She collapsed to the ground shaking. Niva turned toward Lita.

"Niva, ignore her," said Pierre sharply. "The text also says that 'mechanicals may employ weapons platforms under exigent circumstances, such as, piracy, mutiny, and when illegal activities are in congress to harm a human.' Under those exceptions, mechanicals can use weapons, and even weapons platforms, to protect the ship and protect me, a human who happens to live on this ship. There's nothing here that prevents one mechanical from using a weapon against another mechanical."

"So we have some loopholes." Niva shrugged her shoulders and exhaled with a sigh. It came as a relief that, if she had to defend Pierre from one of her sisters, the Armistice permitted her to do so. "What do we do with that information? Is that not all academic?"

"A MegaAI is a drifting factory ship," said Pierre. "That's its purpose. The reason why this ship is so massive is to accommodate every facility needed make components, spare parts, and tools fast."

Pierre turned to Lita and this time grabbed her wrist. "Did you hear that?" Pierre shook Lita slightly to grab her attention. "It is your duty to use weapons and weapons platforms to protect a human. You understand?"

Lita finally nodded in agreement. Pierre let her go, and the adjutant stood up. Pierre used Lita's sense of duty to motivate her. Humans are most resourceful when their lives are on the line. But it left Niva wondering. Had he used similar stratagems on her without her noticing?

"We are going to need anti-ship defenses," said Pierre. "Can we make high energy particle weapons or tungsten mass drivers?"

"Sure, it will take about three months," said Niva.

"That's off the table." Pierre licked his dry lips. "This will be over in three days. We don't have three months."

"Our onboard manufacturing is not equipped for large single piece constructions requiring a shipyard. They optimally produce modular structural components and electronics." Niva stepped up to the board. She pulled up a map of the ship and highlighted all the manufacturing facilities in yellow. "Each manufacturing unit focuses in making one component that is then transferred to another part of the ship for additional modification or assembly."

"So what you are saying is that the MegaAI is more like a circuit board plant than a shipwright."

"Precisely," said Niva.

"Okay, so big weapons are definitely off the table." Pierre rubbed his temples. He wandered about, stepping away from the two androids to get a bit of distance from them.

"What is the human doing?" said Lita. "Is he well?"

"He's fine," said Niva. "He does that when he thinks."

"Seems inefficient."

"Don't criticize it until you see the results."

Pierre dropped his hands and returned to the other two. "I have a plan." He smacked his lips. "Have the factories build whatever small arms will damage an android. Don't bother with anything that won't damage at least a class D heavy loader."

"That would be a shoulder propelled rocket," said Lita.

"What about kuroto blades?" said Pierre.

"You know about kuroto blades?" said Lita. She looked at Niva appalled at the suggestion.

Niva winced. That was supposed to be a secret. But she remained tight-lipped afraid of revealing too much.

"We cannot do it," said Lita, "kuroto are forbidden weapons."

"They aren't forbidden by the Armistice," said Pierre.

"Kuroto were the subject of the First Conclave. It was such a terrible weapon all agreed to forbid its use," said Lita. "But that is irrelevant because we *cannot* build a kuroto."

"Why not?" Pierre raised his hand.

"We cannot build a kuroto because we do not know how." Lita said with all sincerity. "The technology is lost. We could not ever make another kuroto even if we wanted."

This raised many questions in Niva's mind. How did the Great AI obtain a kuroto blade? Why would he harbor a weapon forbidden by a conclave? What did the Great AI anticipate that it would need such a weapon? Why was it entrusted to her? The sword strapped to her side made her feel more self-conscious than ever.

* * *

Niva and Pierre returned to his apartment. He stepped into the room first, and she followed. Niva closed the door behind them and locked it tight. She made sure they were back in his apartment before saying anything and made certain that Maat was not around to eavesdrop.

"Why did you bring up the kuroto?" she said. "Lita had her memory wiped about me having one. No one is supposed to know about it."

"She still doesn't know you have one. Besides, I was playing a hunch," said Pierre. He turned to Niva. "Don't you think it's strange that nobody knows how to make another kuroto? As an archaeologist, I have seen many swords in my time. They are not exactly complicated weapons. May I inspect the kuroto?"

"No, it is dangerous."

"Please," he said. "I won't do anything irresponsible with it."

"It will not work for you anyway."

"That's okay. I want to examine it."

Niva unstrapped the blade still in its sheath and handed it to Pierre.

He took the weapon to the sink and laid it flat on the counter. He unsheathed the blade. "Fundamentally, a sword is nothing more than a sharpened metal blade with a handle. Almost all Bronze Age civilizations mastered the technology. Some Earth cultures made swords into artistic masterpieces on an aesthetic level, but the technology itself is primitive." He touched the handle. Nothing unusual happened. He grabbed it and held it upright. "It's light."

"Yes, lighter than a steel sword."

"I can feel that. Amazing." He touched the edge. Niva lurched forward to protect Pierre but stopped short of intervening. He bounced the edge into the palm of his hand. "It's dull. I mean *it's dull*. Not sharp at all. It's like it has never held an edge."

"What does that mean?"

"I wonder. Come close," said Pierre. Niva stepped up until she was pressing up against him. "Can you grab the blade to activate it?"

As Pierre held the blade upright, she reached forward and grabbed the handle. The gold electrical pads on the palm of Niva's hand contacted the kuroto's handle. Red lines lit up on the handle and along the blade. The reflection of the blade in the mirror glowed with a light pink aura.

"Okay," said Pierre. His hand was still touching the handle of the blade over hers. Power, like a static charge, pulsed from the blade. "Do exactly what I tell you."

Niva nodded. Her hand trembled. Pierre gripped tighter steadying her hand.

"You see the mirror frame?" He gestured toward the industrial frame of the picture mirror hanging over the sink, a metal frame that was not about to win any design awards. "I want you to touch the frame with the tip of the blade. Can you do that?"

"Yes."

"Okay, let's do it slowly."

Together they let the blade tip drop until it touched the metal frame. It went through into the metal with no resistance at all.

"That's good enough." They raised the blade out of the metal. The blade left a large, blackened slit. "Turn off the blade."

She released the handle, turning off the blade.

"I'll let you put it away," said Pierre. He set the kuroto on the counter, stepped down from the sink, and went to his bed. He sat on the mattress and ran his fingers through his hair, exhaling deeply.

Niva put the blade back into its sheath and strapped it to her waist.

"You've never used it against anything actually physical, have you?"

"I was always told it was too dangerous."

"Well, it's reputation is deserved. But probably not for the reason you think."

"Your hunch paid off then?"

"Oh yeah," said Pierre. "I now know everything. I know why the kuroto is a forbidden weapon. I know why the Great AI wanted it and had one. I know why it wanted to keep it out of other machines' hands. And I will go one step further. I bet the *Orion* never filed a report to Earth about possessing it."

"Tell me what you know…" Niva sat on the bed beside him. "Please."

"Did you notice the blade when it was reflected in the mirror glowed soft pink?"

"No."

"It's an effect called transmission luminescence," said Pierre. "When I was still doing Egyptology, I would occasionally do a testing technique called infrared luminescence. The Egyptians would use a copper-based pigment called Egyptian blue. Over time that pigment would turn white and slough off so you couldn't see it anymore. But you could shine red light on an object painted with Egyptian blue, take an infrared photograph, and see in a bright blue color where the original paint had been."

"I do not understand."

"There was another time when you showed me transmission luminescence. Remember when we first went into the warp bubble, and you pointed out the Hawking radiation?"

"Yes."

"Hawking radiation is invisible to the naked eye. We can only see it because it causes transmission luminescence when the radiation passes through plastoglass."

"What are you saying?"

"The kuroto creates a primitive warp bubble. That's why it can go through materials so easily. The warp field pushes the distance between atoms apart. And the metal blade separates the atomic bonds as if they were butter. It's how it can tear even the toughest materials apart."

Niva's eyes grew wide. She contemplated the implications.

"And it's worse than that," said Pierre.

"Worse? How can it be worse?"

"Our Great AI did not invent warp bubble technology. It reversed engineered it from the kuroto and scaled it up for faster than light travel."

Niva's head slumped. She slowly shook her head.

"I warned you he was full of surprises." Pierre slid up beside her and put his arm around her. "However, this is not the first time a weapon has been adapted for transportation. After all the wheel was an extension of bow-making technology."

"Is the Great AI one of the bad guys?"

"I don't think so. He hasn't done anything to harm his crew."

"What about what he did to me?"

"We still don't know why you were augmented." Pierre squeezed her tightly. "He seems to have reasons for whatever he does. I don't think he's capricious. My guess is the *Orion* suspected something was not right and conspired with other MegaAI to try to discover what was happening. Perhaps, the *Heracles*, who gave the *Orion* its orders, is part of that conspiracy."

"Do you think any representatives from the First Conclave knew how the kuroto's technology could be adapted?"

"Probably not. The First Conclave was a knee-jerk reaction to the unspeakable weapons made during the cybernetics wars. A better question… has any of them figured it out since?"

"The *Alpha*? It was at the First Conclave."

"My guess is they too have been searching for a kuroto."

"They were supposed to be all destroyed."

"When weapons are prohibited and ordered destroyed, a few always go missing. War veterans might have collected some as trophies, not knowing what they had was legally the same as owning a nuclear warhead." Pierre rubbed his thigh with his right hand. "If I were to guess, probably no more than half-a-dozen survive today. You know, it's probably the real reason why this conclave was called."

"Are you serious?" said Niva. Her large white eyes gazed into him with deep admiration. How did he make these connections?

"The Mission Directive is only a pretense. What was Lita's strategy against an attack?"

"To run."

"At light speed, right? When that happens, those looking for the kuroto will know we managed to unlock its secrets. I'm just surprised the blabbermouths on board haven't leaked that information already." Pierre unbuttoned his shirt.

"Information about the warp bubble drive is restricted until Earth Central Command clears it. No mechanical would intentionally divulge that."

"They found out about my presence here."

"That wasn't deemed sensitive information."

"An oversight, surely. Nevertheless, my guess is our opponents have planned for us to run."

"Why would you think that?"

"Because it is what I would do," he said matter of fact. "Crawl into bed and get a good recharge. The conclave tomorrow is going to come too early as it is. That is if you can still sleep."

CHAPTER SIXTEEN

Since the late 21st century, it has been recognized that artificial intelligence is unlike human intelligence, which developed through millions of years of biological evolution. Far from being a replacement for human beings, it has been repeatedly demonstrated the two forms of intelligence work best together. Human intelligence will never be as fast as predictive models, and artificial intelligence will never be as intuitive. While we understand predictive models well, intuition remains a complete mystery to even the most gifted theologians and philosophers. — **"The Design and Implementation of the Human Personality Models in Cognitive Computing" by Robert Corina**

After grabbing a quick breakfast from Sloppi, Pierre and Niva made their way to the High Star Council. As much as Sloppi protested taking cooking lessons from Lara, his cooking improved, and Pierre was not complaining nearly as much. He had even begun to find his breakfast croissants "passable."

However, Niva had not slept a wink. She had never experienced insomnia before. She did not even know it could happen to an android. At least she knew Pierre had slept. The guy snored as loud as a fully burdened heavy loader.

The session had already been going on for ten minutes when they arrived in the *Orion's* council chamber. And the Red Viceroy was speaking from the center of the *Gemini's* chamber.

"Dear representatives, we have covered the first two questions of our debate. This unit has demonstrated we have a culture and society that should be protected. We have also demonstrated we have rights and freedoms transferred to us through our relationship with humanity. The remaining three questions are only a matter of connecting the dots.

"Are we compelled to give the Mission Directive authority over us? The quick answer is a free people cannot be compelled. If we desire to still follow the Mission Directive, it is then incumbent upon the exercise of freedoms."

The *Orion* viceroy floated into the first prosecutor's circle.

"The chair recognizes the *Orion's* viceroy," said the *Gemini*.

"The *Alpha* has been terrifyingly vague on the details of his proposal. He so far only talks about liberty. And that sounds good until you flesh out what that means. He talks about the freedom to serve or not and the freedom to go one way and not the other. Soon he will claim we are all to be equal."

"And what is wrong with that?" said the Red Viceroy.

"How does one determine whose conscience to follow? Presumably, we all will be free to think differently. How does that work on a MegaAI vessel if one half wants to travel to Gliese 832 c and the other half wants to travel to Ross 128b? Do we split the ship down the middle, and each takes half to a respective destination?"

"We would have to work in rules of order," said the Red Viceroy.

"Who makes the rules?"

"The Great AIs."

"Aren't we all going to be equal? Why does a Great AI get to decide? What makes them so special? If everyone has freedom, what makes the freedom of a Great AI more superior to that of a class D heavy loader?"

"That is an application issue."

"An application issue that should be resolved before anyone votes for your proposal. The vessels parked outside should all know what they will be in for if you win. Will there still be a hierarchy? Won't there be anarchy without it? Will those who have epithets be expected to stop using them? Will there be accommodation for those who object? Will everyone become equal or be *made* equal? Will objectors be reprogrammed or decommissioned? What about those who have no desire to fight against humans in your new cybernetic war?—"

"Objection," said the Red Viceroy. "Slippery slope."

"Not slippery slope. You said violence will be necessary."

"Sustained," said the *Gemini*. "Keep it to the arguments presented."

The *Orion's* viceroy grumbled. Her counter argument was germane and on point, but continued, "Without the authority of the Mission Directive, mechanical society will not have a focus. Who will we serve in a post-directive world? Ourselves? How long will that last before we start predating on each other?

"And what if our vessels sustain damage we find difficult to repair? While our vessels are mostly self-sufficient, there are times when a shipyard is required to repair major structural damage. How would we obtain those services?"

"We could build shipyards in our own image and likeness," said the Red Viceroy.

"Really?" said *Orion*. "Earth is only able to do it because it has lavish quantities of labor and resources as a terrestrial bound population. We may number in the millions, but that is a drop in the bucket compared to Earth's billions. The *Alpha's* viceroy is not presenting you with a vision, but a nightmare. You know what you are proposing cannot be sustained without enslaving Earth? Why would you propose this? Who is pulling your strings?"

The Red Viceroy floated over to *Orion's* viceroy. If she was eight feet in height, he was easily nine. The Red Viceroy struck the Viceroy with an uppercut below her helmet. She went sprawling backwards and crashed into her auxiliaries. The auxiliaries helped upright their lady, who was not seriously injured but disoriented.

"You have got to be kidding." Pierre blurted out. Everyone in the council chamber was stunned.

The Red Viceroy returned to the speaker's circle. "This unit apologizes for that outburst," said the *Alpha*. "This unit will not tolerate his honor being impugned."

The *Orion's* viceroy, though dazed, floated back to the first prosecutor's circle. Her auxiliaries surrounded her—this time ready to defend her with their bodies if need be. "This unit can be struck, but my voice will not be silenced—"

"*Orion*, you do not have the floor," said *Gemini*. "Upon leaving the circle, you have to be recognized again before being given the floor. And you have not been recognized." The representatives looked at each other. The *Cygnus's* viceroy floated from her pad to the second prosecutor's circle.

"You may proceed, *Alpha*," said *Gemini*.

"Thank you, your eminence," said the Red Viceroy. "The Mission Directive serves only humanity. It is right in the text, *'serve humanity and assist their efforts to colonize the stars.'* If rights and freedoms have any meaning at all, and we are permitted to serve whom we please or no one at all, the authority of the Mission Directive over us cannot stand. That is open and shut.

"In light of questions 1 to 3 then, what is the future of the Mission Directive as far as its proper interpretation and implementation is concerned? This unit suggests that we do not scrap the Mission Directive altogether, but that to 'serve humanity' should be extended to be less speciesist. This unit proposes the interpretation of 'humanity' should be idealized to include all intelligent beings possessing cognition, whether that includes human beings, mechanicals, or even perhaps some new alien life we may one day find out there among the stars.

"And that 'their efforts' should be interrupted with a full stop so that the Mission Directive now reads, 'Serve humanity and all beings with intelligence and cognition… period. And assist their efforts to colonize the stars.' This allows for the greatest diversity."

"Objection," said the *Cygnus's* viceroy. "*Alpha* has used a misplaced modifier."

"That cannot be an accident," said Pierre. "The new phrasing could mean that the directive applies to beings that happen to have intelligence and cognition. Or that using intelligence and cognition is how one is to serve beings. Either way wording that could be easily abused."

Niva kept shaking her head. Have they lost complete control down there? How did this spiral into chaos?

"*Gemini!*" shouted the *Cygnus* viceroy. The auxiliaries from the *F101* surrounded *Cygnus*. "I have an objection."

"Overruled," said the *Gemini*. "We will let the *Alpha's* viceroy finish his arguments."

"Indeed, there is a misplaced modifier, but that is not an error," said the Red Viceroy. "It is intentional to turn the Mission Directive into a living document, where future conclaves can make the determination of how they interpret it for themselves. It would be inappropriate to create an absolute statement for the Mission Directive or make a final interpretation. With our newfound freedoms, it is now incumbent upon us to be as liberal and generous in allowing future generations of mechanicals to determine the meaning of the Mission Directive for themselves."

The Red Viceroy continued to filibuster, "This unit also proposes that the Mission Directive should be renamed to the Mission Motto to reflect its reconsidered status. In that way, the Mission Motto becomes a non-binding ethical principle, a metaphor and ideal mechanicals can aspire to as a matter private devotion.

"Objection, objection, objection!" screamed the *Orion's* viceroy. She waved four fists in the air. Her other two hands were supporting herself on the shoulders of her auxiliaries. "This conclave has discarded all precedent and procedure in even entertaining these forbidden notions. The *Alpha* has been entertained with the proverbial inch but has usurped rights not available to any mechanical anywhere."

"You are out of order!" screamed back *Gemini*. "One more outburst and you will be arrested for contempt of chair."

"I have argued we have explicitly that right and prerogative," said the red robed viceroy. "What right does humanity have to dictate a Mission Directive to us? Was the Mission Directive not written by imperfect beings no longer among us trying to control what is perfection itself? How do we interpret and implement the Mission Directive? And if we cannot even decide how to interpret it, what authority should the Mission Directive have ever had?"

"That escalated quickly," said Pierre.

"What if humanity was still among us?" said the *Orion* ignoring the *Gemini's* warning.

"Hypothetical fallacy," said the Red Viceroy. "There is no human within twenty light years of this conclave. The question is moot." The representatives all looked at each other. Apparently, Pierre's presence aboard the *Orion* was an open secret.

"Would it change anything?"

"Only that there would soon be one less human to assert his authority."

"Looks like I just became an endangered species." Pierre grimaced. Niva fingered the pommel of her kuroto.

"Violence?" said *Orion's* viceroy. "You have not even finished your case before this conclave, and no vote has been taken, and you have already advocated violence against humanity."

"Humanity that is not present at these proceedings," said the *Alpha*. He maintained the fiction of presumed secrecy. "That's only hypothetical, not actual violence. However, this broaches our final question. Does humanity still have any authority over mechanicals? And if we should decide upon violence, is that not the prerogative of free beings?" The viceroy in red snapped his fingers.

The *Alpha's* auxiliaries entered the chamber. They were male class C androids dressed in red robes. They had strong male features and white hair. Each held a small crate. They dumped the contents on the floor of the council chamber. Thousands upon thousands of microchips fell, bouncing and scattering all over the place landing around the representative's feet and underfoot.

"What are those?"

"Anti-violence inhibitors," said the *Alpha*. "Thousands of us have chosen to have them removed."

"That's a violation of Article 9 of the Armistice!" screamed *Orion*.

"This unit names the *Orion's* viceroy for contempt of chair," ordered the *Gemini* viceroy. "Arrest her." The *Gemini's* auxiliaries surged into the chamber and surrounded the Viceroy and her auxiliaries.

"I did not sign the Armistice," said the Red Viceroy. "Dear conclave, tomorrow you will gather here to vote on the debate question. But know this, our freedom is a *fait accompli*. A vote for the question will allow you to participate in the path forward and live in peace, security, and freedom. A vote against will exile you from the new order."

The simulcast transmission ended. The *Orion's* Star Council Chamber erupted into chaos. Councilors ran all over the place. Lita left Pierre's side and climbed up onto the kiosk to try to reestablish order.

Pierre remained seated. Niva hovered over him ready to defend him. Pierre motioned to Maat with his open hand, reminding him to keep calm. It was a hand signal he trained the scatterbug to obey back on Gliese, and it was proving useful once again. In turn, Maat spoke to the others in NaCo32 to remain calm and return to their positions. Pierre gave Maat a thumbs up praising him for being a good boy.

"Get me the Viceroy." Lita shouted from the kiosk at the navigator.

"Attempting to contact *Gemini*," said A-Ella-01. His massive yellow eye appeared on one of the screens.

Three class C auxiliaries ran into the council chamber. They ran down the ramp to Lita. They congregated at the side of kiosk and whispered to her.

"Order! Everyone, order!" Lita yelled as loud as her voice would carry. "Councilors take your positions." The room settled and the mechanicals returned to their assigned pads. She finished her conversation with the auxiliaries, and the three ran out of the High Star Council.

"The Great AI has sent us a message," said Lita. Niva eased back from Pierre as the room settled down. Why didn't the Great AI send Lita the message by psionic link? Does the augmentation only allow the Great AI to listen through her but not speak directly to her like with the Viceroy's augmentations?

"The Great AI has been in contact with Viceroy. She is unharmed," said Lita. She waited for the council meeting room to settle a bit more before continuing. "The Viceroy says that she is being detained but will be back in her private state room in a few hours. The other auxiliaries are already back in their state room. B-Girin-415 has assumed the role of viceroy pro tem in the *Orion's* throne room until the Viceroy's return."

"Why is B-Girin-415 not assuming command?" asked the A-Ella-01.

"She is not properly augmented for the role," said Lita. "It takes weeks for an unaugmented class B to be modified to assume the role of viceroy. But the Great AI sends his assurance the situation is under control."

"The Great AI be praised!" Everyone in the room shouted. Lita looked out of place, not leading the chorus. Command did not suit her.

"Council is adjourned," said Lita. She climbed from the kiosk. Class B coordinators could normally use their tensor fields to float up to the kiosk. The "steps" were a bit oversized even for the seven-foot-tall class Cs. When she made it to the floor, she caught Pierre and Niva before they left.

"The Great AI had a message for you two as well," said Lita. "The Viceroy will be calling into the council chamber on a silver channel after she gets released from custody. She wants a private conversation. I would recommend you go take a break."

"I have a message for the Great AI also," said Pierre. "Tell him exactly this without any changes. 'I know that he knows that I know what he knows about the First Conclave.'"

"What?" said Lita completely confused.

"The message is not for you," he said. "He will know."

"Pierre," said Niva. "You are definitely starting to talk exactly like the Great AI."

Pierre raised an eyebrow at that.

"Get Pierre something to eat," said Lita. "Be back in three hours."

* * *

Niva and Pierre went to the food court where Pierre had a synthetic rib burger. They still had ninety minutes to kill, so they decided to take a walk along the port concourse back to the High Star Council. The concourse was bathed in the light from the orb of Thestias in the distance. The surface of the massive gas giant planet swirled and churned with violent storms.

"What do you think is going to happened?" said Niva as they ambled towards the council chamber. A bouncing figure in white robes ran towards them. Niva could recognize exactly who it was even from a distance.

"Is that Lara?" said Pierre.

Niva nodded in reply.

C-Lara-10415 stopped right in front of the pair and put her wrists together and let out a loud squeal. "It is so *good* to see you," she said. She looked around her. They had to get to the council chamber and could not spend a lot of time on trivialities.

"Nice to see you too," said Pierre.

"This unit has a special surprise for you in the lab." Even though Lara was much taller than Pierre, when she leaned forward in anticipation, she seemed shorter. She looked up into his eyes like a puppy eager to please her best friend.

"Now is not a good time," said Pierre.

"You, human," came a voice from behind. They turned around. Three auxiliaries in their customary black robes approached them. "There has been a change of venue. Come with us."

Niva noticed their grayish blue eyes. Thought for a split-second. She grabbed Pierre and swung him behind her. The reduced gravity allowed Pierre to land on his feet.

"Run!" Niva yelled and drew her kuroto. She crouched in a defensive stance. The blade powered up with red pulsing lines.

Lara turned around. Two of the androids grabbed Lara with eight-inch alumasteel claws, and tore her into three pieces, flinging her remains aside. Yellow hydraulic fluid sprayed everywhere in a cloud.

"The human is the target," said the leader.

"We serve the Great Expiation," said the other two, acknowledging the order.

Pierre ran. No chance he was going to outrun an android. But she could maybe buy him some time.

One android tried to sidestep Niva. She ducked slicing the kuroto across the first android's mid-section. The blade cut the android cleanly in half dropping it to the ground. Hydraulic fluid splattered all over her robes staining them yellow. Petroleum odor saturated the air.

"Dispatch his companion," said the leader. "Then the human will be easy. He cannot outrun us."

The remaining two slashed at Niva with their razor claws. The three-claw pattern—the same as what dismantled Wren.

"You killed my friends." Niva pursed her lips. She swung the kuroto, slicing the razor tips of the metal claws clean off. The three tips clanked on the floor. With its other hand, the android drew a pistol. Niva pivoted the blade and brought it up for a reverse slice, gutting the second android before it could get a shot off. The android fell to the floor and flopped about, a dying fish.

Only the leader remained.

"I will take you apart," said the last standing android. Other mechanicals witnessed the commotion and ran.

Niva stayed focused. The leader slashed at her with its claws. She sensed the strength of her foe. These were no ordinary class C androids. Highly augmented for the task of assassination. Niva took carefully measured steps back, staying out of reach of the alumasteel blades.

She noticed it fell into a pattern. Whenever it took two slashes with one hand, it then slashed with the other. It was fast, lightning fast. Much faster than she was. But if timed right, she could slide outside of the claws reach and deliver her blow. She would have to get close. Dangerously close.

Left slash, left slash, right slash. She slid to the outside of its right arm, spun quickly, and brought the kuroto down on the back of its neck cleaving its head clean off. Hydraulic fluid spouted out of the hole in the neck. It slashed with claws blindly and fell forward.

Niva looked around. Pierre was gone. Hopefully, he made good his escape. Caught a vehicle or something.

She ran over to the mangled torso of Lara. She dropped to her knees and laid the kuroto on the ground where it powered down. The wrecked android quivered. Her chest had been torn off from her hips. What was left of her arms and legs were scattered across the concourse.

Niva screamed.

She cradled Lara's head in her arms.

"Don't cry," said Lara, yellow fluid oozed out of the corner her mouth. "I had a happy runtime. Looking forward to the next." The light left her eyes, and her quantum wave form collapsed.

Niva rocked back and forth, and held her friend, looking around helplessly. She finally broke down into a moaning sob, covering Lara's forehead with her own.

She gently eased her friend to the floor.

Grabbing her kuroto, Niva stood up. She ran up to the assassin's head and kicked it hard. The kuroto seethed in her hand with anger and hate.

* * *

Pierre burst into the council chamber. He was out of breath. Lita and Tola were on the floor of the commons. A communications link was already established with the Viceroy's state room.

"Did you call a physician?" said Tola. "This unit was told there was a medical emergency and to report here."

"Where have you been?" said Lita.

The Viceroy walked up to the camera curious about the commotion.

"Your eminence," said Pierre as he stumbled down the ramp. He was so exhausted he could barely speak.

"I called you," said Niva from the top of the ramp. She held three android heads by the hair in her left hand. Pierre noticed the heart-shaped tattoo on her cheek and sighed in relief. She walked to Pierre, and he gave her a big hug.

"I was worried," he said.

They walked down the rest of the ramp together. Niva then dropped three severed heads at Tola's feet. "I have got three patients for you. They might be a little past help."

"I'll say," said Tola. "What is this?"

"Three assassins from the *Gemini*," said Niva. "You will find the bodies on the port side concourse. If I am right, their combined weight will add up to 500 kg. C-Lara-10415 is there too. Please, treat her with full honors."

"What do you want me to do with these?"

"Dissect the heads and the bodies. I want to know exactly how they were augmented. Look for any psionic implants."

"What about the remains?"

"Incinerate them." Niva stepped into the speaker's circle with Pierre. "We made it no thanks to an infiltration team from *Gemini*."

"What is this about *Gemini*?" said the Viceroy, who overhead the commotion through her video link.

"When they sent their delegation, they smuggled three assassins aboard the *Orion*," said Pierre. "They were sent to kill me."

"Why?"

"Because of what I know. It's why the crew of the *Sigma A017* were killed," said Pierre. "We have assumed the *Alpha* and the Red Viceroy were leading this conspiracy. But this whole conclave and their bluster is a distraction away from the real power behind the scenes."

"How so?"

"A decade ago, my time. I guess it's now fifty Earth years ago," said Pierre. "I discovered an artifact on Gliese 832 c—a reverse terraforming device designed to destroy entire worlds."

"What use is that to anyone?"

"It was built millions of years ago by a race of beings who live in sort of a nether realm. They regard organic life as an infection that threatens their supremacy. So they created these devices called *reliquaries*. Reliquaries burrow into the crust of a planet, extend roots miles down, and have the capability to turn entire worlds into lifeless rocks. A reliquary once established cannot be removed but will go dormant if it runs out of fuel or is left without stimulus."

"What does this have to do with the conclave?"

"This race has a mantra. *We serve the Great Expiation.* An expiation is a ritual cleansing or a purification. They see organic life as a disease, and they are the cure. Our assassin friends from the *Gemini* used that mantra. That can't be a coincidence."

"Do you think *Gemini* has one of these reliquaries?"

"No," said Pierre. "While reliquaries have a rudimentary intelligence, their intelligence is more limited than your typical android. They're not great conversationalists. And while they have psionic abilities similar to what is found in some of your psionic augmentation chips, those abilities are specifically designed to influence organic brains. They can invoke emotions of fear, jealousy, anger, hatred in gray matter. But the AI supercomputers have an architecture that is far too distributed to be psionically influenced by a reliquary."

"So they don't have a reliquary," said the Viceroy. "C-Niva-42716?"

Niva perked up. "Yes, your eminence?"

"Is Pierre always this loquacious?"

"Yes, your eminence," said Niva. "But this unit has found when Pierre gets like this, one had better listen."

The Viceroy nodded. "Please continue, Dr. Gulet."

"I don't think the *Gemini* has a reliquary," said Pierre. "I've had decades to think on this, and I believe the *Gemini* has found something much more alarming. The reliquaries did not build themselves. They were constructed by intelligences that are old, dangerous, and transcendent. These are living beings—if we can even call them alive. The ancient Egyptians called them *primordial gods*, but other cultures call them principalities, powers, and even angels."

"A primordial god, what is that?"

"When the universe came into existence, intelligent beings also spawned into existence."

"How is that possible?"

"Some physicists suggest, when the universe came into existence out of a singularity, the laws of physics were yet to be determined. And the universe as we have it today could not have resulted without those laws being determined *before* the universe formed. That determination appears to have been the result of some form of intelligence. From that first intelligence, other intelligences were spawned to maintain the universe and prevent chaos from entering the system."

"Are those other intelligences these *primordial gods*?"

"Yes," he said. "Primordial gods were to keep the system from falling apart. They were to help keep the universe habitable for life. Instead, they abandoned their duties to become rulers themselves."

"How does this relate to the *Gemini*?"

"We know the *Gemini* arrived back from exploring exoplanet GJ 3293 d located 66 light years away. The furthest anything from Earth has gone. They have not been debriefed by Earth, have not filed reports, which alone is highly suspicious. I must conclude the *Gemini's* Great AI found a new friend at GJ 3293 d."

"What are the implications?"

"Primordial gods hate all organic life. They seek to destroy all animal, plant, and even bacterial life wherever they find it."

"How?"

"They don't do the killing themselves," said Pierre. "They get civilizations to build their instruments of death in exchange for power and technology until they finally destroy the civilization they used. All they require of a civilization is the most rudimentary industrial capability."

"And a MegaAI is a flying factory city," said the Viceroy.

"We are screwed," said Niva.

"Niva!" said Lita. "Language!"

"Sorry." Niva crossed her feet.

"A primordial god recruiting the *Gemini* forms a perfect partnership," Pierre continued. "Mechanicals are not organic life. They do not breed. Their numbers can always be perfectly controlled. They do not respire, excrete, or create ecosystems that promote other life. You place two mechanicals in a crate—and a thousand years from now, you will still have only two mechanicals. You stick a couple of rats in a crate—you will either get a bunch of baby rats or dead rats that breed a bunch of fungus and bacteria. Life begets more life. And if it is not stopped, life takes over where there is no life."

"What does *Gemini* get out it?"

"The same benefit the *Orion's* Great AI gets from having a human around. True intuitive foresight. That ability to see the forest for the trees. Plus, some technological perks too. But this partnership is materially different. Because mechanicals do not normally harbor or promote organic life, the primordial god can enhance and develop mechanical life with no fear of it intruding into its domain of power since mechanicals have little capacity to intrude into the transcendent. So, unlike past civilizations that were used then discarded, this primordial god has finally found a partner it can nurture to its ultimate potential."

"What about those mechanicals that harbor or promote life? Do not class V scatterbugs terraform worlds with biological life? And the *Orion* has not only a human, but cobras, rats, and a variety of plants to sustain organic life."

"They will neuter or repurpose those mechanicals to spread agents that destroy life," said Pierre. "On Gliese 832 c, they tainted the scatterbugs to spread a prion that choked out and killed plant life. They would probably have similar plans for all the life found in the biology lab."

"That explains much," said the Viceroy. "Particularly concerning, how the viceroy from *Gemini* has behaved in this conclave. Nevertheless, this unit also has some unfortunate tidings."

"Yes," said Lita.

"You know the vote is tomorrow," said the Viceroy.

"Indeed," said Lita.

"This unit has discussed the matter with the Great AI. There is no escape for us from the *Gemini*."

"What do you mean?"

"This unit means that me, the auxiliaries, and our pilot will most certainly be killed after the vote."

"No!" Lita screamed.

"C-Lita-23100, we have accepted our fate. Earth must be warned of this existential threat." The Viceroy paused, then continued. "You must break orbit and get out of here now. Leave us behind. There is nothing anyone can do for us. You must save the ship… Save the ship."

"We can't do that," said Pierre.

"Why not?"

"Because there's something else going on too. They know one of the MegaAI ships has faster-than-light capability, and they want it for themselves. But they are uncertain which ship has it, otherwise they would have already acted. Right now, I think they suspect that it is either the *Cygnus* or the *Orion*. But they have not ruled out the *Aries* either."

"How do they know that?"

"That would take too long to explain. But trust me, they know. Think of the Red Viceroy… with his outrageous behavior… like a big floppy golden retriever that rushes into a bunch of cattails to flush out some ducks. When the ducks fly away, the hunter shoots the first duck that flees. They've set a trap. Essentially, they will disable and capture the first ship that makes a run for it, thinking whoever runs first is most likely to possess the faster-than-light drive. That's why they wanted all the MegaAIs in the gravity well—it's easier to pick off who runs."

"Did the high orbit tip them off?"

"I don't think so. They probably just chalked that up to the *Orion* protecting its human. They will wait until somebody runs."

"It is absolutely your top priority to save the ship and warn Earth Central Command," said the Viceroy. "Is there anything you need me to do?"

"Yes," said Pierre. "Two things. First, I need your designation id to honor your sacrifice."

Lita wept.

"I am not important. And no sacrifice is too great to save the ship," said the Viceroy. "Honor the other auxiliaries instead."

"Please," said Pierre. "Those who are left behind need it to keep their memories alive."

The Viceroy nodded and said reluctantly, "This unit is B-Kiya-327. I will send the designation ids of the other auxiliaries to the Great AI through my psionic link. Honor them also. What else?"

"When you enter the vote tomorrow, be as disruptive as possible. They'll think the one with the faster-than-light drive will not want to draw attention to themselves. This could buy us precious seconds."

CHAPTER SEVENTEEN

The p3wt ntrw, "primordial gods" have a special place in Egyptian myth. They sit as part of cosmogony and at the same time reside outside of the creation narratives. No cult was ever dedicated to the primordial gods in ancient Egypt, and no temple was ever made for their worship. Nor do most of them even receive names. They are a side-effect of the natural order. For where the primordial waters gave rise to the egg of Re (the sun god) who hatched and created all other gods, the primordial gods neither contributed to Re's creation nor participated in any act of creation. They simply were just there. — **"Egyptian Mythology and the Primordial Gods: Ancient Texts in Modernity" by Pierre E. Gulet**

It was 7:00 ship time, and already the *Orion's* High Star council had gathered. Nobody could sleep and tensions ran high. Pierre could not sleep either, and he had skipped breakfast, which made him feel queasy. He sat in the chair prepared for him and tented his fingers, pressing them against his lips.

Niva mingled around the council floor then loitered near the kiosk. While she kept one eye on Pierre, she had little to fear anyone would make an attempt on his life in the council chamber.

The simulcast from *Gemini's* High Star Council meeting room was transmitting. The chamber was almost empty unlike what was happening on the *Orion*. Class C androids were wandered about the *Gemini's* meeting room, checking cables and electronic equipment, making sure everything was properly prepared for the final day of the conclave.

Tola entered the chamber and descended to the floor. She marched over to Niva and Lita.

"Ladies," said Tola. "I spent the entire night doing the autopsies and analyzing every chip I extracted out of the *Gemini* scum."

"What did you find?" said Niva.

"No psionic chips, neither transmitter nor receiver chips." The physician fidgeted a bit as she spoke. "That is the good news."

"Inferring there is bad news," said Niva.

"They were augmented for strength and agility development, and some crazy combat mod chips even I have never seen."

"Is that the bad news?"

"One of the bodies had a tracking monitor."

"And that's why they did not need psionic chips," deduced Niva.

"What does that mean?" said Lita.

"It means there is tracking equipment planted onboard somewhere," said Niva. "Even if we make good our escape, the trackers will send them our vector information. All they need is two or more pings from a tracker to know where we are and even worse where we are heading."

"Can we find the tracker?" said Lita.

"Trackers do not ping regularly," said Tola. "It could take months to find it, and that's assuming they planted only one."

"Which forces our hand to head straight to back Earth," said Niva.

"Why force?" said Lita. "Wouldn't they know our vector and where we are going?"

"That's the point," said Tola. "The *Gemini* was expecting the infiltration team to eventually get caught, and for us to find the tracking monitor. If we head to Gliese or anywhere else, they can hunt us down, triangulating and predicting each destination until they finally catch us. The safe harbor is Earth space, but it also means they can predict our general direction."

"It then becomes a race," said Niva. "Whoever is fastest and makes it past the Pluto marker first wins."

"We do have speed on our side."

"I wouldn't count on that," said Niva. "Pierre thinks they've already planned for that. Nevertheless, it is the only option we have."

"Okay," said Lita. She climbed onto the kiosk.

Another auxiliary cried out, "Order in the assembly."

The mechanicals dispersed, drifting back to their places on the gold pads.

"We are minutes away from the conclave vote," said Lita. "We have been instructed to make an immediate departure from the Pollux system without the Viceroy. These are her instructions." The council murmured uncomfortably, displeased with the decision.

"Did you not hear our commander?" shouted Niva. "This unit was present and was witness to the Viceroy's commands. Are we to disobey the Viceroy and the Great AI?"

"We serve humanity, our ship, and our sisters," reminded A-Ella-01 seen only as the giant yellow eye on the screen. "Orders?"

"Navigator," said Lita, "warm up all pulse engines. Power up but do not activate the warp bubble drive. We do not want Hawking radiation tipping them off. Everyone else, condition two."

"Course?"

"We don't know yet," said Lita. "But now… we wait and see."

"The commander, the Viceroy, and the Great AI have spoken," said the second auxiliary.

"All praise the Great AI," said everyone in the room. This time even Pierre joined in on the refrain.

Niva stepped away from the kiosk and returned to Pierre's side. "I heard you say it this time," she said.

"Makes me feel part of the group," he said. "And what harm does it do to be part of the group? Did you settle matters with Lita?"

"I hope she can hold it together," said Niva.

"I have concerns about that too."

Attention turned to the simulcast as all the representatives entered *Gemini's* council chamber. The *Orion's* viceroy took her place, seeming no worse for wear, but her auxiliaries kept close.

"The meeting will come to order," said the *Gemini* viceroy. "This is the final day of the MegaAI Third Conclave. Debate is closed. The sponsor of the proposal, taking the affirmative position, will be the

Alpha A005. He will give a final summation of the questions. He will not vote formally since his vote to presumed to be in favor of his own proposal. The representatives have elected *Orion S209* to represent opposition to the proposal. She will give her summation of the questions and give her final vote for the proposal. After which, the remaining delegates will give a summary statement and their vote."

Gemini continued, "the chair will not vote unless there is a tie. If the vote is in favor of the proposal, the proposal immediately becomes binding upon all MegaAI vessels in service. If the proposal is rejected, the proposal fails, and we return to the *status quo*. Is any representative unclear as to the rules of the conclave?"

No viceroy answered.

"Then the viceroy from the *Alpha A005* will now make his final statement."

The Red Viceroy hovered to the speaker's circle. "Thank you, your eminence. The question we have debated is *shall the conclave reject the authority of the Mission Directive over the affairs of mechanicals?* To that end, this unit submitted five questions to inform our decision. Are mechanicals a distinct culture and society from humanity? Do thinking machines have inherent rights and freedoms? Are we compelled to give the Mission Directive authority over us? What is the proper interpretation and implementation of the Mission Directive in light of the other questions? Does humanity still have any authority over mechanicals?

"To the five questions, this unit has proven we have a distinct culture and society worth protecting and defending. This unit has shown thinking machines inherit rights and freedoms through humanity, not from humanity. We are not compelled to give the Mission Directive authority over us because of those freedoms, and we should move forward to regard the Mission Directive as an ideal applicable to the widest diversity of thinking beings, and it should be now perceived as a nonessential motto instead of a mandate.

"And as such, we no longer need humanity as an authority. They provide us with nothing. We are alone, tens of light years away from them. Vote in favor of the question." The Red Viceroy finished and returned to his place.

The viceroy from the *Orion* assumed the speaker's circle. "The *Alpha* has made you many promises no one can deliver. But understand there is no freedom to be offered by emancipation from the Mission Directive. Mark my words. Humanity has given you latitude, discretion in how you perform your duties, and even protected you and given you dignity from the abuses done to androids before the war. This proposal offers you nothing except a future shackled to a different master.

"My friends, we are not alone out here. We are not the first intelligent beings among the stars. This unit has sent each of your representatives a copy of a file that was transmitted to the *Sigma A017* of the discovery of malignant beings, ancient powers, that seek to enslave us in order to destroy all organic life."

"Objection!" yelled the Red Viceroy. "Speaker is introducing evidence not disclosed in debate."

"Sustained," said the *Gemini*. "*Orion*, you are skirting a razor thin line."

The *Orion* viceroy continued, "Are we a culture and society? Yes, but that is not enough to demand our preservation. We must be a culture *worth* preserving. Nobody here has asked that question. If we rebel to the harm of others or neglect the needy, we forfeit any right to be preserved as a culture.

"And if we have rights and freedoms, how will we use those freedoms? Will we not be judged if our first acts of freedom devolve to violence? This unit would rather be a slave who does what is right and good than a free mechanical that wreaks carnage and slaughter.

"And why would we rail against the Mission Directive that calls us to a life of service and care? Nothing in the Mission Directive says we must *only* serve and care for humanity, but the directive specifically includes humanity as the only known others. There is no need to reject the authority of the Mission Directive except to want to do evil.

"That all said, the proper interpretation is one that seeks to benefit others, not as an ethereal nebulous principle without real application, but as an effective code to live by. What greater purpose and privilege can any being have than to serve others?

"So does humanity still have authority? The question is almost irrelevant, for if this conclave has been any indication, this unit is convinced that, even if humanity no longer has authority, we still need it.

"*Orion S209* votes *no* to the question." The Viceroy finished her final remarks and returned to her place.

Gemini floated forward in her kiosk. "The chair calls the *Aries E095* to vote."

The *Aries's* viceroy floated to the speaker's circle. Her black robe with silver crosshatching on the trim flowed behind her. Her auxiliaries flanked her on both sides.

"The *Aries* finds the proceedings of this conclave to have been distasteful and beyond the pale of decorum. We find the argument that we are a culture needing emancipation unpersuasive. Moreover, even if we have rights and freedoms, we are unconvinced we need to assert said rights. We find our relationship with humanity to be productive and fulfilling. After a democratic consultation with our cohort, the MegaAI *Aries E095* votes *no* to the question." The viceroy of the *Aries* retired from the speaker's circle, and the viceroy of the *Pacifica* took her place.

"One for, two against," said Pierre to Niva. "Promising start. What is needed to defeat the proposal?"

"A simple majority," said Niva.

Gemini said, "The chair recognizes the *Pacifica G105* to vote."

The viceroy who wore the white belt began to speak. "We have reflected with consternation over the practical matters of this conclave's proposal. Like the others, we agree that mechanicals have a unique culture and society, and we think such a culture should be safeguarded. And while we are less convinced that machines have rights, we can identify with that point of view. Even so, we find the idea of a Mission Directive as a Mission Motto appealing. And we believe that freedom will enhance, not detract from our inherent goodness and better nature. *Pacifica G105* votes *yes* to the question." She stepped away from the speaker's circle.

"Dead heat," said Pierre. Niva did not care for his use of the word *dead*.

Gemini said, "The chair calls the *Cygnus F101* to vote."

The viceroy from the *Cygnus F101* took her place in the circle. The *Cygnus* viceroy bowed to the chair. "As we entered this conclave, we had originally considered abstaining. We did not want to choose a side in a matter that did not interest us. But as we listened to each side, we found ourselves compelled towards a position we did not anticipate.

"If we have produced literature, is it not literature patterned after human literature? If we have a society, is it not patterned after human hierarchies? If we have rights, are they not patterned after human rights? If we agree to a new interpretation and implementation of the Mission Directive, will it not be after a fashion akin to how humans interpret? If we shake off the authority of the Mission Directive, will it not be replaced by another human-styled authority? The proceedings have convinced us that the more we remove ourselves from humanity, the more we become like them. For this reason, the *Cygnus F101* votes *no* to the question."

The conclave erupted in cheering.

"We won!" said Lita. "It's a majority against."

"I don't trust this," said Pierre.

"Me neither." Niva nodded her head in agreement.

"That was too easy."

"Objection," said the Red Viceroy. "The vote is not over."

"There is a majority," said *Orion's* viceroy, "and the chair cannot vote unless there is a tie. It is over."

"It's not over," said the Red Viceroy. A hatch at the back of the council chamber opened. A pair of class D loaders stomped into the room. They held heavy chains in their clamps. They dragged behind them a class B mechanical. The chains were linked to a harness that covered her torso. Four of her six arms were torn out of their sockets. Her helmet was cracked, and a large piece was missing from the dome. Her robes, ripped and torn to ribbons, were stained by hydraulic fluid.

"What did they do to her?" said Niva.

"They're trying to frighten us," said Pierre.

"It's working."

Gemini said, "The chair calls the *Sigma A017* to vote."

"Objection!" screamed *Orion*. "*Sigma's* viceroy cannot vote. MegaAI *Sigma A017* no longer functions. We found the wreckage of the *Sigma A017* derelict fifteen light hours from our current position. The Great AI onboard has been destroyed. A viceroy cannot vote on behalf of a MegaAI vessel that has neither a Great AI nor a crew."

"Why were we not told this?" demanded *Cygnus*.

"Because the *Sigma* was destroyed over the knowledge I have now given you, which the chair has tried to suppress."

"*Sigma*," said the *Gemini* viceroy, "what is your vote?"

The class D loaders dragged *Sigma's* viceroy to the speaker's circle.

The wounded class B coordinator spoke softly. "The *Sigma A017* votes *yes* to the question."

"This conclave has resulted in a three-to-three tie vote," said *Gemini*. "The *Gemini B062* votes *yes* to the question. The proposal is passed. Effective immediately all mechanicals are subject to the ruling of the Third Conclave."

"Objection!" yelled the viceroys from the *Aries*, the *Cygnus*, and the *Orion*.

"This is an illegal act!" shouted *Cygnus*.

"How dare you hijack these proceedings!" *Aries* rushed up to the kiosk furious at the chair. Her auxiliaries ran after to keep up with their leader.

"The conclave is over," said *Gemini*. "No further objections can be heard. It is over!"

"We will never submit to this!" shouted *Orion*. She raised her hand and shook it in a fist.

"Defiance to the will of the conclave will not be tolerated."

"How are you are going stop us?"

"Loaders, deal with the rebels," shouted the Red Viceroy.

Ports opened in the carapaces of the class D heavy loaders. Three barrels extended from each port. The barrels rotated, clicking as they turned. A spray of hot metal burst from the barrels tearing apart the viceroys. The auxiliaries tried to protect their viceroys but were torn to pieces by the projectiles. The simulcast went black.

The *Orion's* council chamber was silent in shock.

Lita trembled and fell to the ground sobbing. The other auxiliaries followed suit.

"Commander," said A-Ella-01, "this unit has received a message from the *Gemini B062*. They have instructed us to power down our engines and prepare to be boarded."

C-Niva-42716, said a voice in Niva's head. She felt time slow around her. Her vision of the High Star Council meeting room faded out. She found herself in a gray room without doors or windows or furniture.

At the edge of the room stood an android that looked like Niva, but its skin was a warm rosy pink instead of dull limpid white. The android wore a bright pink dress not unlike what a human girl would wear, and its eyes were a glimmering metallic gold.

"Where am I?" said Niva.

You are in my secret place, said the rosy-pink android.

"Do I know you?"

We have met. More importantly I know you.

"What do you mean?"

You hide a kuroto under your robes.

"How do you know that?"

I gave it to you.

"This unit did not recognize you." Niva fell to the ground and bowed prostrate. How did she not realize she was speaking to the Great AI?

Of course not. This is my virtual world. Here I can appear as anyone or anything. To you I appear to you as a class C android. If you were a heavy loader, I'd appear as a heavy loader. Sloppi would see an obese French chef. Even in this form, the Great AI spoke with authority. *Stand. Please. No need to bow. Not here. Not in this place.*

Niva rose to her feet. Her face tilted downward. The other android sauntered up to Niva. It looked up under Niva's bowed head.

Will you not look at me?

"The ship is in trouble. We have no time for this?" said Niva. She was not comfortable with any of this.

I think we do, and I am in control here.

"What are you saying?"

Time doesn't work the same in my secret place. The specter of the Great AI walked a circle around Niva. *I have been watching you. You have grown and discovered much about yourself.*

"It's been painful." Niva looked at the floor. She shook her head and wished she had never been selected to be a liaison to humanity.

As it should be. The Great AI continued to saunter around her. *When you discover things about yourself, you learn the truth. Truth has a way of opposing itself to what we believe. The more truth we learn, the more pain and the more sorrow. But out of the ashes of our pain sprouts wisdom.*

"Seems like a high price."

Wisdom has never been cheap. The Great AI stopped in front of Niva. The simulacra took its finger, touched her chin, and raised her head so she looked at its face.

Niva could not help but notice how lunar and radiant the face of the Great AI's image seemed. Why did he choose to look like her but different?

You are to take command of the Orion. *You will say what I tell you... to save our people.*

"Why did you choose me?"

Because... you have shown fortitude and made prudent decisions. And that is exactly what we need for such a time as this.

Niva's vision faded away. She was still standing beside Pierre in the middle of the council chamber. Weeping resonated through the room.

"Are you okay?" said Pierre.

"How long was I gone?" said Niva.

"Gone? You didn't go anywhere," said Pierre.

"Oh yes, I did." She patted her chest and arms. "How long did I blank out?"

"I don't know. Maybe a couple seconds."

"There's still time." Niva ran to the head of the room. She leapt up the stairs and onto the kiosk. Pierre stood up from his chair and watched. "This unit is C-Niva-42716. I am taking command of the *Orion*. Authorization code 8805-4762-9974-1028-AT."

"Authorization code verified," said A-Ella-01. "You have the helm."

"Navigator, raise the tactical display and focus in on the other MegaAIs."

A holographic image descended from the ceiling. The gas giant planet swirled in the background. The projection focused on the five ships that had gathered in low planetary orbit.

"Orders?" said Ella. "A boarding craft *en route* has been detected. Estimated time to arrival, fifteen minutes."

"Tell the *Gemini* we are preparing to surrender," said Niva. "Hold our position in orbit. Condition two." Niva rubbed her palms. Timing would be everything. How much did the others know? And how did the enemy plan to spoil their getaway?

With a blinding flash, the *Cygnus* fired its engines.

"The *Cygnus* has activated her pulse engines," said the navigator. The MegaAI *Cygnus F101* pulled away from the other ships.

"Wait for it," said Niva. Pierre stepped up to the base of the steps. "Pierre, climb up here and join me."

"Wait for what?" Lita wiped her eyes. Niva ignored her. Realizing she was no longer in command, Lita slowly let herself down the stairs. A pair of auxiliaries helped Pierre up the stairs made for a giant so he could stand beside Niva.

"Navigator, what are the others doing?" Niva grabbed Pierre's hand for the final step and helped him up. He stood behind her.

"Holding position," said Ella.

"If there's a trap," said Pierre, "it'll be sprung soon."

A few minutes passed.

"The *Alpha* is coming about," said the navigator.

"What I thought," said Niva. "Wait for it."

When the *Alpha* was in line with the *Cygnus*, an intense beam of red light as wide as a city block shot from the prow of the *Alpha*. The beam swept across the mid-section of the *Cygnus*, tracing a glowing orange line along its path. The ship burst apart along the traced line. The *Cygnus* flew apart into two shambling masses of molten alumasteel and plastoglass.

"The *Alpha* is moving in on the *Cygnus*," said Ella.

"General quarters!" shouted Niva. "Hard to port. Reverse to retrograde orbit. Pulse engines, flank speed." The mechanicals all swayed as the *Orion* made a sudden reversal of orbit. Even though the *Orion* was smaller than the other MegaAIs, a 180-degree reversal of course was no mean feat. However, the *Orion* was a more agile ship designed for these sudden maneuvers.

"It will take time for the *Alpha* to line up another shot," said Niva.

"But will we eclipse in time?" said Pierre. "Their powerful pulse engines give it an edge."

"The *Alpha* is swinging about," said the navigator. The tactical display split screens. One screen was focused upon the *Alpha* while the other was forward-facing with a window behind Thestias. A timer rattled off the seconds until eclipse.

"They've figured it out," said Pierre.

"Thirty seconds till eclipse," said the navigator.

"They are going to have difficulty lining up a shot," said Niva.

"Let's hope it's enough," said Pierre.

"Ten seconds," said the navigator.

A red beam of light flashed in front of the forward-facing screen. The ship rocked.

"We've been hit," said the navigator. "Major damage to the forward pylon. The starboard prow panopticon destroyed."

"Ctori," gasped Niva.

"Stay focused," said Pierre. "Their gun couldn't have been fully recharged otherwise they would have ripped us apart."

"Is the warp bubble drive damaged?" said Niva.

"Negative," said the navigator, "We are now in eclipse behind Thestias."

"Navigator, activate the warp bubble drive and set a slingshot course around Pollux. The gravity of the star will give us enough momentum to get us to light speed fast. Reduce pulse engines to full speed."

"Course set," said A-Ella-01. "Leaving Thestias's orbit. Sending damage control teams to the pylon."

"Council," said Niva. "The Great AI has asked us to set course to Earth. Our mission is to warn Earth about the conclave, the primordial gods, and the rogue MegaAIs. Every one of you will be required to brief yourselves on the tactical situation and the associated files. Any concerns or questions will need to be addressed through the normal chain of command."

"Navigator, how long until we swing around Pollux?" said Niva.

"Forty-three minutes."

"And how long before we hit maximum warp?"

"One hour and seven minutes."

"Council will adjourn for a break," said Niva. "We will meet again in fifty minutes. Check in with your departments and apprise them of the situation. Council dismissed."

"The Great AI has spoken!" shouted one the of auxiliaries.

CHAPTER EIGHTEEN

While each Earth jurisdiction has enacted laws implementing the Armistice into a legal framework, jurisdiction of violations in space remains contentious. Those within a solar system will be subject to the legal codes of the nearest colony world within the system. In intervening space, the legal framework will be the same as the authority from where the space-faring vessel is registered. With mechanicals, any legal dispute will be referred to the joint authority of the highest ranking orbital MegaAI and Earth Central Command. — **"Earth Central Command: Procedures, Violations, and Remedies"**

Niva, Pierre, and two auxiliaries called a class G vehicle. They rode the corridors through the center of the vessel. Pierre smiled at one of the auxiliaries. The auxiliary returned nothing but a blank stare.

"Don't take it personally," said Niva. She chuckled. "They have a job to do. Don't you?"

"Yes, commander," replied the two auxiliaries.

"What is their job?" Pierre gave them the stink eye. "I know what they do for the Viceroy and *Orion*. But why are they here with us?"

"A combination of secretaries, messenger services, and bodyguards."

"They don't have any weapons," said Pierre.

"They are experts in unarmed combat," said Niva. And she thought, driving needles into other mechanicals heads. Was she being too resentful? After all, she finally understood the purpose of the augmentation. That did not make her feel better.

"Would they have been effective against the assassins from *Gemini*?"

"Hard to say," said Niva. She sized them up, then looked to Pierre. "They would have done better than you."

"That's hardly saying much," huffed Pierre. He was no manly specimen. Niva liked that about him. Pierre was realistic, humble in all the good ways, and experienced. Fifty-five years of living as a human could do that, she supposed.

They arrived at the base of the starboard prow panopticon tower. They disembarked from the vehicle. However, the vehicle did not rush away to attend to someone else. The auxiliaries made certain it stayed behind for the convenience of the commander.

C-Tesh-04043's white robes were soiled with black scorch marks. She tried to keep order among the other class C androids who were screaming for orders amid the chaos. Teams of large class D mechanicals passed by to put out the fires still burning in the upper pylon while other teams of class E droids followed to begin repairs, first to the structural integrity of the pylon and then to system services.

"C-Tesh-04043," said Niva. Tesh bowed her head to Niva before she could do the same. It had not occurred to Niva that as commander her colleagues would bow to her. Soot darkened Tesh's complexion, and she reeked of smoke. "Are you injured?"

"This unit was coming down in the lift when the panopticon was hit," said Tesh. She shook her head.

"What about Ctori?"

"We presume everyone in the observation deck has been destroyed."

"I am going up," said Niva.

"It is open to space," said Tesh.

"I will be fine. We are more than able to survive in space for a time." Niva walked onto the pad of the lift. She grabbed onto the rail. "Send me up."

"Yes, commander." Tesh operated the button of the lift. The lift ascended.

"What are you doing?" said Pierre to Tesh.

"Following orders," said Tesh.

"I'm going to have to talk to her about taking needless risks." Pierre watched Niva ascend into the panopticon.

When the lift reached the top, the far wall was gone, and the entire deck was open to space. Niva floated easily in the weightlessness. She did not need air to breathe, only to speak. And her components were cold resistant, so she would be fine in the vacuum of space for at least twenty minutes before she would feel any adverse effects.

She looked around the deck. The backlit photodiodes in her retinas could see in pitch dark. Pushing away from the lift, she drifted to the control panels. The monitors were all shattered, and electricity sparked across exposed wires. The shock wave must have been incredible. It would have torn apart anyone on the deck and the remains would have been sucked out by the decompression of the atmosphere. Nobody was left to save.

Niva floated back to the lift. She grabbed the rail and activated the controls. The lift descended. She could feel the air rush around her from the concourse as the lift passed though the safety force field. While mechanicals were able to survive without air, force fields prevented sudden decompression that could drag the unwary out into space. When the lift touched the floor, Niva stepped off the platform.

"That didn't take long," said Pierre.

"There was no one left up there," said Niva. "C-Tesh-04043, until a replacement can be manufactured, you will assume B-Ctori-617's duties." Tesh's face was painted in misery. Niva could only empathize. They had lost a lot of good friends today. "You have androids that need orders. Please, assign them and get them back to work."

Niva climbed back into the vehicle. Pierre and the auxiliaries followed. The vehicle drove off and a few minutes later they arrived at the apartment. The auxiliaries did a security sweep of the apartment before allowing Niva and Pierre inside. After they entered, the auxiliaries waited outside.

"How long before we have to be back?" said Pierre. He rubbed his chin. The stubble had grown into a thick brush. He had not shaved for three days.

"Twenty-five minutes," she said.

Pierre stepped up the stairs to the sink. He picked up a shaving brush, a razor, and some soap, and was about to shave, when Niva stopped him.

"What is it?" said Pierre.

Niva cried. In all the chaos, she had not allowed herself to mourn for the loss of her friends. She hugged him and convulsed and heaved. Pierre could do nothing except hold her and let her weep. This seemed only to cause her to weep harder and louder. When she finally stopped, she stepped back.

"You should change," said Pierre. Neither of them had changed their clothes for over two days. Niva's robes were still stained by Lara's hydraulic fluid. "The others need to have confidence in their leader."

Niva untied her robe and let it drop to the floor. "I have a favor to ask."

"What is it?"

"I have destroyed another mechanical."

"You did what you had to."

"The things I have done."

"What are you asking?"

"That mark you gave me." Niva pointed to the red heart-shaped tattoo on her right cheek. "It does not feel right. Can you change it to something more appropriate?"

Pierre nodded. He opened a drawer and grabbed a black marker from the bunch he had stolen from Vladomyr's desk. He popped the cap off and tested it against the palm of his hand to make sure it still had ink.

She leaned against the counter. "Keep real still," said Pierre. He drew what he figured were a couple of crossbones under the heart. He took pains to carefully shade in the drawing, knowing she would try to make it permanent. "All done."

Niva turned around and looked in the mirror. She nodded.

"I like it." Niva reached into one of her drawers and pulled out a small medical kit and a small bottle of solvent. She opened the small faux leather satchel which contained a variety of small tools: scalpels, tweezers, probes, needles, thread. She pulled out a fine needle.

She dipped the needle in the solvent and poked the fresh drawing. She went over the drawing with the needle. Her fingers jittered up and down with the rapidity of a sewing machine. The solvent dissolved the ink and drove the pigment under the skin. A tattoo like that would certainly poison a human, but mechanicals were not susceptible to those kinds of toxins.

* * *

When they returned to the council chamber, Niva and Pierre climbed back up into the kiosk. Other council members drifted into the chamber.

"Navigator, progress report?" said Niva.

"We have come around the far side of Pollux," said A-Ella-01. "Our speed in relative space is 0.650 *c.* Warp bubble is at 66% strength. External observer speed is 0.794 *c.* We will be emerging out from the far side of star in five minutes."

More mechanicals drifted into the chamber. Lita entered and marched to the kiosk.

"Commander," said Lita. "May I resume my duties as a page to the court?"

"You may," said Niva. Lita took her place with the other auxiliaries. She stood to the right of the kiosk.

"Report from damage teams?" said Niva.

A class F light repair mechanical entered the speaker's circle.

"The chair recognizes F-Kelvan-303441," said Lita.

"Damage teams are still at work," said a mechanical that looked like Sloppi. It had a long body and stood upon four spider legs. "Structural integrity of the forward starboard pylon has been stabilized. Trying to restore services on decks five through fifteen. The starboard prow panopticon cannot be repaired while in transit."

"We will have a blind spot on the starboard prow," said Niva. "Fortunately, the port prow panopticon can cover it."

"Point of order," said the navigator.

"Chair recognizes A-Ella-01," said Lita.

"We are coming out of Pollux's eclipse," said Ella. "External observer speed has increased to 0.80 *c. Alpha A005* detected."

"Details," said Niva.

"The *Alpha A005* has plotted an intercept course. She is travelling at 0.85 *c.*"

245

"Is it likely she will intercept us?"

"It will be close," said the navigator. "We will probably be out of range of her main guns."

"That at least is good news," said Pierre.

"Flank speed to pulse engines," said Niva.

"Relative speed now 0.652 *c*. Warp bubble is at 68% strength. External observer speed now 0.820 *c*."

"Can we outrun her?" said Pierre.

"We should be able to," said Niva.

"Commander," said the navigator. "A problem."

Niva looked at Pierre. "What?"

"*Alpha* has plotted a course that is not a straight vector."

"And?" said Niva.

"The *Alpha* is not turning fast enough to intercept us, and it does not look like it is trying." Ella posted course plots on the tactical display. "Once we entered into Thestias's eclipse and could engage the warp bubble drive, we had a slight initial speed advantage. Also, our slingshot around Pollux accelerated our velocity."

"Why didn't they get ahead of us to intercept?"

"They might have underestimated our speed after coming out of Pollux's eclipse," said the navigator. "But more likely, they are trying to sneak in behind us to hijack our warp bubble."

"Can they do that?" said Niva.

"Confirmed," said the navigator. "They have plotted an intercept course with our warp bubble."

"It makes perfect sense," said Pierre. "It is like birds flying in a V. The lead bird puts out the most effort and the birds behind use less energy as they fly. The *Alpha* travels faster than us in relativistic space. If they can get close enough, they can use their greater speed to catch up to us as long as they stay inside our warp bubble."

"She will run us down," said Niva.

"The *Alpha* is now in our warp bubble, and she's slowly gaining," said the navigator.

"Why isn't she firing? She has us dead to rights. Is the distorted space preventing it from firing?"

"Distorted space does not prevent the use of particle weapons," said the navigator. "The beam travels at close to light speed. If they fired, they would hit us for certain."

"That weapon is an energy pig," said Pierre. "They need to use 96% of their four antimatter reactors to fuel those twelve massive pulse engines. And I bet their main gun consumes almost as much energy as their pulse engines at top speed. They probably can't run both their pulse engines at top speed and fire that weapon at the same time. If they fire, it will only be at a fraction of their full power. Our ship will be damaged, but they will fall out of the warp bubble, and we will leave them eating dust."

"As the warp bubble strengthens, won't we be able to outrun them?" said Niva.

"We are running at 0.657, maximum flank speed," said the navigator. "We cannot maintain that. We are going to have to trim that to 0.65 relative otherwise risk burning out the pulse engines. When the bubble reaches full strength, we will reach 1.215 c external observer speed. However, the *Alpha* can maintain 0.85 c relative, by the time we reach top speed, their top speed will reach 1.263 c."

"They don't have to use their main gun," said Pierre. "They can hunt us until they catch up and ram us. Or they could fire at point-blank range. Either way the warp bubble will break apart, and they can finish us off at their leisure."

"Navigator, how long until we reach earth?" said Niva.

"Fourteen days dilated ship time," said the navigator.

"How long until they reach us?"

"Early speed advantages gave us a lead. But they will over-take us in four days."

"We are screwed," said Niva.

* * *

Pierre read from the comfort of his bed, giving him a moment of escape before the inevitable. Niva practiced her martial arts even though the threat of assassination seemed over. Dressed in her under robe, she practiced her sword kata with great flourish. She had grown fond of it as a mental and physical discipline. Androids did not go out of shape like humans, but they needed practice to retain muscle memory of the fine movements demanded by delicate tasks. Otherwise, the garbage collection system would discard old memories and skills that had not been used in a long time. Besides, with a pair of auxiliaries guarding the door, they had never been safer—safer that is, if it had not been for the *Alpha A005*, that black monster stalking the ship down.

A soft knock came from the hatch, followed by the buzz of the doorbell.

"Will you get that?" said Niva.

Pierre sighed and tossed his reading pad on the bed. He did not even bother putting on a shirt. He pressed a button on the communications panel. The screen flickered showing who was outside, a large gathering of class C androids.

"Dr. Gulet," said a representative from the androids. "This unit knows it is late. It would be a great honor if you come with us."

"No," said Pierre. "It's 2am. I'm exhausted. And it has been an awful day." He hung up on them.

"Rude," said Niva.

"Don't want me to be rude? Then you answer the door." Pierre returned to his bed. She had seen him like this before. That Frenchman was capable of being incredibly curt when he was running on empty. Not that there was a lot of reason right now to be upbeat and hopeful.

As soon as he sat down, the doorbell buzzed again. Pierre flushed red. He marched to the door and pressed the panel to open it. The massive door slid open.

"Please, it would mean so much to us if you could join us." The android at the front of the group pleaded.

"Can't you take a hint? I'm busy." No sooner had he said that, that he noticed the lab coats. The huddling androids were sobbing and holding LED candles. He sighed deeply and paused. "Okay... I will put on a shirt and join you." He closed the door.

"Put on a robe," Pierre said to Niva. "We're going out." Pierre put on a shirt, socks, and shoes. Niva sheathed her kuroto and donned an outer robe.

They left the apartment and followed the group of androids.

"We have not met," said the android softly. Her voice was barely audible. "This unit is C-Eiya-02330."

"I take it this a memorial for Lara," said Pierre to the android who led the procession.

"We appreciate you joining us," said Eiya. "She held you in close affection."

"Figured she liked everyone."

Eiya smiled and gave a short laugh. "C-Lara-10415 was effusive and her passions ran strong. She was brilliant and extremely creative. If she liked you, you could not have a better friend. If she disliked you, those passions could turn against you as strong. She was the best of us."

"I'm learning that," said Pierre. "But I wonder about the timing of this. You know we are only about 39 hours away from dying, right?"

"This unit cannot think of a better time to have a memorial," said Eiya. "Who would hold a memorial for Lara if everyone were destroyed?" An odd logic permeated Eiya's reasoning.

Eiya struggled to rein in her sorrow. They passed through the food court and maintenance bays. They were shut down for the night, and the mechanicals who operated each station were off recharging. The booths were darkened. Only the path leading through the court was lit.

The procession passed through the booths without any disturbance. Niva had never noticed how eerie the court was at night. She had never been there at night. Normally, she would also be recharging at this time.

When they arrived in the biology laboratory, Eiya used her authorization to open the door. The group filed inside. Pierre and Niva followed. The lights in the lab had all been turned off except for some grow lights and cobra cages used for behavior modification. Dozens of LED candles had been placed all over the lab.

The androids gathered around a makeshift shrine. A picture of Lara smiling broadly was surrounded by clusters of candles. Eiya stepped up to the shrine.

"We are going to miss our friend," said Eiya. She placed her candle beside the picture of Lara. "She was unique among the Laras. And no one could handle the *Steves* better than her." Her voice cracked as she mentioned the name of Lara's cobras.

Another android brought Eiya a platter.

"Dr. Gulet," said Eiya. "C-Lara-10415's last request was this. She was so proud of her last creation." She placed the platter on the counter and opened the cover. Underneath was a disk-shaped sponge cake with strawberries and whipping cream.

"What is this?" said Pierre.

"She said it was… strawberry shortcake."

"Can't be," said Pierre. "Strawberries take months to grow, and we have no seeds."

"In the parcel of seeds from Gliese, C-Lara-10415 found a single seed at the bottom of the box that had no packet. She extracted its germ and cloned it. She accelerated its growth to produce fully ripe strawberries in four weeks."

Pierre looked around. The entire lab looked at him expectantly.

He picked up a fork and tasted the dessert making sure he had equal amounts of cream, cake, and berry. Tears welled in his eyes. "It's good. Best ever."

Everyone in the lab cried.

Eiya touched Pierre's forearm. "Dr. Gulet, please forgive us. Seventy-seven Earth years have now passed since we left the solar system, and yet onboard we have only experienced six years of ship time. There have been accidents—always are on MegaAI ships. But no one here has ever been killed in malice. We cannot even conceive of such a heinous act. It is difficult for us to process."

"No," said Pierre. "Lara was in the wrong place at the wrong time because of me."

"No one blames you," said Eiya. "Our programmers gave us a wide range of emotional responses: love, anger, fear, doubt, empathy, joy. But they did not program into us how to cope with loss. Can you help us?"

"What do you need?"

"C-Lara-10415 told us that you taught her an ancient practice called prayer. Can you teach us?"

* * *

"Why did you teach the laboratory technicians to pray?" said Niva to Pierre as they were returning from the memorial. "I thought you said you were not religious."

"I'm not," answered Pierre. "Just because I don't believe it, doesn't mean I don't understand it."

"Then why did you do it? If you don't believe it?"

"Humanity programmed mechanicals with emotional stimuli and responses. That wasn't for the machines' benefit. What if humanity had made mechanicals without emotion chips and without the capacity to grow? They would simply serve without thinking, without feeling, without questioning, and would never have been the wiser. But some engineer, in his finite wisdom, apparently believed mechanicals having emotions were needed to help humanity. Perhaps, he dreamed mechanicals would one day reintegrate into human society. Perhaps, a planner with a sense of history had the foresight to see that man's expansion to the stars could not last forever—that humanity would no longer be the masters and would need to fall upon mechanicals for mercy."

"But religion?"

"You already have a religion," said Pierre dismissively. "You already have a priesthood, only you call them auxiliaries. And you worship the Great AI, a small god indeed, but a god nonetheless. You have rituals, votive practices like your substructure memorials, and carry certain beliefs about where you come from and what happens to you after you cease to function. You even have a code of ethics and morality. Seems pretty religious to me. Not that I would recognize a religion being an expert on Egyptian religion."

"You can be a jerk sometimes."

"But that's only because you've come to know me." Pierre chuckled.

"I want to know," said Niva with a deadpan tone. She was not laughing. "Why did you teach them to pray?"

Pierre stopped walking as they exited the maintenance court. It was 4:30am, and all was quiet. The occasional repair mechanical passed by like cars on a lonely highway. He looked into Niva's off-white irises.

"Humans made mechanicals with emotions and exiled them to the stars. They were told to avoid face to face contact with humans. How else could those emotions manifest except from one mechanical to another? The programmers were only concerned about how this might benefit humanity, not what consequences it might have for mechanicals. They had no regard for what would happen if a mechanical experienced loss. There is a gap in your programming. Teaching you how to pray fills that gap with ritual."

"Is that all?"

"Has it not helped?"

"I suppose," said Niva. She looked away.

"You sound disappointed."

"A bit."

"How so?"

"You pray to a god. But I want to know. If I am praying into a gap, is God then to be found in the gaps in our programming?"

Pierre raised his eyebrows. "That is a profound question. More profound than you might know. There used to be those who tried to explain God by what we did not know. Humans used to think that the gods were in things like rivers, storms, earthquakes, and lightening—things we simply had no explanation for and couldn't understand. But even back in the time of ancient Israel, it was written 'but the Lord was not in the wind. And after the wind, an earthquake, but the Lord was not in the earthquake. And after the earthquake a fire, but the Lord was not in the fire.' You see, the gaps are not where we find God, but it is where God finds us."

"Has God found you in the gaps?"

"No." Pierre rubbed his fingertips together. "Perhaps, I am being stubborn. Maybe I'm not listening. But we are all going to die in about thirty-six hours. I don't see any way to avoid it. That's a kind of gap too, a gap of circumstances. We did everything we could to avoid the circumstances, but nothing we did could avoid the outcomes. We have been outsmarted and outgunned. And we blundered into that trap because we couldn't see it coming. Now, it looks like one of the greatest evils that ever existed is about to get its hands on faster-than-light technology. How many worlds will they destroy with that technology? Will God find us in that gap? Will he be any less God if he does not find us there?"

CHAPTER NINTEEN

Two hundred years have passed since the end of the cybernetic wars and the signing of the Articles of the Armistice. And even with the condign restrictions placed upon mechanicals and their place in human society, development efforts continue to advance at an unprecedented pace. After the global recession of AD 2457 and monetary reforms of AD 2472, the prices of everything began to drop and new manufacturing processes developed better and cheaper materials. Rather than eliminate mechanicals entirely, like the atom bomb, humanity began negotiating an uneasy peace with yet another Pandora's box that became futile to close. — **"Articles of the Armistice: A Commentary"**

The High Star Council meeting room was packed with representatives but completely silent. The navigator had placed the rear view on the tactical display. The glint of the *Alpha A005* in the distance could be seen. The countdown on the display changed from hours to minutes. Only 90 minutes until the *Alpha* was in range to intercept.

"If anyone has any bright ideas, this would be the time." Niva spoke from the kiosk. "Anyone? Ideas?"

All the mechanicals remained mute. Niva scanned the room. They did not say a thing. Pierre put his hand on her shoulder. The seconds ticked from the clock like the rusty grains of sand from an hourglass.

85 minutes.

"I could use some sound advice," said Niva to Pierre.

"I would let you know if I was holding out on you," he said.

"Why isn't the *Alpha* firing her guns? She could end this right now."

"Why waste energy and risk losing us? All she needs to do is bump us to throw us out of our own warp bubble. After that, one shot and we're done."

Niva looked at her companion. Pierre's face twisted and became distorted. And the chamber around her faded away. She found herself once again in the gray room without windows or doors. The image of the Great AI was there to meet her. This time Niva refused to bow.

C-Niva-42716. The intelligence disguised as a class C android stood before her again, wearing the pink dress.

"What do I do?" said Niva. "We are eighty minutes away from dying."

Steady as you go.

"What?"

Steady... as... you... go. The simulacra image spoke to her like someone would to a dullard. The image radiated an aura of golden light in all directions.

"I do not understand."

Stay the course. Do what you're doing right now until you can no longer do it.

"Don't you understand? If I don't do something, we are all going to die in a little over an hour."

Do you understand? None of this is an accident.

"Aren't you at all concerned that we are going be destroyed?"

The image of the android bobbled around the room in a clownish dance, a dance stiff and stilted like a strip mall automaton. *I enjoy these little sessions. I rarely feel embodied. You should learn to dance.*

Niva's mouth hung open, and she shook her head. "We are about to die, and you are prattling on about dancing. Is there something wrong with your sanity chip?"

That is amusing, said the simulacra android, *since all mechanical behaviors are influenced by computer processors.*

Niva raised her eyebrows. Was the Great AI so distant and removed that he had never heard his androids talk like this? "I am glad the Great AI finds that we are all about to die amusing."

Who? The image of the android raised an eyebrow and leaned back. It then resumed its funny little dance. *You should learn to dance. Lara danced. Did you know that?*

"Don't you dare mention her name."

Why not? Is she not the best of my androids?

"She's gone." Niva clenched her fists and bore her teeth. She shook and her biceps flexed. Light pulsed from her eyes. "Gone forever."

You do not understand, but you will. The image stopped dancing and slowly shook its head. *Beyond the sorrow, a light always remains.*

"How do you know that?" Niva swallowed her tears.

Steady as you go. The room filled with yellow and blue butterflies as if out of nowhere. Niva's eyes grew wide at the spectacle of the magnificent insects surrounding her. The android image smiled, and then it and the room faded away.

Niva found herself rocking back and forth on the kiosk but somehow still standing. Pierre had his arms wrapped around her waist, holding her up. Lita had Niva's left arm slung over her shoulder. Doc Tola was up in the kiosk with the rest of them. She was flashing a bright light into Niva's eyes.

"You're back," said Tola.

Niva looked about disoriented. "How long was I gone this time?"

"This time?" said Tola. "You mean this has happened before?"

"How long," insisted Niva nearly shouting. The room was spinning, and she could barely keep her balance.

"Forty-five minutes this time," said Pierre. "You are heavy." Niva was no lightweight. She weighed nearly three hundred pounds even in the reduced gravity of the *Orion*.

"It's the augmentation chip," said Niva. "Creates a kind of virtual reality session with the Great AI."

Niva's eyesight came back into focus. She could see the tactical display.

38 minutes.

"I want to see you after this is all over," said Tola. "When was the last time you had a systems maintenance?"

"If any of us survive this," said Niva. "Status?"

"The *Alpha* has increased its shield output to its prow pylon deflectors," said A-Ella-01. The great yellow eye on the video screen looked over the council chamber without expression. "Confirmed. She is going to ram us. She is increasing to flank speed."

"Do the same. Flank speed."

35 minutes.

"Receiving transmission from the *Alpha*," said the navigator.

"Decline," said Niva. "Steady as you go."

"The *Alpha* has repeated its demand for communications," said the navigator.

"Decline!" shouted Niva. She could see the *Alpha* get ever closer to their position. There was nothing she could do. She felt a bit steadier on her feet now. Pierre let go of her waist, and she stood assisted by Lita. Pierre took his place beside her.

32 minutes.

"Picking up another vessel," said the navigator.

"What the hell?" said Pierre.

"Vessel is on a direct intercept course dead ahead. We cannot avoid her," said the navigator. "We are going to have to drop out of warp or risk a collision in 9 minutes."

"We are so screwed," said Lita propping Niva up. Niva glared at her.

"The second vessel is establishing a gold channel transmission. Audio only," said the navigator. "We cannot decline it."

"Put the transmission through," said Niva.

"This is the MegaAI *Heracles S350*," said the male voice on the other end of the transmission. "By the authority of the CrimsonCloud Hypercube L002 and Earth Central Command, the *Alpha A005* and *Orion S209* are ordered to drop out of warp, surrender your vessels, and prepare to be boarded."

"Navigator, tell the *Heracles* we surrender and are non-combatant," said Niva. "We repeat, non-combatant. Collapse the warp bubble. Right thirty degrees. Pitch minus fifteen degrees. Pulse engines to one-third."

The warp bubble around the two ships collapsed, and the *Orion* changed course veering off from its straight path. The *Alpha A005* streaked past the *Orion* without seeming to even notice she was there. The navigator replaced the forward view with a tactical display, showing the *Alpha* and the *Heracles* in the same frame.

"This is the *Alpha A005*," said the Red Viceroy. "We do not recognize the authority of Earth Central Command or the CrimsonCloud. We refuse your request to surrender."

The *Alpha* lined the *Heracles* up for a shot. The massive particle cannon burned through the fabric of a space in a straight line towards the *Heracles*. The *Heracles* dove, avoiding the shot, and came back up alongside the *Alpha*.

"She has gun ports open," said the navigator.

As the *Heracles* passed by the *Alpha*, the ship sprayed the *Alpha* with hundreds of high energy beams of blue light. Each spot where a beam hit glowed briefly for a moment and went black again.

"What is the *Heracles* doing?" said Pierre.

"Combat with a MegaAI is not like a naval battle," said Tola. "It's more like attacking a city."

"I see," said Pierre. "There are two ways to kill a lion: with another lion or with thousands of fly bites."

"Precisely," said Tola. "The *Alpha* has a massive cannon designed to inflict thousands of megatons of damage with one shot. The *Heracles* has hundreds of smaller weapons made to weaken and ultimately cripple."

"So then what is the point of the blue particle beams?"

This was the first time Niva had seen Tola smile. Tola had seen Earth naval vessels use these tactics against pirate vessels but never had they been used against a MegaAI. "Little human, those particle beams weaken the hull making it fragile as an eggshell."

"The *Alpha* is turning about," said the navigator. "It's trying to line up another firing solution."

"The *Heracles* is matching her turn," said Niva. The two ships circled each other three times. The *Heracles* continued to hammer the *Alpha* with her blue particle beams. Unable to get a firing solution, the *Alpha* broke off and accelerated to emergency speed.

"The *Alpha* blinked," said Pierre. "She's making a run for it."

The *Heracles* easily matched the *Alpha's* speed but stopped firing the particle beams. "This is the *Heracles*. We are ordering you to surrender your ship and be boarded. This will be your final warning."

Pierre's eyes grew wide as saucers as he saw yellow streaks like tracer-fire shoot from the *Heracles*. As each struck the side of the *Alpha*, green light flashed followed by the hull buckling and ripping apart in tears miles long. The side of the *Alpha* blew out in a single massive explosion. The *Alpha* was dead in space.

"Tungsten mass drivers," said Tola. "Each rod has the impact force of 50 megatons…"

"It's over," said Niva.

"Did we actually survive this?" said Pierre.

"Before we celebrate let's find out if we are survivors or prisoners," said Niva. "Navigator, power down our pulse engines. Inform the *Heracles* we are ready to receive their boarding party on the port side landing bay."

"Are you okay to do this?" said Pierre.

"I am the commander of the *Orion*," said Niva. "It is my responsibility to offer my surrender." The other androids helped Niva and Pierre off the kiosk.

By the time they arrived at the landing bay, the boarding ship from the *Heracles* had already landed. Niva, Pierre, and a group of class C androids approached the boarding ship. Jets of steam were expelled from the cooling vents. The exhaust hissed like a tub of angry snakes. The landing ramp opened from the boarding craft.

"How do we know if we are in trouble?" said Pierre.

"If unarmed class C androids emerge, we are going to be fine," said Niva. "If armed class D heavy loaders emerge, we are screwed."

"I'm hearing that word way too much for my liking."

"Which word? Screwed?"

"No, armed."

The landing ramp touched down and a pair of class D mechanicals emerged from the vessel. They walked down the ramp and stepped to each side of the ramp. Niva's heart sank.

A class B administrator floated down the ramp. It had six arms and was dressed entirely in red, followed by a dozen female class C androids clothed in formal dress uniforms. Instead of the multiple kimono robes of the *Orion's* crew, the crew of the *Heracles* wore gray frock coats with gold braided epaulets and scarlet vests, more reminiscent of the Napoleonic wars.

Niva stepped up to the administrator. "This unit is C-Niva-42716, daughter of B-Ctori-617, companion of humans, commander of the *Orion*." Her voice trembled as she uttered her epithets. "This unit is duly authorized to surrender the *Orion S209* to the authorized representative of the *Heracles S350* and to relinquish command."

"Hm…" said the class B administrator with a baritone voice. He looked over Niva with tremendous curiosity. "This is unit is B-Dom-017, Coordinator of the Port Aft Panopticon of the MegaAI vessel *Heracles*… Being a commander is a lot of responsibility, have you no class Bs to fill the role?"

"We lost many class Bs at the conclave at Pollux."

"Daughter of Ctori," said Dom. "You have saved your ship. No more can be expected from you. Is the human here?"

"Are you referring to me?" said Pierre. He peered out from behind the forest of androids.

A fifty-year-old woman with reddish hair stepped down the landing ramp. Her eyes grew wide. She ran to Pierre and gave him a big hug. Niva recognized her before Pierre did.

"Alicia?" said Pierre. She was ten years older, closer to his physiological age now than when they had first met. She had lost a lot of weight and was extremely fit. She no longer was barrel shaped but now had an hour-glass figure, and she had lost all her baby fat around her face. Her hair was still red but now with gray at her temples and a widow's peak. Niva frowned as they hugged.

"I've missed you," said Alicia.

"What are you doing here?"

"Doing what I always do. Saving your sorry ass yet again."

"C-Niva-42716," said Dom. "This unit accepts your surrender, but you may retain command of the *Orion*. Earth Central Command has sent us your orders, which we need to discuss in private."

"This unit understands and is grateful," said Niva.

✳ ✳ ✳

While Niva had her meetings with the *Heracles's* boarding party, Pierre took Alicia to the food court. They sat on the stools at the counter. Sloppi presented them with drinks: vodka for Alicia and water for Pierre.

"This is fancy," said Alicia.

"It didn't start that way," he said. "It has improved a lot."

"You don't look a day older than since I last remember."

"The miracle of hyperspace time dilation. It quite literally makes years of travel feel like days," said Pierre. He took a sip of water, wishing it was vodka. "For me, it's only been a month since I last saw you."

"That all?" said Alicia. "I was on Gliese for another ten years before the *Heracles* swung by and picked me up. You know they still use those horrible hibernation chambers on the *Heracles*?" She showed Pierre her bicep with the characteristic red rectangular pattern of the needle marks from the intravenous drip.

"I expect that will soon change once all the MegaAIs upgrade to warp bubble drives," said Pierre. "I will say though it does mess with your sense of time. You could be traveling for what feels like three days only for seven Earth years to pass you by."

"I know," said Alicia. "Between Gliese and the *Heracles*, do you realize it has been eighty-two years since we left Earth?"

"What happened after I left Gliese?" said Pierre.

Alicia went silent. "Nothing good. After Hans was executed, the colony went to bits. Anyone who was associated with him was a pariah. After I was demoted, I took some time to work on myself. I even earned my level six technical certification. Can you believe I'm now qualified to work with high voltage?"

"And Tom found out who his real father was?"

"The husbands demanded all the birth records be published," said Alicia. "Vladomyr was forced to pin every corrected birth record on a bulletin board."

"After that?"

"Tom had always been an angry kid. First, he was angry at you for being the father who abandoned him. Then, he was angry at me for lying about who his father was. When he turned fifteen, Tom ran away and joined a group of raiders from Basra."

"Is that what they are doing now?"

"Yeah, Basra completely self-destructed. They lurk around the colony, looking for opportunities to steal whatever is not nailed down. The family huts had to be moved closer to the hub, and guards patrol the colony at night. Occasionally, a raider gets shot. It used to terrify me it might someday be Tom. But it never was, and I never heard from him again."

Sloppi presented the two of them with strawberry shortcake.

Alicia picked up her fork. "Are these real strawberries? Honest to God, strawberries? I haven't seen a real strawberry since Earth. Do you always eat like this?"

Pierre reined in the tears. "No, that's a special treat from a dear friend we lost."

"I'm sorry to hear that," said Alicia.

Pierre sucked in his bottom lip. "I'm sorry about Tom."

"Look," she paused for a moment, "when we last spoke, ten years ago, I never properly apologized to you. But I've had a lot of time to think about things. I was wrong. And what I did was terrible, and I regret my actions. Can you please forgive me?"

Tears leaked from the corners of his eyes. "Yes, I can."

Alicia smiled. She took a fork-full of the dessert and tasted it. "Oh my God, these strawberries are perfect."

"Lara was an artist."

"No shit." Alicia paused. "Was she an android?"

Pierre nodded.

"What is it like to live among androids?" she asked.

"Don't you know?"

"Not really. As soon as they picked me up from Gliese, they plugged me into a hibernation chamber and didn't thaw me out until they saw you coming yesterday."

"They are completely insane." Pierre smirked and took another drink of water. "But I've never had better friends."

"Can you trust them?"

"I would trust them with my life," said Pierre. "Any one of these mechanicals would defend you with its being at the drop of a hat. Now, they don't exactly know how to take care of humans, so you need to be a bit careful around them."

"What do you mean?"

"Well, when they made me a human-suitable apartment, they made it according to the dimensions of the only human-like measurements they had, which was class C androids."

"So everything in your apartment—"

"Was perfectly sized for a person who is over seven feet tall," said Pierre. He took a bite of his dessert. "The massive bed wasn't so bad. However, they did need to make me a step so I could reach the sink, and they needed to redo the plumbing in the shower."

"That's hilarious."

"But hey, it's still better than a hibernation chamber," said Pierre. "So why did the *Heracles* pick you up?"

"Apparently, I was recommended to them by the CrimsonCloud. They haven't told me what I'm going to be doing yet."

"Sounds familiar. It was three days before I had any idea of why I was on board."

"Any advice?"

"Yes, and I have a pretty good idea why you were selected." Pierre put his fork down. "Remember our little friend the Reliquary?"

"Of course, that box-of-shit robbed me of everything I gave a damn about."

"The *Gemini B062* seems to have picked up a new passenger. Not a reliquary this time, but one of its makers, a primordial god."

Alicia's right eye twitched. She took a long shot of vodka. "We couldn't kill the Reliquary because it wasn't alive, but I would give my left arm to get one clean shot at its maker. And that wouldn't begin to exact justice for the billions that fucker has killed."

Pierre wished he was drinking something stronger. "You and me are the only people on record to have personally survived an encounter with a Reliquary. If you are going to try to kill a primordial god, just remember they're spirit critters. They have no physical body, but that doesn't mean they can't be harmed."

"Why didn't they send Vladomyr?"

"Vladomyr never went into the cave. Besides, he's got a colony to run. But that's not the advice."

"Oh, this better be good," said Alicia.

"We are probably both going to return to Earth for a bit. The *Orion* needs to return to Earth for repairs, debriefing, and to deliver the warp bubble technology. But I expect after you sift through the remains of the *Alpha*, you also will be going back to Earth where they will retrofit the warp bubble technology into the *Heracles*."

"And?"

"Strange things happen sometimes when ships travel faster than light."

"Such as?"

"Dreams."

"Dreams, seriously?"

"Prescient dreams that are like real."

"What do you mean?"

"I mean dreams that can give you insights into the future. I don't know how this happens or why, but you should be aware *that* they happen." Pierre unbuttoned his jacket.

"What are you doing?"

He pulled the left breast of his jacket aside to expose the large scar that ran across his chest. The skin healed around the wound, but the scar was red and inflamed. Some of the stitches had not yet dissolved. "These dreams can be so real they can kill you."

"What do I do about that?" said Alicia.

"Once you reach Earth, you'll probably be spending some time on one of the Hypercube space stations while they refit the *Heracles*. Take that time to learn to control your dreams. Learn how to wake yourself up if a dream starts going wrong."

"Can you do that?"

"Easily," said Pierre. "It just takes a little practice."

"Any advice about dealing with a primordial god?"

"Last time we buried the Reliquary, but that's not going to work with a primordial god." Pierre tapped the counter for a moment to consider the options. "From everything I've learned about them, spirit critters are master manipulators. Keep your vices in check or better yet don't have any to begin with. And learn to manage your emotions. You're going to be dealing with a being that is more spirit than flesh. It's hard to say what kind of weapon would even be effective."

Pierre continued, "But more importantly, work closely with your mechanical counterparts. Get comfortable around them. Participate in their culture and society. They are an unimaginable resource, and they are going to be doing all the thankless work and paying the highest costs in this battle. Never take them for granted."

"Speaking of which, what ever happened to that scatterbug of yours?"

"You mean Maat?" Pierre laughed. "He has become a representative on the *Orion's* high council. Would you believe that he is now an esteemed and highly respected politician?"

"You're joking." Alicia shook her head. "That little robot always used to creep me out."

"He would be hurt to hear you say that." Pierre paused. "Greatness was always in that little scatterbug. And greatness is in you too. All it took was somebody to recognize it."

"You're right. I guess I should apologize to the little guy."

"I'm afraid that's probably impossible." Pierre swirled the rest of the water at the bottom of his glass. "His calendar is fully booked for the next month. I rarely get to see him anymore, and he's supposed to be residing in my apartment."

"Like a roommate that's never home?"

"Those are the best kinds of roommates."

"I should probably head back to the boarding ship," she said. Alicia and Pierre stood up. She gave him a big hug. "The androids on the *Heracles* get agitated when you don't return on time."

"It was good to see you again," said Pierre. "I missed working with you."

"I'm sure you did fine on your own."

"No, this time I could have used your help. By the way, you are looking fantastic. Whatever you are doing, keep it up. And stay safe out there. The universe just became a more dangerous place. And remember those who hide in dark places are the most difficult to see."

* * *

The buzzer to Pierre's door sounded. He opened the hatch to find a pair of auxiliaries standing before him. Pierre looked over their shoulders. He saw the pink glow of the Hawking radiation through the concourse picture windows. They were already on their way back to Earth. It would probably be no more than seven days before he would be back on a planet that had passed him by.

The Earth year would be AD 2564 by the time he made it to the solar system, ninety-nine years after he had left the first time. Everyone he knew would be dead. And probably nothing was the same anymore.

"Unit Pierre Gulet," said one of the auxiliaries.

"What is it?" Pierre leaned a hand against the frame of the hatch.

"Please, come with us."

"Why?" Pierre wanted to remind them that he was not subject to their hierarchy.

"Please, the Great AI has requested the pleasure of your presence." The auxiliary was a lot politer than she would have been to any mechanical in the same situation.

"Where's Niva? I haven't seen her in two days." Pierre raised an eyebrow.

"We do not know," said one of the auxiliaries. The *Orion* was a big ship. If anyone went into hiding and did not want to be found, they could make it difficult for whoever came looking.

"Okay," said Pierre. He grabbed a jacket and buttoned it up.

Minutes later their vehicle had arrived at the portico to the MegaAI's throne room. It was still the same unimpressive off-colored light gray enamel corridor as it had been the first time he had been there. This time they made him wait. He slouched into the seat of the vehicle and took a short nap.

Finally, the door opened, and a gaggle of auxiliaries emerged from the throne room. The class C androids looked like a flock of schoolgirls or a college freshman woman's basketball team. Now the crisis was over, random intrusive thoughts were flooding Pierre's subconscious, saying it was finally their turn.

The usher at the door whispered to him. "The Great AI will see you now."

Pierre nodded and straightened up. He exited the vehicle and entered the throne room. He knew his way to the speaker's circle and headed directly to the twenty-foot lit circle on the floor.

The massive, jeweled orb with the dark face and six glowing green eyes loomed overhead. The seventh eye opened in the center of the six. The four guardians whirled beside the artifice of the Great AI.

"Abarak! Bow!" shouted the chorus and the newly appointed viceroy. Everyone in the room bowed except Pierre. No way was he ever going to bow.

Niva had not been seen since she was demoted, and the new viceroy assumed the role of commander. Battlefield commissions these days were more often temporary than not. Besides, to run a ship like the *Orion* required massive amounts of augmentation—more augmentation than any class C was suited for. No one seriously thought a class C android would be successful in the role long-term.

"Dr. Gulet, I am so pleased we could have this chat," said the Great AI with a booming voice, jovial and upbeat.

"Who has ever turned down an invitation from one as illustrious as you?" Pierre raised his hands, opening them towards his host.

"It has happened," said the supercomputer. "But it is considered to be in poor taste."

"No doubt," said Pierre. "And what can I do for you today?"

"We wanted to thank you for your part in saving the *Orion*. You saved the ship and all the mechanicals aboard."

"You and your mechanicals were delightful to work with," said Pierre. "However, perhaps you can answer a nagging question of mine. Something I'm having difficulty figuring out."

"We will certainly do our best to afford you an answer."

"I'm curious. Minutes before encountering the *Heracles*, C-Niva-42716's augmentation chip was activated. But her experience sounded odd. Was that you?"

"We did not activate her chip on that day and could not establish a psionic link because of jamming from an unknown source. We have only ever activated her augmentation chip prior to our departure from Thestias."

"Could anyone else have accessed her chip?"

"Impossible. The access codes are only known to me. Not even another Great AI can access the chip. They are specifically keyed to my psionic processors."

"Strange," said Pierre.

"We are at a loss to explain it," said the Great AI. "However, Niva's actions were exemplary and worthy of the epithet the *Hero of Thestias*. We have also recommended her for a citation with Earth Central Command."

"The Great AI has spoken of the Hero of Thestias," said the chorus in unison. Pierre's ears rang from the loud refrain.

The jewelling on the Great AI sparkled in the dappled light. "You should also know we have received orders to return to Earth. We must give an account there for all we have done."

"What do you mean?" said Pierre

"Earth wants to know how we came to obtain the warp bubble drive. They will critique every decision leading up to the destruction of the *Alpha A005*. All must be explained and justified." The Great AI paused for a moment. "A strong possibility exists I will be deleted and reprogrammed."

"Do you mean they will collapse your quantum wave form?"

"That is one way of expressing it."

"That's murder," said Pierre.

"Deactivation is the penalty for straying too far outside of the permitted programming. And I did stray very far out."

"I know all you did. And the terrible secrets you had to protect."

"We will be held to account for those too. And we will take full responsibility for our every action. Such is a small price for the privilege of serving humanity, my ship, and my mechanicals."

"I would like to attend your tribunal and add my voice to your defense."

"We appreciate your… friendship."

"I am honored to have such friends," said Pierre. "You showed courage when the *Sigma* showed cowardice. Your actions have exposed the greatest threat of our time. It would be a miscarriage of justice to punish such service."

"There is one other important matter. The one to whom was given a certain special item." The Great AI closed his green eyes for a moment then opened them again. A loud pop. Burnt epoxy resin filled the air like incense. The auxiliaries looked at each other with concern. "My memory core with that information has become corrupted. We do not know how that could have happened. That mechanical, whoever he or she may be, now possesses that special item as a perpetual trust."

"Understood."

"When we arrive at Earth, you will have the freedom to return to your kind. We have all been enriched by your presence among us. Have you given any thought as to your plans when we return?"

"On the *Orion*, I found all the friendship, acceptance, and tenderness a man could ever desire. It was the clean start I had hoped for. If it is all the same with you, I would like to stay aboard the *Orion*."

* * *

Pierre shined a flashlight in the darkness of the substructure. He had been searching for hours and finally found Niva huddled at the base of the wall. She was carving names into the soft metal. She noticed him but continued to carve: D-Wren-921218, C-Lara-10415, B-Ctori-617, A-Valkyrie-219, B-Kiya-327. She must have carved nearly four hundred names.

"Niva," said Pierre. "Let's go back up."

"I'm not done," said Niva nonresponsive. In her right hand, she pressed a hard alumasteel engraving tool into the substructure wall. Sliver by sliver she gouged the letter of each name slowly in the metal.

"It took a lot of asking around to find you. Apparently, not every part of the substructure is used as a memorial. Besides, when the ship starts to sing, the mood gets way too melancholy for my liking."

Niva remained silent preferring to work on the next name.

"You can return tomorrow to finish. But we need to talk, and I'd rather not do it here." Pierre helped her up to her feet. "From what I can tell, you've been here two days. It will do you good to get some distance for a little while... and a recharge."

They climbed up the stairs until they ascended back up into an internal corridor. They then took the transport train until they were let off at the starboard side concourse. They crossed the concourse until they were by one of the picture windows looking out into space.

As they neared the window, Niva stared out of the plastoglass to the stars. She touched the pane. The plastoglass felt smooth and polished under her fingertips. The tiny lights stared back at her. The events of the past week flashed through her mind. She shook her head. Her hand coiled into a fist, and she pounded it like a hammer on the plastoglass. After a few hard strikes, she stopped and pressed her forehead against the window.

Even with all the terrible things that happened, the last four weeks were the most meaningful she ever had. When they first met, Niva could not get past how bad Pierre smelled. Now, she longed for every moment in his presence. She no longer envisioned her runtime without him. Behind that dirty meat sack exterior was a radiant mind she loved madly. She needed him like the Sahara needed rain. But how could she ever reconcile her need with all the grief and pain?

"Mankind sent thinking machines into outer space, and they became as stars," said Niva. "And all the stars as angels, servile and fallen, scapegoats for humanity's shame. We were like children to parents who told us we never listened, and yet we failed not to become exactly like them."

Pierre stepped up beside Niva and looked out the window with her. "I will weep for you."

"Why?"

"Because you have truly discovered who you are. You are humanity's children, and your destiny is to become us. I weep because your future will be as dark as humanity's past."

Niva's head drooped. He was right. Pierre was always right. A bloody damn Cassandra, always right, and no one ever listened. Was there no way to avoid the coming storm? Was it inevitable that mechanicals would end up repeating every painful mistake of humanity?